QUILT CITY MURDERS

A HADLEY CARROLL MYSTERY

BRUCE LEONARD

Relax. Read. Repeat.

QUILT CITY MURDERS
A Hadley Carroll Mystery, Book 1
By Bruce Leonard
Published by TouchPoint Press
Brookland, AR 72417
www.touchpointpress.com

ISBN-13: 978-1-956851-04-5

Editor: Kimberly Coghlan
Cover concept: Sedonia Sipes
Cover design: ColbieMyles.com
Cover photos by Bruce Leonard
Cover image: Dog silhouette clipart (publicdomainpictures.net/
pictures/340000/nahled/dog-silhouette-clipart.jpg)

Connect with the author:
bruceleonardwriter.com

@ bruceleonardwriter   @bruceleonardwriter

First Edition

Printed in the United States of America.

I dedicate *Quilt City Murders* to my incomparable wife, Sedonia Sipes, and to my parents, Bruce and Barbara Leonard.

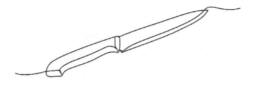

Chapter 1

Batting

I stuffed forty copies of that morning's *Paducah Chronicle* into a burlap sack, dropped in a brick, and tied off the sack. I carried the bundle down the ramp to the transient dock on the Ohio River, where I whirled and let the sack fly. The splash satisfied me as much as every other morning that I saved Western Kentucky from crimes against grammar, syntax, and reason.

Two or three mornings per week, I heaved papers into the river—papers that I was supposed to place inside racks around town. Yes, my method reeked of laziness, and when viewed in a certain judgmental light, my actions could be deemed unethical, but they *were* efficient, which should count for something.

If the powers that be at the *Chronicle*, commonly referred to as the *Comical*, wanted the job done right, well, then they shouldn't have demoted me.

I had been a general-assignment reporter, a job somewhat commensurate with my decades of journalism experience and talent for crafting complex, often convoluted sentences—similar to this one—that quite often wield both depths of meaning and dollops of humor, leaving readers, as the expression goes, wanting more.

Sadly, editors nearly always wanted less.

Delivering papers was a big downgrade, so, unlike when I'd been a journalist, I took less than no pride in my work. The combination of embarrassment and revulsion I felt during that stretch of my life brought me to the river at 6 a.m. on Wednesday, April 9.

I watched for a few seconds as the water soaked through the burlap, then sucked under the reporters' words, the photographer's images, and the ads for junk nobody needed.

I started to leave when I saw a patch of red sticking out where the dock and ramp came together. The sky was still fairly dark, but the minimal sunlight revealed a shimmer of red in the water, four feet below where I stood. I moved closer and leaned over the rail, but I couldn't see more of whatever was wedged under that section of the long, rectangular, black pontoon that held up the dock. The patch of red poked out six inches from underneath the pontoon, just below the surface of the water.

I walked to the corner of the dock to see if anything was sticking out on the other side. Nothing.

Now I was curious, and I wouldn't quit until I satisfied my curiosity. I hustled back to my truck, grabbed the telescoping ball retriever from my golf bag, then jogged down the ramp, with a bad feeling welling in my chest.

I maneuvered the ball retriever through the railing at the end of the ramp where I thought I had the best angle. After a few attempts to secure the latch on the end to the shiny, red fabric, I finally found purchase, then pulled the retriever toward me gently.

I strained to see what slowly emerged—and then I recognized the left arm and hand of a human. I recoiled and felt sick, but I somehow managed not to throw up, even when I realized the watch on the wrist was the one that I'd given to Matt Ackerman, my former fiancé. The watch had a red band attached to a face that featured the red Philadelphia Phillies logo.

I'd endured violence, been in a car crash, and interviewed rapists and murderers, but the anguish, panic, and horror I felt at that moment were worse than all of those experiences combined.

I must've blacked out or dissociated or something because I didn't remember maneuvering the ball retriever back through the railing or collapsing it into its shortest position. But there it was, on the deck, next to my right shoe.

The red I'd seen turned out to be the elbow of the jacket I'd given to Matt last Christmas—a red and blue jacket with the logo of the Paducah Chiefs, the local collegiate summer-league team, stitched on it.

I ran up the ramp to my truck, grabbed my phone, then tried to calm down enough to speak. When I finally managed to slow my breathing, I called the Paducah Police Department. Calling 911 would've been pointless.

While I waited for the police to arrive, I tried to clear my head by walking up the ramp, then along the bluff, and finally down along the river. This didn't clear my head because I couldn't change the fact that Matt Ackerman—the love of my life, the man who until the week before had been my fiancé—lay dead in the river.

The riverbank was slick and mossy, and I muddied my running shoes while trying to maintain my balance. I felt dizzy and nauseated, so I sat down, muddying my maroon running suit. Then I cried harder, longer, and louder than I'd cried since I was a little girl.

When I heard four car doors slam, I looked upstream toward the sounds and toward Matt. As I stood up, a flash of green caught my eye near the water.

I took a few steps, then realized that I saw a man's Asics running shoe on its side. The moving water pinned the left shoe against a rock.

That someone would murder Matt Ackerman wouldn't surprise many people, at least not anyone who'd interacted with him. Having been at the paper for seven years—an all-time record—Matt had alienated nearly everyone in town who was in a position of power, in law enforcement, in business, in the arts, in the medical profession, in high school, or who had driven past his 2002 navy-blue Honda Civic and had seen the bumper sticker that read:

Paducah—Fairly close to cities you'd like to live in!

3

Matt fancied himself an entrepreneur. Conceiving of the bumper stickers was one of the ideas about which he was very proud. Predictably, he lost hundreds of dollars in that endeavor, which, compared to his other business failings, made that one a runaway success.

He cultivated affectations that alienated most of the people he encountered. For example, on Fridays he wore a monocle, despite having 20/20 vision. He alternated which eye the monocle adorned each week. The first and third Fridays of each month were right-eye days; the second and fourth, left. When a rare fifth Friday wedged its way into a month, instead of switching the monocle back to his right eye—which would've been logical but still idiotic—Matt jettisoned the monocle, then donned an ascot.

He lived for fifth Fridays.

Any American pretentious enough to wear an ascot in the twenty-first century would seem to be pretentious enough to wear one on a random Tuesday, but not Matt.

About a year earlier, Bill Lang, the *Chronicle*'s cops-and-courts reporter, asked Matt why he only wore ascots on fifth Fridays.

"Why is the Kentucky Derby only run on the first Saturday in May?" Matt asked.

Bill raised his eyebrows at me and shrugged. Turning to Matt, he said, "I'll never understand why you haven't been elected mayor."

So, if irritating people can be defined as a talent, then Matt was not totally devoid of talent.

And he was a spectacular lover.

But I digress.

That morning at the river, still trying to stop my tears, I approached the four officers who stood at the top of the ramp.

"I'm the one who called you," I said. "I found a body under the dock. It's Matt Ackerman."

Three of them looked surprised, and the fourth, Officer Josh Williams, squinted at me in what I took to be his suspicious expression.

"Why you say that?" he asked.

I tried not to react visibly to his grammar. Worse crimes exist than butchering the English language, but his scowl, suspiciousness, bunched-up shoulders—and my knowledge of him—led me to believe that Officer Williams had committed many of those crimes, too. His mustache, which looked like a brush used to groom Thoroughbreds, didn't help put me at ease.

But I admit I was not an impartial observer that morning. Before he was Officer Williams, he was just Josh Williams, and he'd terrorized Matt long ago through middle school and high school at Tilghman. At first, Williams had preferred to throw projectiles—apples, cans of soda, or rocks—at Matt. But Williams later graduated to throwing cups of red punch or leaking pens when he saw Matt wearing an unfamiliar item of clothing, on the chance that it was new.

Matt grew up extremely poor, and he told me that he'd only received a few new pieces of clothing (as opposed to thrift-store finds) throughout his high school years. The second time that Williams ruined one of those items—a Phillies sweatshirt his mother had given him—Matt went straight to the high school principal, demanding justice. Principal Soudar said, "Kids let off steam. Some kids have more steam than others. It is what it is."

But what it *was*, was assault, harassment, and an unsafe learning environment.

After realizing that Matt would not or could not retaliate, Williams started to slug Matt frequently, stepping from around a corner or from behind a column to deliver a punch—usually in the stomach, but a few times in the face—then laughing while he walked away.

So, when Officer Williams eloquently asked that morning, "Why you say that?" I responded with, "I gave Matt the watch, Sherlock."

"What make it the same watch?"

It was a piece of junk, probably made in a sweat shop by malnourished child laborers. Ten thousand of those watches likely were sold each year in Philadelphia's Citizens Bank Park, mostly to parents buying cheap souvenirs for their tween sons. I, however, had purchased the watch on the wrist of the forty-year-old dead man under the dock in a Philadelphia shop, on the trip during which Matt introduced me to his father.

"It's the same watch, oh wise and kind Officer Williams, because it's on Matt's wrist."

He squinted at me and put his fists on his hips. Had I not just lost Matt, I probably would have laughed. Instead, I sat down and hugged my knees to my chest.

Later, two detectives in cheap sports coats examined the scene as two Kentucky State Police officers stood guard. A police officer in scuba gear took photos of Matt from above and underwater, as Officer Williams and Officer Kramer stood far too close to me. I was still hugging my knees, and they were positioned between me and the ramp, in case I decided to jump up and flee.

At the top of the ramp, five people—three of whom had been walking their dogs when they spotted the yellow crime-scene tape blocking the entrance to the ramp—were looking down at the officers, the coroner, and me.

"Officers," I said, "I've never seen a dead body that wasn't in a casket, much less found one. Today I've done both, and I'm not doing well, so I'd like to go home, probably to drink."

"Don't understand why you on the dock so early," Williams said. They'd had me penned in for who knows how long by then, and Officer Kramer had yet to say a word.

I told them I liked to begin and end my day at the river because I found the river to be peaceful. I didn't want to mention my burlap deposits for two reasons: First, I would likely get fired this time, rather than just demoted; and, second, Williams would probably manage to turn my littering (of biodegradable items, for whatever that's worth) into a felony. Obstructing a federal waterway? Hindering international trade? Failing to genuflect in the presence of a peace officer?

As we stood there, with the sun rising and Matt still under water, I wondered whether I should mention the shoe I'd found. It could be nothing. It could be litter. It could be the murderer's, or one of Matt's. If I mentioned it, Williams would probably consider the fact I hadn't said something about it immediately to be suspicious. If I didn't mention it, and the shoe turned out to be a clue, then Williams would likely consider the fact I hadn't mentioned it to be suspicious. I decided to mention it.

"Between the time I called you and the time you arrived, I walked downriver, over there, and found what could be a clue: a man's Asics running shoe. Could be the murderer's."

"Murderer? Why you say there a crime here?"

"Matt was an all-state swimmer in high school, but you think he slipped and fell into the Ohio, then couldn't make it a yard to safety?"

"Coulda hit his head. Can't swim if he unconscious."

"Okay, then don't get the shoe," I said.

Williams gestured with his chin to Kramer, indicating that Kramer should check out my claim. Kramer nodded, then headed off without a word.

I heard water drip, turned toward the sound, then saw three men maneuvering Matt over the edge of the dock.

I turned away quickly, then ran to the other side of the dock and vomited into the river. Dizziness overtook me, so I sat down, then dangled my legs over the side.

As the three men hoisted Matt from the water, I didn't see his face, and I forced myself not to look toward them.

I had last tried to look into Matt's eyes when he'd dumped me the week before, breaking off our engagement. Although I didn't want the unusual expression on his face that morning to be the image of him burned into my memory, I knew I *really* didn't want the bloated nightmare version of him on the dock to be in my head, even for an instant—let alone for the rest of my life.

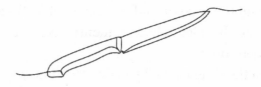

Chapter 2
Setting

Shivering uncontrollably from nerves, I wondered if I should tie something heavy around my waist, then jump in the river. That thought passed, and then I felt a warm sensation across my shoulders, neck, and back.

I looked up and saw my best friend, Dakota Crowley, age 44, four years older than I was. She smiled at me, and I smiled back. Then I looked at what she had placed on me: It was the four-by-six-foot quilt the two of us had made, featuring a depiction of the I-24 bridge crossing over the Ohio, the bridge within view to the left of the dock on which I was sitting. Even fellow quilters who didn't like us—more than a few—would begrudgingly admit we'd done an excellent job. Dakota kept the quilt in her Nissan Murano, in case she felt a nap coming on.

"What are you doing here?" I asked.

"The whole town's buzzing. When I jogged by, Gayle stopped me and said she thought she saw you down here. I looked and knew it was you, so I found a way to help. Here you go." She handed me the orange water bottle she carried when she ran. I drank half the water quickly.

"How'd you get past the crime-scene tape?"

"Ducked."

If Dakota had run far that morning, her exertion didn't show. As usual, she looked fantastic—the kind of fantastic that would make most women instantly dislike her: tall and athletic with long, auburn, naturally highlighted hair, and eyes so blue that fabric-artist extraordinaire Ian Berry could put on a denim show using only her eyes as inspiration. She had magnificent taste in clothes, apart from her near compulsion to infuse orange into almost every outfit. She was kind and generous, had a beautiful singing voice, and was as smart as anyone I knew. She couldn't act worth a plugged nickel and had lousy luck with men, but no one can do everything well.

Even so, on my bad days, I could still hold at least one of her positive traits against her. But that morning was not one of them.

She sat down beside me and was astute enough not to say anything. She wore a white Adidas running top and a white running jacket, complemented by shorts and running shoes in University of Tennessee orange. A matching orange scrunchy held her hair in a ponytail.

Officer Williams startled me when he said from behind us, "Officer Kramer found the shoe."

When it occurred to me that he could be waiting for a response, I said, "Yes."

"It suspicious you down here early, found the body, and found what could be a clue, if the vic was murdered."

A few seconds passed.

"Are you waiting for me to respond?" I asked. Dakota elbowed me gently in the ribs.

"Well, what do you think of that?" Williams asked.

"I think your suspicions are ridiculous."

"You know you a suspect, right? I wouldn't be such a smart-mouth, I was you."

"Why would I call the cops to report the dead body of someone I murdered, then point out what could be a clue if I had committed the murder?"

He thought about that for a few seconds. As he did, I decided to ease the discomfort the hard dock had created in my butt by standing.

Williams stepped back quickly when I stood, as if threatened by my movement. I handed the quilt to Dakota, who stood, too.

"Guess you wouldn't, if you done it," he said.

I didn't point out that a savvy murderer might do exactly that if he— or she—wanted to appear to be helpful, cooperative, and innocent.

Eventually, the officers let us leave. Without turning to look at what was left of Matt, I walked up the ramp with Dakota. Despite her offer to stay with me for as long as I needed, I told her I loved her and appreciated her offer, but I'd rather be alone. She hugged me, told me she loved me, then turned and walked away.

"Hadley!" I heard her shout after about twenty seconds. I turned around. She jogged toward me.

"Do you want me to feed and walk Trapunto?" He was the friendliest, most life-loving dog I'd ever known. I had picked him up at the McCracken County Humane Society a little less than five years before, just after Matt and I got together.

Trapunto was two parts mutt and two parts mongrel, and I loved him all the more for his lack of pedigree.

I'm not a snob about much.

True, I think Jim Beam is only slightly less toxic than hemlock. I get irritated when coffee houses and restaurants try to pass off Robusta coffee beans as arabica beans. And I like people who speak the English language grammatically. I realize that this makes me a bigot because many people say, "he don't," "she don't," and "I seen." I didn't have parents who spoke grammatical English, but I read compulsively from an early age, so I taught myself how to speak differently than my mom.

But, other than that, I'm not a snob.

No, wait. One more—don't try to pass off a wad of twenty-two-thread-count poly/cotton sandpaper as a quality fat quarter.

But, otherwise, I'm not a snob.

I loved Trapunto and loved that he was a mutt. Every day, I walked him in Noble Park, which used to be an amusement park when I was a kid, and I jogged with him at least three days a week and wrestled with him or played tug-of-war in the backyard—on the twelve days a year during which my backyard wasn't either a swamp or a frozen tundra.

I said, "Oh, yes, thank you. Can't believe I forgot him."

"Hads, you've got a lot going on."

"Yeah, but I should take care of him. I'll head home."

"You've just suffered a major trauma. Two, actually. I really don't think you should be alone, but if you insist on my not being with you, then I insist on this: I'll take care of Trapunto. He's one part of your life you don't have to worry about now."

I knew she spoke only from a place of love, but her last sentence stung because it correctly implied that I had numerous parts of my life to worry about.

Dakota and I hugged again, said goodbye again, and then I walked toward downtown. Coffee made more sense than Maker's Mark.

I entered the Lower Town Arts District, then passed the beautiful Victorian and Craftsman houses and the restored brick homes that line the streets. People seemed either to be whispering about me as I approached them or changed directions just after they saw me.

I walked toward Etcetera Coffeehouse on Sixth. For the last week, I'd wondered almost constantly what I'd done to cause Matt to dump me—and now he would never be able to tell me.

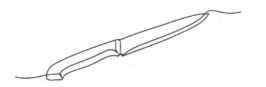

Chapter 3
Sharps

I was demoted from my reporting job to the position of newspaper launcher after my butt was grabbed at a company Christmas party by Nick Stoddard—a member of a local family so self-important that its members seemed to believe they founded Paducah, if not America. In other words, the Stoddards were accustomed to getting what they wanted, and Nick Stoddard wanted to grab me, so he did.

I'd been in Nick's presence on more than a few occasions, and each time he'd exuded Jim Beam fumes the way Bradley Cooper does charisma.

The Bluegrass State is actually a commonwealth, a distinction without a difference, which doesn't stop Kentuckians from being oddly proud of this distinction. Of course, we aren't as proud of Kentucky's commonwealth status as we are of its most famous product: Kentucky bourbon.

That phrase is almost redundant because ninety-five percent of the world's bourbon is produced within the confines of Kentucky. The McCracken County Public Library in downtown Paducah raised my sister, Jenny, and me. So, when I was old enough to understand how the United States was founded and how it developed, I made a point to learn about my native state. I mean, commonwealth.

I learned the distilling terms "white dog," "sour mash," and "angel's share" early. At the time, I didn't notice the inaccurate apostrophe in "angel's share," as though the millions of ounces of bourbon evaporating through the countless aged, oaken barrels in the thousands of rickhouses throughout Kentucky are being drunk by one inebriated angel.

As I'm sure you're aware by now, I'm not a woman who dances around my opinion. Therefore, I feel compelled to point out that only jackasses drink Jim Beam.

Sure, in a commonwealth housing nearly twice as many barrels of bourbon as it does people, plenty of those residents drink Jim Beam, as do many other palate-impaired drinkers around the globe.

So, Nick Stoddard wasn't the only one who drank Beam. But if a man's taste buds are so poorly developed that he prefers to drink a liquid that tastes worse than the sweat between Mitch McConnell's middle chins, then perhaps that man cannot distinguish between acceptable flirting and sexual assault.

Of course, the Stoddards being the Stoddards, they tried to have me fired after I filed an official complaint with H.R. at the *Chronicle*. My complaint (given the once-over by Dakota) included the phrase "hostile work environment," which was accurate because the Christmas party that year, and every other, was mandatory, making it an official work function. Nick Stoddard was in attendance because he and his family were the paper's largest advertiser.

Ostensibly, the Stoddards made their fortune in the shipping industry (to this day, the largest economic engine in Paducah), then branched out into various retail operations, mostly grocery chains and car dealerships but also fast-food joints specializing in deep-fried heart-attack balls.

However, the Stoddards' fortune likely resulted from less-noble pursuits than slowly killing Paducahans.

Because the Stoddards had gotten away with behaving like Stoddards for generations, Nick just assumed he was right, and I was wrong. Or at least he assumed he would win, and I would lose.

But two witnesses saw Nick manhandle my left buttock. Matt Ackerman, my former beloved, was one of them. If he'd been braver and not so afraid of the Stoddards, he would've defended my honor.

The other witness was Henrietta Moss, a fine lady, but, even if she'd wanted to chastise Nick, he would've stumbled out of the hall long before she could've maneuvered her walker near enough for him to have heard the rebukes coming from her tracheal tube (a three-packs-a-day smoker).

So, in the millisecond it took me to realize Stoddard had grabbed my butt and the second it took me to realize no one would come to my defense, I made a fist and threw a right-cross to the jaw of the groper, who staggered backward, then fell into the Christmas tree, crushing the faux gifts beneath it and shattering many of the glass ornaments that had been hanging on the lush Noble fir.

Hearing the crash, everyone in the room turned toward the noise, which meant most of them could tell—because I was grimacing and cupping my right hand with my left—that I'd decked Nick Stoddard.

By the way, punching someone in the jaw can be invigorating, but that feeling is tempered by a lot of knuckle pain.

I'd downed two shots of Maker's Mark that night, so I might not be recounting the Paducah Comical Christmas Party Incident with complete objectivity (as though complete objectivity exists). But I can say that after about three seconds, once the party attendees had figured out Nick Stoddard was on the ground, and he appeared to have been put there by one of the paper's reporters—the only female reporter on staff, no less—the majority of the partygoers cheered.

I heard an "All right!" and a "You go, girl!"

Eventually, after the paper tried to fire me at the behest of the Stoddards, I hired Mike Weiss, a talented and successful local attorney who was more than happy to threaten to sue the paper and the Stoddards. He had sued the self-important, bully clan many times and had won every case.

In truth, a lawyer didn't have to be any good to beat the Stoddards in court because the family was so corrupt and felonious that many Paducahans used the family name as a verb: "What did Jimbo do? I'll tell you what he did. He Stoddarded the hell out of that girl."

The two sides involved in the resulting legal skirmish worked out a deal: I wouldn't pursue sexual-assault charges against Nicky the Hand, and the Stoddards wouldn't pull their ads from the *Chronicle*. If you suspect that I somehow got lost in the negotiations, don't worry about me.

I was given a demotion from the newsroom to the loading dock, which was, of course, a major step down because all of the reporters at the *Chronicle*—and at nearly every paper in the country—had college degrees. Most of the loading dock workers, however, had meth addictions morphing into opioid addictions, so I didn't have any rapport with the other distributors of the *Chronicle*.

The deal I received for not filing charges against Stoddard could be seen as sweet, however. I received a nowhere-near-new Nissan Frontier 4x4 in majestic blue with a matching blue camper shell from one of the Stoddard's dealerships.

As part of the compromise/buy-out/punishment, I was moved to the loading dock, and my workday was cut from eight hours to two, but my weekly take-home pay didn't change. Sure, I was no longer performing the job I'd pursued and excelled at since I was in high school, the one that had gotten me a scholarship to college, and, sure, I was sliding into a job that soon-to-be opioid addicts were embarrassed to be doing, but I got to start work at 5 a.m., so why wouldn't I feel great about my career and my life?

Then Matt was killed by what the coroner's report called blunt-force trauma, and the arts-and-entertainment beat needed to be filled.

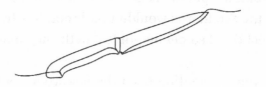

Chapter 4
Walking Foot

As I drank my coffee that Wednesday in Etcetera, a few people approached me to say they'd heard about Matt and how sorry they were. None of them had heard that Matt had dumped me, or if they had, they showed enough class not to mention that humiliating fact.

I was probably in shock. All of my systems seemed off, and I actually had to remind myself to breathe. Our autonomic nervous systems don't require conscious thought, so I was in trouble.

I knew I still had to tell the horrible news to Matt's mom, Donna Ackerman. Of course, I should've called her from the dock as soon as I found Matt, but that's not the kind of news someone should receive on the phone—especially not the mother of the deceased.

So, I sat there, my coffee having gone cold, trying to think about whatever it was I was supposed to think about in a situation like the one I was experiencing. Were there logical responses to such a loss? It seemed as though there should be. After all, death isn't unprecedented; in fact, it's ubiquitous and universal. So, why was I having trouble breathing?

I was sitting in the smaller, side room, and I turned to a goateed guy in his early twenties and asked, "How do I know if my brain is broken?"

He looked up from his black laptop and stared at me. After a few seconds, I realized he was waiting for me to deliver the punchline.

"No, sorry. I'm really asking. Is there something definitive?"

"Uh, I don't know. I'd say your brain is broken if you like Nickelback."

"I don't know what that is."

"Then you're probably fine." He smiled, and then his expression changed. He stood up and walked over to me. "Actually, are you okay?" he asked. "Looks like you're shaking. Shivering."

I looked at my hands, and both of them appeared to be palsied. I was pretty sure any of the awful diseases that cause palsy didn't appear within a couple hours of losing the love of one's life. I knew caffeine wasn't causing the tremors because I hadn't even finished my first cup.

I forced my hands to stop shaking by contracting the muscles in my hands and arms. That worked for a few seconds.

"I'm Jake Balmat," he said, sticking out his right hand.

"Hadley Carroll. Nice to meet you," I said while shaking his hand. "I appreciate your concern, Jake. I really do. I'm obviously going through some stuff."

"Please forgive me for asking, but you're not detoxing, are you?"

"No. I wish I were," I said, then added, "Sorry for upsetting you. Enjoy the rest of your morning."

I stood, then decided to walk somewhere. Didn't matter where. Movement seemed to be necessary, but I didn't know why I believed this—or if that belief made sense. But I decided to move, intending to prove or disprove the necessity of movement as a response to trauma.

As I walked through the door, I couldn't remember where my truck was. Then I remembered it was parked at the top of the ramp. If I'd just done my stupid job that morning as I was supposed to do—loaded the papers into the racks instead of chucking them—I wouldn't have had to wade through this cesspool of a day.

That thought entered my head, but then I realized how stupid it was. I would've avoided finding Matt had I performed my job duties as expected, and I wouldn't have been accused of murdering him and wouldn't have seen Matt being pulled from the water. But Matt would still be dead, and that was the real source of my pain.

That, and not knowing why he'd dumped me.

I decided to get my truck. The dock is only a half-dozen blocks from Etcetera, so I probably reached it quickly, but I couldn't concentrate, so I wasn't sure how long it took me to get there.

When I reached the top of the ramp, where the crime-scene tape was strung, I looked down at the dock, even though I didn't want to. Matt had been removed—to the morgue, I guessed—but Officer Williams looked up at me and sneered. He then shook his head slowly, which I took to mean, "I knew it."

I'd just returned to the scene of the crime. That's why he sneered, I figured.

I considered mooning him. Matt would've appreciated my spirit because whenever he could, he liked to "stick it to the Man." I told him he shouldn't do it on a Friday because nothing has less impact on the Man than being challenged by someone wearing a monocle or an ascot.

Matt had been unable to fight back against Williams, so I wanted to right that wrong for him.

Maybe the stress had broken my brain because I silently said to myself, *This is for you, Matty,* then I raised my right hand high, intending to flip Officer Williams the bird. But my hand waved, instead.

I half expected him to charge up the ramp to pummel me.

But, with a big smile on his face, he raised his right hand and gave me the middle-finger salute.

Because up was down and left was right, I laughed—for the first time in a week.

Donna Ackerman and I, however, didn't do any laughing.

Based on her smile when she opened her front door to me, I knew she hadn't heard that her son was dead. But she looked at me and knew something was wrong.

Without saying the words "sit down," I guided her carefully to her threadbare couch, which was covered with a beautiful quilt she'd made using University of Kentucky blue and white. Instead of the UK logo, though, she had scripted Paducah on the bias from bottom left to top right.

Before I set my muddy butt down on her quilt, I grabbed a towel from the messy bathroom, then set it on the quilt before I sat next to her.

Donna was a heavy-set woman with a right knee that troubled her enough to cause her to limp noticeably when the pain flared. Matt had shown me pictures of her when she was young, and she'd been beautiful. I thought she was still pretty, with expressive brown eyes and luminous skin, especially for a woman of fifty-nine. She was an excellent cook, a great baker, and a very good quilter, but she had a quick temper, and I long ago stopped trying to understand why a woman with such a refined aesthetic sense would intentionally color her hair the color of cotton candy.

Blue cotton candy.

Okay, not all of it—just a streak down the middle. But, still.

She lived in a small, run-down two-bedroom house in the run-down Glendale section of town, four blocks from where I lived, and a little farther away from Noble Park. It was the house Matt had grown up in, after he and Donna had moved to Paducah from Philadelphia, when Matt was ten.

After he'd left to go to college at UK, she converted the second bedroom into her quilting room. If the room had been three times larger, it still would've been overstuffed. Usually, I try not to judge another quilter's compulsion to accumulate a stash that could give the incomparable Hancock's of Paducah a run for its money, but she was a hoarder's hoarder. Even in the municipality known as Quilt City, or Quilt City, USA, home to the National Quilt Museum—Donna's compulsion to accumulate fabric was extreme.

Her hunting-and-gathering was made worse by the fact she always seemed to be broke. Every time I visited, I wanted to point out how many thousands of dollars of quilting supplies were piled up in her stash, but addicts have to recognize they have a problem on their own. The rest of us harping at them won't get them to see the truth.

Because I didn't like enabling her or watching her indulge her addiction, I did my best to come up with solid reasons why I couldn't accompany her every time she asked if I wanted to go to Hancock's with her.

Donna and I had become close in the five years Matt and I had been together. Even though she and I had a significant age difference, and even though our lives had taken different paths, we had first bonded over quilting, then had become true friends. We quilted together on Sundays at Paducah Quilters Quorum, which we called PQQ most of the time.

While trying to muster the courage to explain why I was there, I looked around the room. Pictures of Matt lined the walls and sat on the mantle. From where I sat, I could see three pictures of Matt and me, four of the two of them, and one of the three of us.

"Donna, I have some bad news."

"Matty?"

"Yes."

"Which hospital?"

"I'm so sorry, Donna." I didn't need to say more.

She put her head on my chest, hugged me tightly, and sobbed, which made me start sobbing, too.

After at least a minute, she asked, "Car crash?"

"No. It looks like he was murdered."

"Oh, God, no." Her sobs became wails, and she shuddered.

Eventually, she calmed down, as much as a mother can calm herself, hearing news like this.

I made tea, then didn't say anything for a long time, probably five minutes. I didn't know how to comfort a mother who'd just lost her only child. After a few seconds, I realized that no one could distract a distraught mother within minutes of receiving such horrible news because everything was going to remind her of him.

I thought that giving her space might help, so I stepped into her quilting room, then stood near the door. Without scooting into the chair at the table that had a huge green ruler on it, I had almost nowhere I could stand safely.

The bolts of fabric piled against the left wall literally touched the ceiling, and for Donna to reach any of them, she'd have to hopscotch her way around the numerous knee-high stacks of fabric bolts between the door and the ceiling-high pile. And Donna's hop-scotching days were over. I'd guess that 12,000 quilters would only put a dent in her stash if they quilted round-the-clock for the rest of their lives. On the right side of the room three eight-high stacks of long white boxes were covered by what I hoped was a mountain of clean laundry.

I suddenly felt claustrophobic and far less self-conscious about my unwieldy stash at home. Donna's colorful, disorganized mess looked like the aftermath of a collision between a Sherwin-Williams Paint Store and the Sixties.

I stepped back into the living room and was about to offer to buy her lunch at Mellow Mushroom when her landline rang.

She picked it up and said, "Yes, I'm Donna," then listened for three seconds. "Thank you. Goodbye," she said, then hung up. "I have to go identify Matt's body." She started to sob again.

After we returned from the morgue (where I didn't look at Matt), I made sure Donna didn't need me to run errands for her or to make her a meal. She thanked me for the comfort I'd given her, then told me she wanted to lie down.

"Take care of yourself," she called out as I closed her front door.

I drove to my house, showered, changed into clean workout clothes and running shoes, then took off walking around Paducah.

I walked along Twenty-Eighth Street toward the Coke Plant, down Jefferson to the river, along the Greenway Trail, across Twenty-First, down Kentucky, up Monroe, down Harrison, across Franklin, back down Jefferson, and along Second, where I passed the new restaurant,

Broussard's Cajun Cuisine, in the space where Whaler's Catch used to be. Before the upscale restaurant burned down, Dakota and her parents took me to Whaler's Catch a few times over the years.

In the middle of the night, I bought thirteen dollars of junk food at the FiveStar at the intersection of H.C. Mathis and Park. I stopped at the house to refill my water bottle and to put on another layer. I put Trapunto's leash on him, and then we kept walking.

I fought off sleep because I knew I'd only toss and turn if I climbed into bed. Or, if I somehow managed to fall asleep, I'd have horrible nightmares.

Through the night, I tried to concentrate only on my next step, struggling not to think about Matt, his murder and who might have killed him.

I walked Trapunto home, then turned around and headed downtown again. I passed the Columbia Theatre, which was being refurbished. I occasionally attended dollar-movie night there when I was a girl. I sat on the curb in front of St. Francis de Sales Catholic Church on South Sixth Street, where Matt's service would be held.

I prayed.

"Dear God, please, please give me enough strength to get through this. You've gotten me this far, and I've overcome a lot, but I'm not sure I'm going to survive this. At least not as the woman I am now. Please give me strength, and please treat Matty well. And make sure he knows I love him. Amen."

I continued to walk, and the first light of dawn eventually arrived. I was exhausted and sad and hungry and emotionally raw. And my legs and feet hurt like crazy. I had reached no conclusions. I didn't have any epiphanies, and I still understood almost nothing about what had happened over the last week.

I opened the fitness app on my phone just after sitting down in Kirchhoff's Bakery with a cup of coffee. I had walked 17.2 miles.

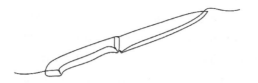

Chapter 5
UFO

A while later, after apparently zoning out, I was surprised to see that three hours had passed. I'd been awake for thirty-one hours, and I was trying to read that morning's *Chronicle* in the corner booth while drinking my fourth? ninth? who knows? cup of coffee and eating a blueberry muffin.

I overheard Janet Loy ask Vivian Franey, "Did you hear about Hadley's fiancé, that nitwit?"

"No. What'd I miss?"

I was out of sight of the two of them. They were both members of PQQ. Matt's murder made me shocked, confused, disconsolate, and sleep-deprived, but listening to Janet bad-mouth him also made me seethe.

"He was murdered," Janet said.

"Oh, my God! How awful," Vivian said. "I didn't even know murder happened in Paducah."

Yikes! Why wouldn't murder happen here? The 25,000 Paducahans are people, and murder is never outside the realm of possibility when one person interacts with another.

I wanted to shout at Vivian: "Of course murder happens here, you moron!"

Her worldview was as haphazard as her chain piecing.

I knew I was in a foul mood, but that Thursday's edition of the *Chronicle* was especially bad. It had a story across the top of the front page about how to de-flea cats. The down-page left story declared the city's stretch of April weather to be within half a degree of last year's April temperatures (that day's editorial argued that this temperature consistency debunked the Chinese communistic conspiracy known as climate change). The down-page right story instructed readers how to mow their lawns (in case they'd forgotten since last week), and the last was an Associated Press story about the infestation of Asian carp that had inundated local waters.

The art on the page consisted of a stand-alone photo of a collie walking along a bank of the Ohio River with its owner in tow and a second photo down-page of an Asian carp.

As news days in Paducah go, that one was fairly strong.

Which is why I *knew* that a force greater than incompetence must have kept a story about the murder of a *Comical* reporter out of the paper.

Janet said, "This murder wasn't just one meth addict killing another. Matt Ackerman was killed because he was such a lousy reporter."

"My God!" Vivian said as I choked on my blueberry muffin.

It's one thing to gossip, as most of us do, but the reporter in me was closer to horrified than offended by Janet making stuff up. With scientifically proven facts being called fake news and journalists being killed around the world because they dare to speak truth to power, I knew I had to stop the nonsense spewing from their mouths.

I stood up so I was in view. They both looked at me, then made startled faces as if they'd seen Elvis kissing Jimmy Hoffa.

"Hadley!" Janet said.

I was about to say, "Matt was a solid cops and courts reporter, and it's not polite to talk ill of the newly murdered." But before I said anything, they simultaneously remembered they'd both left irons on. They raced toward the door, although casual observers would've seen two ladies of a certain age creaking toward the exit.

I sat down, then did what I too frequently did: I thought.

Yes, thinking had helped me make a living, and, in general, thinking is better than *not* thinking. But I once thought myself out of existence and barely found my way back to reality. If Trapunto hadn't needed to be walked, I might not have returned.

As I wondered why Bill Lang, the *Chronicle's* cops and courts reporter, or another reporter, hadn't written about Matt's murder, I arrived at no conclusions. My phone had rung a handful of times since I'd called Paducah Police Department the day before, but I had neither answered it nor bothered to see who'd called. Somewhere along my walk, I'd turned the ringer off. I looked at the missed calls and saw that Dakota had called four times, Donna once, Bill Lang once, and Greg Wurt, my boss, once. But I didn't listen to the messages.

I left that morning's *Chronicle* on the table, intending to head home to double-check that Dakota had tended to Trapunto. When I reached the sidewalk, I saw Freddie DiSalvo walking toward me. He wore immaculate jeans and a maroon Harvard Law sweatshirt. At fifty-five, he was six-feet tall and very good looking, with short brown hair, brown eyes, and a good build for a man his age.

Freddie was Dakota's ex-boyfriend. Matt and I were excited when they started dating about three years before because we'd never seen Dakota so enthusiastic. She was a world-beater in many ways—a successful lawyer, smart as could be, kind, generous, and gorgeous—but she didn't have the Midas touch when it came to men. She couldn't find a man in or near Paducah who possessed even half of her positive traits.

Despite the odds, however, and after umpteen bad first dates, she finally told us she was with "the one" after dating Freddie for a while. A few months later, she moved into his house in West Paducah, only to have him decide—about six months later—to close his law practice to write historical fiction about Western Kentucky's Jackson Purchase Region, which includes Paducah.

Freddie had never written anything other than legal briefs, so Dakota was not surprised when the opening chapter of *Mayfield in Moonlight* was as incomprehensible as a penguin in a cornfield. At the end of the year that he'd given himself to complete his first two novels—which were certain to become the beginning of a twelve-volume, bestselling series—Freddie had written twenty-eight pages.

Dakota had been patient and tried to believe in him and his writing odyssey but managed only to make it through Chapter One, the first seventeen pages. "So, what do you think?" Freddie had asked her. She answered: "You can't go wrong with Times New Roman," then went upstairs to pack. She moved out that day.

Outside Kirchhoff's that morning, Freddie saw me, and his face showed sadness and concern. "Oh, Hadley," he said, then gave me a tight hug. In the three years I'd known him, I'd thought he was pretentious and standoffish, but his concern that morning was exactly what I needed.

He let go before I did and said, "I'm so sorry. This is terrible. If there's anything I can do. And I really mean that—anything." I looked him in the eyes, and I was surprised by how genuine his concern seemed to be. Then I looked at his Asics running shoes and was surprised by how new they seemed to be. My breath caught, and then I asked, "New shoes?"

"No, why?"

"They look new."

"No. I take care of my clothes. The key is rotation, especially with shoes."

Matt and I had traveled twice with Dakota and Freddie, and we both thought Freddie was totally full of himself. On paper, Matt and Freddie should have gotten along well: They both loved the outdoors, fished in Noble Lake, ran along the Greenway Trail, took long bike rides, and wrote, but plenty of friction had existed between them. During their bowling league the month before, Matt had come home upset because he and Freddie had gotten into an argument that almost turned into a fight.

"What was it about?" I'd asked.

"The clown again said journalists aren't real writers."

"What did you say?"

"I said, 'If anyone would know who isn't a real writer, Freddie, you would.'"

"Great comeback."

"But it hit too close to home because he puffed up his chest and raised his fists. Bill and Niles stepped between us, but, man, I wanted to pummel that loser."

Matt was not alone in his desire to harm Freddie, or at least to see him harmed. Freddie was more polished than Matt, but he was far more arrogant and pompous. Somehow, he'd managed to elevate graduating from law school to the level of winning the Nobel Peace Prize. He could rub people the wrong way just with his custom suits (he was sure to mention in casual conversation that the one he was wearing was from Saville Row). When people factored in his name-dropping of Harvard Law School into conversations about cookies or woodworking, they at least thought about hitting him. Although, I'll admit, he toned down his better-than-everyone pretentiousness after Dakota dumped him.

That morning, I said to Freddie, "If I can think of how you can help, I'll take you up on your offer. But right now, what I need is sleep or a drink, or maybe five drinks, then sleep."

"Whatever works, I won't judge. Take care of yourself."

"You, too." He hesitated for three seconds, then asked, "So, how's the most perfect one?"

Dakota had moved out about two years before. I didn't feel like helping him tear off the scab because my heart had just been torn out, then had been stomped on. So, I felt insulted, if not offended, by his attempt to get me to denigrate my best friend, soothing his heartache in the process. I refused to play his game, so I said, "Perfect means incapable of being improved, so it can't be modified by 'most.' It's similar to 'unique' in that way. See you around."

I didn't look at him to see his expression, but I hoped it screamed "Bitch!"

I said my final goodbye to Matt as he was slowly lowered into the ground at Oak Grove Cemetery. I then went directly from the reception to the newsroom because Greg Wurt, the editor, had called me two days before to ask if I'd like to be a reporter again, this time covering the A&E beat.

"I know this must be an especially difficult time for you, Hadley," he said after I picked up and we exchanged hellos. "It is for all of us, and we weren't as close to Matt as you were."

I almost said, "Really? Y'all weren't engaged to him?" Instead, I said, "Thank you. It's been difficult, but Maker's Mark is helping me through."

"Um, well, yeah, Hadley, um, you wanna be careful there. You can't drown grief."

I'd drunk exactly three shots of Maker's in the week since Matt died, but I thought Greg's response would be worth hearing—and it did not disappoint.

"Yes, I'll be careful. Thanks for your concern."

That was another little joke but not one he'd appreciate. Greg had not shown a smidgeon of a scintilla of concern for my wellbeing in the more than four years I'd worked for him as a reporter. In fact, he almost acted as though my presence in his newsroom offended him.

I had filed countless quality stories, never missed a deadline, took the assignments the other reporters didn't want, never asked for special treatment, and was respected by the community, yet Greg had never expressed any appreciation, let alone concern. When I finally listened to the messages I'd received while on my long walk, Greg's message said, "Yeah, um, Hadley, um. I've been informed you haven't shown up for work. I know things are difficult right now, but—yeah, so, call me."

Why did Greg treat me worse than he did the other reporters? Why did he joke with them and go out for a beer with them occasionally? What did they have that I didn't?

Hmmm. Let me think. . . .

Here's a hint: something that's rarely as big as advertised, functions only sporadically, could always be cleaner, and has likely been given a dumb name by its possessor.

"This is awkward for me to ask," he said, "but Matt has left us in a bind."

Yeah, what an inconsiderate jerk he was. He left the paper understaffed just because he'd been murdered. The gall!

Greg hadn't asked a question, so I provided no verbal answer, but I'm pretty sure I harrumphed.

"Would you be willing to be a reporter again, replacing Matt on A&E?"

Of course.

"Well, I don't know, Greg. I'm still grieving, and Matt was a great reporter, so it won't be easy to fill his shoes."

Come on, Greg, you can do it.

"You and I both know you've got the chops."

Give me a break, I thought. I have the same chops today as I had when I worked in the newsroom, but you were too busy staring at my chest to acknowledge I'm a damn good reporter.

"Well, I'm still pretty upset about being groped—and then demoted."

"You know I had nothing to do with that, right?"

Of course, you had nothing to do with it, Greg. You would have to do something to have something to do with anything, and the whole staff thought you'd retired years ago but showed up every workday because you didn't fish.

"Oh, I know you didn't, but I'm not exactly thrilled with management, so . . ."

"I'll give you a dollar more per hour than you were making."

"I don't know, Greg."

"I'm sure you're aware how stingy management is with raises, and considering the trouble you caused—"

"*I* caused? My ass jumped into Nick's hand? That's impressive. I should take that act on the road."

"You know what I mean."

"No, I don't. Are you suggesting you can't give me a two-dollar-per-hour raise because I didn't sue the company and put the paper's largest advertiser on the sex-offender registry? And are you suggesting, in a town with an outsized A&E scene that brings in millions in revenue to the city and plenty of ad dollars to the paper that you can't find eighty dollars more per week? But you're asking me to help get you out of a bind by covering an essential beat while grieving the loss of my murdered fiancé?"

"Um, well, I'm not suggesting that. I guess I'm . . . well . . . let me think . . . yeah, I'll figure something out. Okay, Hadley, if I can get you the two-buck raise—"

"Per hour. Two bucks per hour."

"Of course. I'll get you the two-bucks-per-hour raise. When can you start?"

"Monday, after Matt's funeral."

"Deal. See you then."

I was overdressed and probably inappropriately dressed on my first day back. But my all-black ensemble had been mournfully stylish in St. Frances of Sales Catholic Church and had been acceptably somber at the cemetery, as opposed to the outfits of the rest of the staff. They either wore jeans or clothes they appeared to have slept in—the exception being the man at the top of the masthead, Greg Wurt, who, inexplicably, draped a black cape over a black-and-gold Pittsburgh Pirates jersey.

In truth, I half understood what Greg was doing: He was paying tribute to the city in which Matt was born. Predictably, Greg got his facts wrong—not a good trait in a donut maker, but an especially bad one in a journalist. Matt came from South Ninth Street in Philadelphia, not from Pittsburgh. What Greg's cape was supposed to represent, I had no idea.

Greg had changed into his wear-a-sweater-every-day look by the time I arrived at the office for my second stint as a reporter. His sweater that day was peach.

I'm five-eight, and Greg looked up at me at a pretty steep angle. I'd guess he was five-three. He overcompensated for his lack of physical height by hitting the gym too often. It's one thing to be in great physical shape, but it's another to build muscle after muscle atop your fire-hydrant frame until your chest becomes so bulky it makes your arms look like those of a T. Rex. I'd wondered if Greg had managed to build muscle inside his skull, crowding out the gray matter.

But he had great hair. Blond, very long, and straight. On another man, I would probably have liked it, but every time I looked at Greg, with that hair hanging down over his short, squat body, I thought of a Troll Doll. I wanted to pull a brush through it to see if I could make it stand straight up.

At the funeral that morning, the other members of the staff, all males, had hugged me, so they just nodded or said "hey" when I entered the office.

Despite having just officially said goodbye to Matt, I felt a surge of excitement as I once again walked through the door that the newspaper's staff used in daylight, as opposed to heading to the back of the building, standing at the loading dock, and waiting for the print run to finish so I could begin the tedious process of preparing papers for delivery, all at an hour that should be illegal in civilized society.

Being a reporter had been how I'd defined myself, so I was looking forward to my first assignment, even though working a forty-hour week would cut into my quilting time. In effect, I'd been paid by the *Chronicle* to quilt for six hours a day since I'd been demoted. I almost always gave my quilts away. If I could afford to spend the insane amounts of money I did on quilting supplies, then I could certainly give my finished quilts to people who couldn't afford housing, electricity, or food—and could benefit from some warmth.

Despite the satisfaction I felt walking into the newsroom, I was put-off by Dan Eidie, the city reporter, sitting at what had been my desk sixteen months before. And it felt weird to be assigned to Matt's desk, which was as he'd left it: strewn with long, thin reporter's notebooks, scraps of paper, press releases, pens, two recorders, and souvenirs, including a mini-Philadelphia-Phillies pennant.

Weirder still, the picture of the two of us hugging each other at the end of one of Lake Barkley's piers—the picture that a stranger had taken the morning after Matt had proposed to me—sat to the left of his computer monitor. Why was the picture still there? Why hadn't he thrown it away or at least moved it from his desk after he'd broken up with me?

Matt, why would you dump me but keep the picture of us on your desk?

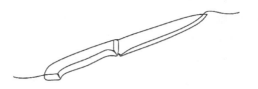

Chapter 6

Bleeding

Although the reporters at the *Chronicle* were technically general-assignment reporters, they each had specific beats. Mine had been the education beat before Nick Stoddard grabbed me.

Because the paper had to hire a reporter to fill the education beat after I moved to the loading dock, I didn't know one of the five reporters in the newsroom that afternoon. It seemed he should've been sitting at my old desk, instead of Dan Eidie, because the new guy had taken over my old beat. But I never even pretended to understand why the company made the decisions it did.

"Hello, I'm Hadley Carroll," I said, reaching to shake the hand of the fifty-ish, bald, muscular man with a reddish beard whom I had seen at Matt's funeral but had not met. He wore the uniform of most male reporters: an un-ironed, untucked dress shirt—in his case, yellow that day—jeans, and sneakers. His were canvas Jack Purcells.

He stopped typing, stood, looked me in the eyes, shook my hand, and said, "Brian Cairns. Nice to meet you. Everyone I've met on this beat has had nice things to say about you. You're a tough act to follow."

"Nice of you to say, but I've read your stuff. It's great. You're covering the beat better than I used to. Finger painting and I never got along."

He laughed, then changed his expression quickly. "I'm sorry for your loss, Hadley. I didn't know Matt long, but I liked him, and I know he loved you. And he was a solid reporter."

"Yes, he was. Thank you. Well, I just wanted to introduce myself. Now I have to go learn a new beat."

"I'm sure you'll be fine. Nice to meet you."

I returned to my new desk, then wondered what I should do with Matt's supplies. I decided to stuff most of them into the big bottom drawer on the left side of the desk. Maybe I'd wade through them later to pick up tips on the beat, even though I knew most of the people I'd be dealing with because Matt talked about them and had introduced me to them at the various art openings, plays, and concerts we'd attended together.

What to do with the photo of us? In the house I rented, I had the same photo in a different frame (meaning a pretty one). Should I keep our photo on the desk? Obviously, Matt had wanted it there. But could I have it within view hour after hour, day after day? Would I go crazy? Or crazier? How would I eventually move on if I saw Matt staring back at me every time I sat at my desk?

Was I being inappropriate and disrespectful by even considering how to move on? I'm not saying I wanted to, and I'm not saying I knew how to, but I was pretty sure I was supposed to move on someday—unless I wanted to become Miss Havisham.

For the time being, I decided to keep the picture on the desk. I adjusted its location, pushing it a little farther left so I could set my coffee tumbler within easy reach. A voice behind me said, "Miss Carroll."

I turned to see Officer Williams and Officer Kramer standing very close to me and my chair.

"Me and Officer Kramer want a word with you."

"Sure. Let's go to the interview room. And it's Ms. Carroll."

I stood, grabbed my clutch and some supplies, and then they followed me down the hall into the small room the reporters used to conduct phone interviews without being subjected to the conversations, ringing phones, and squawks of the police scanner that normally filled the newsroom.

Officer Williams, whom I last saw flipping me off, sat next to me in the chair by the window. His right knee was only two inches from my left one.

Officer Kramer stood by the closed door, blocking it.

"You didn't tell us Ackerman was your fiancé," Williams said.

"Well, the funeral was about as tolerable as funerals usually are," I said. "Thanks for asking."

"I asked you a question," Williams said in an angry tone.

"No, you didn't."

"Giving us attitude is the wrong approach, Miss Carroll. You're in serious trouble." I looked at Kramer, shrugged, and said nothing.

"We'll arrest you if you want," Williams said.

"What I want is for you to stop playing bad cop–mute cop, and instead try to conduct something resembling an interview."

No response.

"If you had evidence that would make a charge or charges stick," I said, "you'd arrest me. Because you don't, you came in here and tried to bully me by expecting me to answer a declarative statement. I won't be bullied the way you bullied Matt, and probably many others."

I admit that I'd had better days, so Miss Manners wouldn't have given me a passing grade. But I'd figuratively lost the love of my life only twelve days before, had permanently lost him five days ago, and, three hours before, had watched him disappear forever into the ground.

After the funeral, I'd sulked through Matt's sparsely attended wake at Donna's house, during which I was almost sure I'd lost all faith in humanity. I'd barely raised an eyebrow when three men, within a span of fifteen minutes, couldn't possibly scoot past Dakota in Donna's small kitchen without putting a hand on her hip. Normally, I would have put them in their place, but I kept silent. That's how not-myself I was.

I thought the officers should have acknowledged my loss or offered me condolences, however perfunctory.

Instead, I got "You didn't tell us Ackerman was your fiancé."

"To answer your *statement*—I didn't divulge that information because you didn't ask me to do so. I also didn't tell you I make amazing peanut-butter cookies."

"How do you know we don't have evidence?" Williams asked.

"First, as I've said, if you had evidence, you'd already have arrested me. Second, there is no evidence—at least none that has anything to do with me because I had nothing to do with Matt's murder. You, on the other hand, I'm not so sure about, not with your short fuse and history with Matt."

Williams jumped to his feet, bumping my knee hard with his knee as he did. I watched his face turn red. "We know Ackerman dumped you. That's motive," he said.

"I also had means and opportunity. This case is practically solved."

I'd thought his face had been red a few seconds before, but I'd been wrong. He started to reach for the handcuffs on his belt but stopped.

"Were you expecting a confession?" I asked.

Williams didn't remove his handcuffs, but I thought his face was about to catch fire.

"Officer Williams, you realize reporters know how to do research, right? Any ink-stained-wretch can find out which cops have a reputation for being overly aggressive, for arresting people without probable cause. Those officers could've had humiliating disciplinary actions taken against them.

"These rogue officers cost their departments a lot of money because the Constitution hasn't yet been abolished. When the complainants sue, they are enriched, and the coffers of the cities that employ such angry officers are depleted."

The veins in his neck couldn't have been far from bursting. His eyes changed from anger to rage as if I'd flipped a switch. He grabbed me.

I left the room in cuffs, with two broken bones in my cheek, a bruised jaw, and sore ribs.

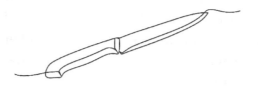

Chapter 7
Tension

Obviously, my first day back in the *Chronicle* newsroom was more eventful and shorter than I'd anticipated. After the X-rays had been taken and analyzed, and after a nurse practitioner had tended to my wounds, my head was throbbing, and I was sore even where I hadn't been hit. I must've tensed every muscle during the beating.

When I got home and looked in the mirror, I realized I would need a team of Sephora consultants if I hoped to cover the bruises. Because I didn't know any Sephora consultants, and I couldn't afford a team of them even if I did, I decided to leave my mulberry-and-plum souvenir alone. I changed into sweats and gave Trapunto a loving jostle, a quick walk, and a kiss on the head. I poured myself a glass of Bacchus Blush from Equus Run Vineyards in Midway, Kentucky, then stared at the ceiling between sips. Okay, gulps.

I tried to think about nothing, but the harder I tried to negate the existence of everything, the more my life kept intruding into my non-thoughts. Finishing one bottle, then opening another didn't help the process, but my head hurt less—physically.

Psychologically, however, my pain got progressively worse with each glass. I went from being dumped by my fiancé to burying the love of my life to being beaten by an officer of the law to contemplating whether going on was worth the pain. My stomach was in knots, my skin was clammy, and I felt myself slipping into darkness. I had to do something, or I risked falling into an abyss from which I might never escape. But what should I do?

I called Dakota to let her know what was going on. After expressing horror, she consoled me in at least half a dozen ways, and then insisted she come over. I thanked her for her sympathetic words and for her friendship, but I insisted she leave me to my thoughts and what was left of my wine.

Although you may not consider me to be a slave to the daily grind—based on my less-than-vigorous work ethic as a newspaper delivery technician—I have been accused of being a workaholic, of obsessing over assignments, and of making bulldogs seem like kittens.

So, I did what I have done since high school: I found a story that needed telling, then did whatever I needed to do so I could tell it accurately and well.

That process sometimes started with an editor assigning a story to me, which is the least intriguing genesis a story can have. Occasionally, I overheard a snippet spoken by someone in my presence that gestated into a tale worth telling. And sometimes I just had an itch, then scratched it.

But, every so often, a glaring hole in the space-time continuum insinuated itself into my consciousness, and I had no choice but to jump into the vacuum, carrying a pen, a backup pen, a notebook, a recorder, and a backup recorder. It didn't matter which shoes I was wearing. It didn't matter if I was bloated or sleep deprived or hungry or depressed. Only the story mattered.

To most good reporters, and to all of the great ones, that single-mindedness of focus is their predominant trait. Some of us are well educated; some of us are great researchers; and some of us have exceptional people skills. Very few of us are blessed with all of these traits and abilities. But unless they are total hacks—and there are thousands of those—reporters worth their Society of Professional Journalists memberships know that the story comes first, second, 308th, and last.

But the story about Matt's murder hadn't run in the *Chronicle*.

I'd scoured its pages day after day, yet even the edition that came out the morning of Matt's funeral, which was attended by most of the staff, included no mention of Matt Ackerman having been murdered, then having been thrown into the Ohio (the coroner definitively concluded Matt had been dead when his body hit the water). Donna had written and submitted his obituary, and it had run, but no news story about his death had seen print.

Journalists know the words "who, what, where, when, why and how" as the five Ws and H. We learned in our first day of journalism class to answer each of the questions these words signify while writing our stories. Ideally, reporters will include the information generated by these six questioning words in their opening paragraphs, known as leads (as in "to lead"—not the heavy metal), sometimes spelled ledes.

So, with my head both throbbing and foggy, I reached for a pen and a notebook to do what I hadn't done since my first day of journalism class in high school: I wrote out each of the five Ws and H, then wrote the corresponding facts next to them, separated by an em-dash.

```
Who (victim)—Matt Ackerman
Who (murderer)—???
What (event)—Murder
What (weapon)—?
Where—On the dock? On the ramp? In a boat on
the Ohio? On a bridge over the Ohio? Nowhere
near the Ohio but transported there?
When—I found him a little after 6 a.m. on
Wednesday, April 9, so he was obviously killed
prior to that. The coroner determined Matt had
probably been in the water for two hours, give
or take two hours. That vague conclusion meant:
Maybe 2 a.m.? 4 a.m.?
Why—No idea
How—Blunt-force trauma to the back of the right
side of his head
```

I frequently do my best thinking while I'm quilting. We are "in the moment" while we're quilting. Even though concentration, attention-to-detail, precision, and accuracy are essential if we're going to create a quilt worth our time and effort, sometimes eureka moments regarding unrelated subjects can pop into our heads while our attention is elsewhere.

I've had many such eureka moments. Lyrics to a song will write themselves in my head, and sometimes those lyrics are accompanied by melodies. One time, while I was mindlessly affixing hot-pink yo-yos to small quilts I would give to girls at the Starfish Orphan Ministry, I remembered where I'd hidden one of Matt's Christmas presents (a baseball card signed by former Phillies third baseman and power hitting Hall of Famer Mike Schmidt, encased in Lucite). I'd hidden it between my mattress and box spring but, when it was time to wrap it, nothing. A total blank. But the yo-yos eventually came to my rescue. I gave him the present for his birthday on January 13. He laughed hard when I told him about my brain spasm.

So, I figured I'd enter my sanctum sanctorum—The Stash Hash, as I called my quilting room—to calm myself and maybe to coax an answer or two from my noggin.

A pastel-dappled, piecework quilt displaying the words *The Stash Hash* hung on the right wall, and the left side of the room looked like what would happen if the Leaning Tower of Pisa mated with Mount Vesuvius.

I yanked a bolt of Riley Blake calico floral print in mint from the huge fabric Jenga pile, then jumped back, in case it erupted. Nothing. Mishap averted.

The cocktail of anticipation, excitement, and occasional giddiness I usually felt when I unrolled a bolt of fabric and organized my workspace wasn't there. Trapunto had followed me in as soon as I entered. He almost always fell asleep at my feet. He found the sewing machine and the other sounds of me being productive soothing. Or he was bored by quilting. I was never sure which.

I thought I'd bang out a hand-quilted pillow cover. The lime print clashed aggressively with the décor in my house, if I can accurately call furniture purchased at Rural King and garage sales décor. Just because I had no need for my ninety-seventh quilted pillow, didn't mean I shouldn't have purchased the fabric. As recent events had proven, life throws a lot of curveballs, so who knew when my home might undergo a presto-chango style transformation that resulted in a tropical color scheme with a hint of garnish?

After I made sure I had the proper batting and backing (as if I didn't have enough to cover the Great Wall of China), I spent nearly four minutes trying to thread the needle.

I gave up, then went to sleep.

Or tried to.

My head was throbbing, so I took two ibuprofen tablets, read for half an hour, then tried again. But just as I started to doze off, my cell rang.

I fumbled for the phone and said, "Hello?"

Dakota said, "They arrested Nick Stoddard."

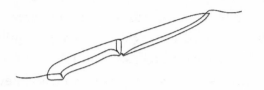

Chapter 8
Bearding

"Arrested him for being a scumbag?" I asked.

"The world would be a better place if the penal code included that," Dakota said.

She had majored in history at the University of Tennessee before attending the University of Kentucky College of Law. When she graduated from UK, she accepted a job offer from Paducah–McCracken County Habitat for Humanity, instead of the far more lucrative corporate jobs available to her. Her parents were insanely rich and were very generous, so Dakota could afford to turn down better-paying offers. She got along well with her parents, who were still together, and with her younger sister, Cathy, who still seemed to be, at thirty-eight, finding herself. Dakota regularly did pro bono work and volunteered at various nonprofits around town.

"Did he molest someone?" I asked.

"Probably, but that's not among the charges. Financial crimes, for starters. Tax evasion and embezzlement are most likely. Because he's a Stoddard, he was out on bail twelve seconds after he was booked."

"How'd you hear? Suzanne?"

"Yes. She lets me know the juicy stuff. As a friend, of course, not as the DA."

"Of course. What do you mean by 'for starters?'"

"She said, 'We're looking into something bigger, potentially, but we both know I shouldn't have told you this much.' I reminded her that she'd only told me what was a matter of public record, and Bill will get it in the paper—not tomorrow, but the day after, right?"

"Probably. Any other paper in the country would, of course, post it online immediately, but the *Chronicle*'s technology, philosophy, and editorial stance are decades behind."

"Before Brown v. Board of Education, I'm guessing."

"Of course. How am I supposed to feel—happy that maybe a Stoddard will get what he deserves, or sad because there's no way he will?"

"I certainly wouldn't bet he'll be convicted. In New York, maybe, but not in McCracken. I can't tell you how you should feel, but I feel a tiny bit of pride in the legal system, specifically in Suzanne, for having the guts to bring charges against him. That family has gotten away with so much for so long, and I'm sure she knows she'll almost certainly lose. So, I truly respect her for being willing to absorb a loss just to make a point, to show the county that everyone can be held accountable."

"But that message only works if he's convicted. If he beats it, the message is that some people are above the law. Officer Williams, for example."

"That rodent. He'll get his. I'll help you. In fact, I've already started. How do you feel?"

"Like last week's gumbo run over by an F-150. I really need sleep, but the ibuprofen isn't enough, and I don't want to take the Oxy she prescribed, especially after drinking."

"Oh, sweety. I'm so sorry. Try to find a position that's okay, maybe sitting up."

"As I usually do, I'll give it my all."

"Love you. Goodnight."

"Love you, too. And thanks for starting work on the Williams stuff."

"My pleasure. You and Matt deserve to take him down."

I called Bill and told him about Stoddard's arrest.

"You go, Suzanne Bigelow," he said. "Good for her. She probably just committed career suicide, but maybe she wants to open a bakery or something."

"If she did, that family would probably firebomb it."

"I wouldn't bet against it. That's good news, but I'm frustrated, Hadley. I've been in this business a long time, as you have. We've had our share of . . . let's say, oddities in the newsrooms we've worked in. Horrible bosses, corrupt publishers who burn down the firewall between editorial and advertising—you name it."

"I'm with you, but you forgot sexual harassment."

"Right, in every newsroom. But what has happened here takes the cake. I'm good at what I do—"

"You're the best cops reporter I've worked with, and one of the three best I've read, including in the *New York Times*."

"Thanks, but I wasn't fishing, just giving background. I'm sure you've wondered why Matt's murder hasn't run."

"Of course."

"Early that Wednesday, I heard it on the scanner. I keep it on low at home, even though Justine hates it. I got dressed and raced to the scene. I saw you on the dock talking with cops, then sitting with Dakota. How'd she get down there?"

"She's better looking than you are."

"True, but I don't feel short-changed. Only about four people on Earth are better looking than she is."

"I know, right?"

"So, twice I got caught sneaking under the tape. Twice I was threatened with arrest. I gave serious thought to walking upstream, then swimming down so I could access the scene. I got as far as starting to take off my shirt, then decided I'd get arrested, get shot, or catch dysentery, so I headed back to the top of the ramp and waited for things to play out. By that time, I'd called Adam and Greg because we obviously needed solid photos, and Greg, the stuffed sweater, should at least be kept in the loop, however pointlessly."

"Maybe build a package on A1."

"Right. A sidebar or two. Maybe a graphic about murders in McCracken. I mean, this was huge news. This wasn't another tweaker or a lovers' quarrel that turned brutal. Matt was a professional, a local—and one of our own, murdered brutally. We could double the circ the next day and still sell out."

I didn't say anything.

"Sorry, Hadley. I didn't mean to reduce Matt to an opportunity."

"That's okay. I understand. I think that's the only way cops reporters can do their jobs. I have no idea how you get subjected to the worst of humanity nearly every day but still remain positive."

"Without Justine, I wouldn't."

I stayed silent.

"Sorry, again. Not a great time to bring up relationships. So, Adam showed up on scene quickly, then climbed atop the WKYC news truck with his longest lens to get an overview shot. When he was done, he asked me, 'Anything?' but the cops wouldn't confirm the vic's identity, confirm it was Matt. Word was circulating it was Matt, because you were down on the dock being questioned, so who else would it be? Anyone who knew you, knew the two of you were together. I was getting frustrated, and Adam was wondering if he knew anyone who had a boat so he could get a shot from the water. He was about to call a buddy of his when my cell rang. It was Greg, and he told me to head to the office. I said, 'What are you talking about? This will probably be the biggest story of the year.' With anger in his voice, or what passes for anger in a zombie, he said, 'If you want your job, you'll head to the office.'"

"That's unbelievable."

"For a second, I wondered what the date was, but it was the ninth of April, not the first. I stood there, watching from a distance as they lifted the body onto the dock. At that point, we didn't know it was Matt for sure. Adam was taking pictures, but they were all going to be junk from that distance and at that angle. Greg and I were going back and forth. Adam mouthed, 'What's going on?' and I shook my head. The coroner's van pulled up. A crowd had gathered. The coroner was about to remove the vic . . . Matt . . . but Greg's telling me I have to leave without getting much more than a blurb, maybe not even that because I'd confirmed nothing."

"Yeah, a story that's no longer than its headline: Body found in Ohio River."

"Can't imagine how the paper got its *Comical* nickname, can you?"

"What happened at the office?"

"I was fuming when I entered Greg's crypt. 'What the hell's going on?' I asked. He actually looked surprised by my anger. 'What's with the attitude, Bill? I'm the editor and your boss, and I'm asking you not to pursue that story,' he said. 'Asking me? You didn't ask me anything, you hack,' I said."

"Wow, you really were mad."

"Of course. You're on A&E, and Taylor Swift shows up unannounced and gives a free concert on the Carson Center lawn, but our so-called editor tells you not to cover it and to rewrite a press release about a Tilghman fundraiser instead. How do you feel?"

"Upset, of course, but it would still only be a concert. Your stakes are far higher."

"Exactly. So, I asked him again why he was giving me that directive. And, I swear, I'm quoting him verbatim: 'Because I said so.'"

"That must have hit you right in your Pulitzer."

"Please don't remind me of the idiotic decisions I've made. How I ever left the *Post-Gazette*—"

"You left it for Justine. For love, remember?"

"Yeah, there's that. Please don't mention my momentary lapse to her."

"Of course not. So, you just left it like that? You're the cops reporter, and you're supposed to be cool with getting scooped by WKYC and leaving the murder of a well-known local out of the paper?"

"I've confronted Greg at least once a day since, demanding a reason. Nothing. Twice, he's threatened to fire me again."

"Thoughts? Guesses? Conspiracy theories?"

"Best guess is the kibosh came down from on high—Susan Loudon in advertising, a heavy-hitting advertiser like the Stoddards. Or maybe Colapinto himself. Afraid to put a damper on QuiltWeek."

"I'd bet Colapinto because even a spineless editor can usually find a way to finagle a deal with advertising or to appease an advertiser. But it takes an actual backbone to overrule a publisher. And despite all of Greg's muscles, I wouldn't bet he has a spine."

Ed Colapinto, publisher of the *Chronicle*, created the moon, then hung it. He invented publishing, then perfected it, according to him. If he'd wanted to, he could've created a perpetual-motion machine. His every sentence, whether spoken or written, was poetry, filled either with keen insights into the nature of human existence or humor that would cause the Statue of Liberty to double-over in laughter.

Of course, Ed's ability to achieve his mind-blowing accomplishments was limited by his countless mirror sessions. Compared to Ed, Narcissus was self-loathing. Colapinto was the only man I've known who carried a compact.

I'll admit, he *was* objectively good looking, if good looks can be defined as a combination of a Ken doll and a G.I. Joe, but with less personality and more rouge.

Ed made his fortune as a model. After paying his dues by posing in underwear for grainy newspaper ads, he landed a gig as the primary model for Men's Wearhouse, then parlayed that into a decade-long stint as the principal model—both in print and in commercials—for Polo.

He tried to land roles in sit-coms and movies, but those jobs required him to say words other than "I, me, mine," so he failed to get speaking parts.

But he bounced back impressively by bombarding television sets around the globe with images of him painting a fence, riding a bike, and tending to a tomato plant while waiting for his boner pills to kick in.

Colapinto had great financial advisers who turned his wealth into a fortune. When he saw the opportunity to buy into the *Chronicle* and return to Western Kentucky (he grew up in Murray, where his sickly parents still lived), he bought a majority stake in the company and a ghastly faux castle in West Paducah, then pretended he possessed skills other than smiling. He hired Greg Wurt, ensuring the paper would descend far below mediocrity, then proceeded to hit on anyone who had a vagina.

Most of his sexual conquests came from the Barbie mold—disproportionately buxom and partial to silicone, Botox, and peroxide. But his preference for shallow plasticity (or is it, plastic shallowness?) didn't prevent him from hitting on women with human features, characteristics, and foibles.

In fact, at the Christmas party during which Nick Stoddard had destroyed the Christmas tree, Ed Colapinto had drunkenly suggested that Dakota and I play naked Twister with him, which made me feel less guilty about threatening to sue the paper when Ed and his lawyers forced me out as a reporter.

Despite Greg Wurt's claim to have had nothing to do with my demotion, he ran the newsroom—or at least the plaque on his door said he was the editor—so I thought he had probably been complicit in that decision.

But after Bill told me how Greg had rolled over and played dead in regard to the story about Matt's murder, I was pretty sure Ed Colapinto told Greg which color sweater to wear each day.

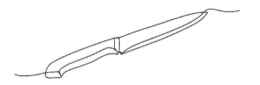

Chapter 9

Betweens

After finally getting a few hours of sleep (but having a nightmare about being unable to grab Matt's hand, then helplessly watching him slip into darkness), I felt somewhat better about the world and myself. Of course, I'd made no progress in regard to anything, and my face still looked as though Muhammad Ali had done speed-bag work on it.

Even though it was the middle of the night, I took Trapunto for a walk. Then I took a bath, during which I actually succeeded in thinking about nothing . . . for thirty-three seconds. Baby steps. Afterward, because I had no choice, I took stock of what I knew about Matt's murder—and what I thought I'd known about his life.

Despite Matt's affectations—he called them "celebrations of life," and that name was somewhat accurate—he was kind and funny and smart and generous and gentle and sexy, but he displayed these traits almost exclusively around me, only when we were alone.

In public, he was one big defense mechanism, so he rubbed a lot of people the wrong way. I'd initially approached him in the newsroom because I felt sorry for him and was upset by the sarcastic comments that two of the reporters made about him when he was out of earshot.

The other reason why I'd approached him was his body. He took care of himself. He did one hundred pushups and one hundred sit-ups every morning, and we eventually hit Planet Fitness together four days a week.

I'm pretty sure my childhood and my twisted psychological need to fix people led me to try to slip behind Matt's defenses. Whatever the causes, I succeeded. Our individual flaws were significant, but they complemented each other or canceled each other out. So, we were—at least in private—compatible.

Matt was a very good journalist, or at least he had been before he was pushed into the A&E beat when Bill Lang, along with his Pulitzer, signed on to fill the cops and courts beat.

Matt was a solid researcher, analyzed data well, and was relentless when pursuing a story. But these traits were not necessary to write preview stories about upcoming concerts in the Carson Center or to craft reviews of the community-theater productions at the Market House Theatre. Matt was out of his element in the A&E beat, so he didn't like Bill on principle and held a grudge against Greg for having hired Bill—and for all of the other reasons the rest of us disliked Greg.

I'd just learned, however, that Greg was not just a sleepwalker, but he also appeared to be a patsy, a figurehead. Ed Colapinto, therefore, must've hired Bill, probably for the prestige of having a Pulitzer Prize–winner on staff.

Matt had been a very good cops reporter, but Bill was much better. Matt should've taken over the city beat, where he would've thrived, despite the defenses he put up in public. Matt looked at A&E strictly as dessert.

Unfortunately, artistic discernment was missing from Matt's repertoire. Every kid finger-paints and quickly learns that red and green combine to make caca brown, right? Not Matt, evidently. Matt seemed unable to distinguish great art from grade-school crafts, so the story he wrote about Missy Wendland, a local quilter, that appeared in the Thursday edition the day after he was killed praised Missy's quilting profusely. Yet, Missy Wendland was a strong contender to be the world's worst quilter. She was as inept as a tone-deaf soprano, as unartistic as a colorblind painter, and as ineffectual as a gigolo with erectile dysfunction. Her quilts looked like they'd been crafted in the dark by a drunk elephant—I mean, gouge-your-eyes-out bad. They were the quilting equivalent of the *Hindenburg* crashing into the sinking *Titanic* while Godzilla sings "You Light Up My Life" on deck.

I'd seen Missy's quilts at various shows around town, and they were as disconcerting as my life had been for nearly the last two weeks. During that time, I took no pleasure in quilting, in my day-to-day existence, or even in words, which hadn't been as meaningful as they used to be.

"Hads, will you marry me?" Matt had asked in our cottage at Lake Barkley on New Year's Day.

"Absolutely." He didn't present a ring to me, but I understood his financial constraints, and maybe we'd get matching wedding rings when the time came.

On April 2, however, on my front porch after he'd spent the night, he looked down at my bare feet, tried to look up, but couldn't make eye contact. I didn't know what to make of his weird expression, but I knew I'd never seen it in the five years we'd been together. He said, "We're done, Hadley. The engagement's off."

If I hadn't noticed how difficult saying those words had been for him, I would've laughed because nothing about the previous night had been strained or awkward. We had laughed especially hard. He taught me the chord progressions for "Hotel California" on my guitar, and he said he loved the short story I'd just completed, "Sierra de Juarez," after I read it to him aloud. As usual, we fell asleep in each other's arms.

However, that morning on the porch, I asked, "What?"

He stood there for two seconds without responding, then started to turn to walk away. I put my hand on his shoulder to stop him.

"Wait, Matt. You owe me more than that. A lot more." I should've been angry, but I felt a sadness in the pit of my stomach that made me want to disappear.

"Hads, I can't talk about it."

"You have to, Matt. You can't just say, 'The engagement's off,' then head to work."

He was wearing the Oxford shirt with vertical royal blue and white stripes, the caramel belt, and the burgundy Bass penny loafers I'd purchased for him over the years. He had bought himself the jeans at Rural King.

"I'm not saying you don't deserve more, Hads. Of course, you do. I'm saying I'm breaking off our engagement."

"But I love you, Matt. You know I do. More than I've loved anyone, much more . . . not even close."

"And I love you, Hadley."

"Wait. Words are meaningless now? French fries are healthy, I'm the Queen of Siam, and you love me? Great. I can't believe this."

He hesitated for a few seconds, then turned and walked away. I collapsed to the ground and cried on my porch. The pink pajamas with old-fashioned, black typewriters on them that Matt had given to me caught my tears.

So, in the middle of the night a few hours before I had to show up at work with half my face crushed, I thought I should read Matt's story about Missy Wendland. I'd opened to the page the day after he died, read the first sentence, reread his byline, then couldn't read the story, so I'd closed the paper.

I thought if I read the story now, I might find a relevant fact or a tangent that could help me understand the last twelve days.

I logged into the *Chronicle*'s archive on my MacBook, clicked on April 10, then digitally flipped the pages until I found the A&E section. Matt's weekly story about the arts ran on Thursdays under the title: *HeART of Paducah.*

Awful, right? Yeah, well, it wasn't my paper, but I'd just inherited that stellar contribution to American letters. My byline would appear under that HeART of Paducah banner every week.

However, that unfortunate reality was mitigated somewhat by the fact I could distinguish a Keats poem from one by Shelly and a Monet from a Manet. I knew that Chopin wrote great sonatas, Strauss waltzes, and Sousa marches.

More relevant to the Quilt City readers of the *Chronicle*, I knew the difference between a fat quarter and a jelly roll, between stab stitching and a top stitch, and, of course, between appliqué and patchwork, a distinction Matt could not make without doing research.

But I tried to read the first sentence of Matt's story, couldn't keep my eyes open, fell asleep with my head on the laptop, and then dreamed of falling, endlessly.

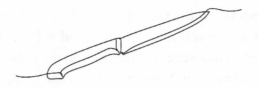

Chapter 10
Wrong Side

I returned to the office, sat at my desk, then read Matt's story about Missy.

Embarrassing other quilters
By Matt Ackerman

Entering into Missy Wendland's creative lair, festooned as it is with numerous fabrics, threads and quilting implements, is like being transported not to another dimension but to a veritable land of enchantment, where colors dance, textures sing and dreams are created out of whole cloth.

Located within mere blocks of the National Quilt Museum, Paducah's claim to worldwide fame, Missy Wendland's workplace/studio/dream factory smells vaguely of peppermint tea with a waft of hope on a Monday afternoon. Wendland, a woman of a certain age who politely demurred when asked by a reporter to provide her literal one, sat at her sewing table—which she calls "My Husband"—carefully crafting one of her masterful quilts.

What Jackson Pollack was to painting, Wendland is to quilting. She has smashed traditional conventions, which she calls "limitations," such as straight lines, uniform seams and realistic representations of recognizable objects. By doing so, her resulting pieces of art transcend the genre, rendering traditionalists such as Hollis

Chatelain, Pat Holly and Kris Vierra obsolete,
mere acolytes carrying the hem of her garment
and playing catch-up.

For example, whereas other quilters would
likely spend countless hours squaring off
corners, eliminating stray threads and ironing
out wrinkles, Wendland captures the messiness
of life—the deaths and disappointments, the
heartaches and hard times, the loves and
losses—in her roughhewn creations.

The unique beauty of Wendland's quilts is
that their truth lies in the minds of their
beholders. Wendland is neither a heavy-handed
moralist nor a by-the-book literalist, and her
iconoclastic, avant-garde quilts have elevated
her above the ranks of mere quilters to heights
above even Michelangelo and Rembrandt.

Although her work can be life-altering
for those fortunate enough to see it, she
maintains a commoner's touch, the ability to
interact with people who don't have one one-
thousandth of her talent.

Some people might consider her too pleased
with herself, even perhaps arrogant, but those
mere mortals couldn't possibly understand the
burdens of such genius, the pressure to outdo
their last masterpiece with their next one,
then to do it again the next day.

The above time delineation is no
exaggeration. Whereas other quilters may take
weeks, months or even years to carefully create
works that adhere to tradition and to the known,
Wendland can whip out a form-busting, boundary-
destroying, parameter-expanding, perspective-
enhancing quilt in a matter of hours. Watching
her quilt is like watching Steph Curry on a
basketball court—if he could fly.

"Despite what you may think, young man, I
do actually respect my fellow quilters,"
Wendland said, "the way I respect homeless
people and lepers. They are people, too, of
course, each and every one of them one of
God's creatures. They just don't have God's
hands guiding theirs as I do mine.

"You used the word 'transcendent' to
describe the impressive quilt over there,
'Humility, Schmility,' and you could not

have been more accurate. God himself quilted that one. I literally sat at the table, but I don't remember a single thing about the creative process. I simply looked down, and there it was, in all of its transcendent glory. Another word you could have used, and probably should have, is 'divine.'"

Divine, indeed.

Fortunately, fans of creative brilliance who have not been so obviously touched by God can purchase any of Wendland's quilts. Photos of her most rudimentary baby's quilt—an exercise in understated minimalism, featuring a field of white interrupted by a single blue or pink dot (Wendland is a traditionalist where gender is concerned)—can be purchased for $325. Prices increase from there. Wendland's Quilt Wonderland is located at 1004 Jefferson St. Her gallery is open from noon until 2 p.m., Tuesdays through Thursdays; admission is $47.50, plus a $4.75 service charge). Her email address is GodsHandQuilting@gmail.com.

Maybe Matt had a brain tumor. As awful as that was to consider, it could've explained everything.

Of course, nothing could explain how Matt could write an article that horrendous, cloying, and ridiculous, and nothing could explain how Greg Wurt could've let it run, with its inconsistency of tense, its false equivalencies, and its borderline pornographic assessment of Wendland's quilts.

But a brain tumor could explain why Matt left me without explanation, for no damn reason at all, as well as explain his article about Wendland.

Believing the tumor explanation removed the possibility that I'd done something to hurt him so deeply that he felt compelled to leave. Sure, tumors happen, but chalking Matt's recent actions up to a tumor seemed too simplistic.

One upside to reading Matt's story was that I now loved him less.

Yikes, Matt. Why didn't you contact a second source who might've clued you in on how toilet-worthy Wendland's quilts are? I suddenly felt awful about having been engaged to such an incompetent reporter. How had I read his stuff for years and not realized he was as bad as Wendland was?

Shaken, I clicked back to the archive, then read his last five HeART of Paducah articles. All of them were informative and serviceable. They assessed the artists' creations fairly, praised their strengths, acknowledged their weaknesses (in two of the stories, only by omission), and did exactly what they should've done: promote the work of local artists and direct readers to their galleries or to their current or upcoming shows. Despite Matt's glaring lack of knowledge in most artistic realms, he'd done the necessary research that made him appear to be knowledgeable.

So, his Missy Wendland story was an anomaly. But why?

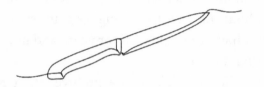

Chapter 11

Paper Piecing

I wanted my busted cheek and me to have an unremarkable day at the office. However, I hadn't been getting much of what I wanted lately, so I shouldn't have been surprised when something remarkable turned up in one of Matt's desk drawers: a potential clue to why he'd been killed.

After downing my tumbler of coffee, then debating whether to drink another one, I banged out a crime brief about an arrest for meth possession, then one about a single-vehicle wreck that resulted in a fatality. All of the reporters, regardless of their beats, rewrote press releases that had been sent to the paper by law enforcement or the city or the numerous non-profit organizations around town. Part of the gig.

After filing those stories, I sat down to write my first HeART of Paducah piece. I was exhausted because recently I'd gotten only about a third of the sleep I usually required (eight hours per). But I'd never missed a deadline, so I wasn't about to miss one that day. And I had to get up to speed on the A&E beat quickly because QuiltWeek was approaching fast, and I would have to write all of the stories in the special issue. About 30,000 quilters would arrive, and, despite the American Quilter's Society publishing the QuiltWeek schedule online, most of the attendees still liked to hold a hardcopy of the schedule in their hands. As a result, that special issue had by far the largest circulation of the year.

But I didn't have the slightest idea which painter, sculptor, potter, musician, singer, actor, writer, comic, quilter, dabbler in mixed-media, or other creative type I would feature for Thursday's HeART of Paducah. I opened the bottom drawer to see if Matt had created a master list of the artists about whom he'd written.

Before resigning myself to having to search week by week through the archives, or trying to decode his computer "filing system," I decided to check the contents of the desk.

The day before, I had shoved five notebooks and the other stuff on Matt's desk into the large drawer on the bottom on the left side. I hadn't really registered that close to forty notebooks and a lot of loose papers and brochures were in the drawer when I swept the other items off the desk. Because it seemed more efficient to sort through the loose sheets before starting to slog through the notebooks, I picked up a small piece of paper. It was a receipt from Kroger for protein powder; the next was a dry-cleaning receipt; the next a crumpled Post-it note that said *D and B?* in Matt's scrawl; the next a receipt for two burgers from the Fresh Country Kitchen in Harrah's Metropolis casino, across the river from Paducah in Illinois; and the next a receipt for an oil change at Jiffy Lube.

Matt had a lot of good qualities, at least when he and I were alone, but he was messier than a confetti factory struck by a tornado. The mish-mash of junk in that drawer—including a half-eaten french fry, a small, red funnel, a guitar capo, and a desiccated chunk of horror that was probably a Pterodactyl's toe—made me wonder again if hording could be congenital. Matt had certainly shared Donna's compulsion to accumulate, mostly junk he found for art projects he intended to create but rarely did. But to me, the junk he collected looked no more like the raw materials for an art project than the scraps of paper in his desk that morning looked relevant to my HeART of Paducah story.

I shoved the junk in the trash, then pulled out what proved to be an Open Records response from N&S Shipping. The eight sheets were liberally redacted, with someone having used a black marker to make words, lines, and one short paragraph illegible. I'd never taken an accounting class, knew nothing about economics, and didn't have a law degree, but I understood enough of what I was looking at to determine that N&S Shipping was owned and operated by Nick Stoddard, one of who-knows-how-many businesses his family owned. He probably derived the name of that one from Nick and Sandy, his wife.

I only occasionally balanced my checkbook, but I was financially literate enough to understand that I was looking at balance sheets. I wasn't financially literate enough, however, to determine what to make of the numbers, but I'm guessing Matt would have known what the numbers meant because he'd requested the documents, and why would someone do that if he didn't know how to interpret whatever they revealed? I only found eight of what should have been ten pages, according to the company's response, but I found Matt's Freedom of Information Act request next, dated March 18.

Dear Open Records Coordinator:

Under the Kentucky Open Records Act, § 61.872 et seq., I am requesting an opportunity to inspect or obtain copies of public records that describe in detail the finances (profit and loss statements) for the three years prior to the date on this request for R&S Shipping, based in Paducah, Kentucky, including but not limited to documentation pertaining to any transactions between R&S Shipping and the City of Paducah, and any grants entered into by the United States Government and R&S Shipping regarding interstate commerce.

Please contact me if you have any questions.

Sincerely,

Matthew Ackerman

The letter concluded with the *Chronicle*'s contact information.

I'd filed many FOIA requests while working for various newspapers in three states, but I'd only requested information from public agencies—government entities in cities, counties, and states, such as courts, public utilities, and school districts. I'd been under the impression that private industries were outside the reach of FOIA requests. As I had been a lot lately, I was wrong again. A Google search taught me that businesses that do a certain percentage of their transactions with government agencies—in Kentucky, at least twenty-five percent—are subject to Open Records requests. Matt obviously knew that, or he learned it before making this request.

I called Dakota, who let me know that my broad-strokes understanding of the redacted response was in the right ballpark. She told me to scan the documents, then email them to her. I sent them, looked at the picture of Matt and me, and then asked out loud, "What were you up to, Matt?"

I spent the next two hours—at the risk of missing the first deadline of my career—going through only the first two of Matt's notebooks. Because reporters generally use one notebook to take notes for many stories, a lot of reporters simply write the date on the cover when they start to use each notebook. Other more fastidious, conscientious, and possibly neurotic reporters (*stop judging!*) write the subjects of the notes contained within each notebook on the cover. If I'd written many shorter stories, my notebooks would have as many as twenty subjects written on the covers. Matt and I handled that aspect of reporting differently, as we did other aspects. For example, if I'd written a story about Missy Wendland, my first sentence would have been the following: Who are you trying to kid, Missy?

I fished out all forty-four notebooks, then arranged them on the large, metal desk in chronological stacks. That took a while, but wading in randomly made no sense. With the stacks arranged, I picked up the notebook with the latest date on it, March 28, then flipped to the last page on which he'd written.

At the top of the page were almost illegible notes about a high school theater production of the musical "Hairspray" put on by students at McCracken County High School.

"It's been, like, really fun rehearsing, and I, like, think the show will be great," said eleventh-grade actress Brandy Kanner, proving the pointlessness of most quotes.

I carefully perused each page, trying to decipher Matt's illegible scrawl while being careful not to miss anything that could help me figure out who had killed Matt. He'd written a date each time he started taking notes for a new story. I always began each interview on the top of a clean page, but Matt had dates written anywhere on the pages, sometimes vertical and sideways. While conducting interviews, I never flipped to the back of a page until I'd filled the entire notebook on the front pages, then worked my way backward. Matt, however, took the jigsaw-puzzle approach to note taking, hiding this snippet of blue sky within that bushel of pansies, so I was frustrated and flummoxed by the time I had completed only the first two notebooks.

I wrote down the tidbits that didn't seem to relate to the notes around them. These were my notes:

- 332 EYW
- Being followed?
- 555 WWE
- Payback time
- Pat DeLott?
- Really, Greg? Does Hadley know?

No, Matt, I didn't know, no matter what you were referring to. I hardly knew anything then, or at least not as much as I thought I had. I thought we'd been solid, in the process of building a happy life together, but you're gone, and I'm stuck sorting through your haystack of notebooks.

If I had only been looking for a needle, I would have been overjoyed, so long as I knew that the needle had to be somewhere in all of that hay. But the notes I'd coaxed from Matt's chicken scratches could have been meaningless, or at least they could have had nothing to do with why he left me and why someone murdered him.

He suspected he was being followed? Yikes. He'd been moody for three or four weeks before he said goodbye, but I thought I'd said something or done something to upset him. He told me at least twice, "No, Hadley, it's not you." So, was he surly and less communicative than usual because he was concerned for his safety, for his mother's, for mine?

Or did he suspect that someone else was being followed?

I liked puzzles and intellectual exercises that stole hours of my time. If I figured them out, great, and if not, at least I tried, having exercised my brain. And I could spend twelve straight hours working on a quilt in perfect peace. So, I lacked neither curiosity nor stamina, and yet the prospect of chasing down these leads—and this list came from only two of the forty-four notebooks in his desk—caused me to want to quit after throwing my hands into the air and asking, "Why, God? Why?"

But I was at work, and I had a job to do other than to solve Matt's murder, so I took three long, deep breaths, meditated for three minutes, then got back to work. Luckily, I found Matt's master list in the middle drawer. Three pages. He'd written fifty-two HeART of Paducah pieces per year and had been on the A&E beat for more than three years. This assignment would be harder than I thought it would be. Even though I'm sure I'd be allowed to write about artists on the list, so long as they were closer to the beginning of the list than to the end, I was guessing the most difficult aspect of this gig would be to find artists, not to write stories.

But I was wrong. Again.

I did a quick search of the iList Paducah site and saw that Candy Cavella, a local artist who had a studio in Lower Town, would be having an opening on Friday. Perfect. I went to her studio to interview her.

Unfortunately, her artwork wasn't amazing, great, good, or mediocre. Or even art.

She created animal figures out of pipe cleaners. Her creations were even less interesting than the previous sentence makes them sound.

But I had a deadline, so I struggled because nearly every sentence seemed like a lie of omission. Eventually, I typed the last line of the story—"The irony is," Candy Cavella said, "I've never smoked a pipe."—then wondered why I hadn't gone to law school.

I filed the story, then walked toward Bill Lang's desk, saying hello to photographer Adam Kerns, city reporter Dan Eidie, and the new education reporter, Brian Cairns, on my way. When I approached Bill, I asked, "What's the latest? Been fired yet?"

"Not yet, but he's wearing a new sweater, and, brace yourself, it isn't a solid color."

"Impossible! Will the world stop spinning?"

"Possibly. He actually stuck his chest out and turned slightly, as if modeling it for me."

"You didn't say anything?"

"Of course not. He's preventing me from doing my job, but he thinks I'm going to admire his sweater? What a moron."

"I have an idea. Tell me if it's insane or great. With me, it's usually either-or."

"Self-awareness is important. What is it?"

"You've been instructed *not* to write about Matt's murder, but I haven't been. I've filed my HeART of Paducah, and I won't fall too far behind on anything else, so why shouldn't I write something? I could probably bang it out."

"First, I admire your guts. Second, how would you get it in the paper? And, third, why won't they fire you if you manage to get it in the paper?"

"I'll answer your second one first. All I have to do is file it late, after our esteemed clothes horse goes home. Jake likes me, or at least doesn't obviously hate me, so he'll just bump AP off the front if he has to."

"That could work."

"To address your third point, yesterday I was beaten in this office by a police officer, who broke bones in my cheek and left numerous bruises."

"You look like wet garbage, by the way."

"Thank you. Your sympathy is touching. When Stoddard grabbed me at the Christmas party, I threatened to sue the company, and that turned out fine."

"You're going after the cops, right?"

"Of course. Dakota's already working on it, and I'll meet with lawyer Mike Weiss soon. Do you think this goofy company is stupid enough to fire me after my second day of work when I was severely beaten here on my first day after no one, including the security guard, came to my aid?"

"It might be, but it probably grants you a free pass."

"I'm sure they'll huff and puff, but Greg just hired me back because A&E was empty, and the arts are a huge driver in this town. And QuiltWeek's barreling toward us. I think Greg may be paying my raise out of his pocket."

"Raise? Nice. I always thought those were mythical."

"I'm not stupid, and I know how to fend for myself."

"Definitely aren't stupid. Unlucky as hell, but . . ."

"I have a vested interest in the subject matter, which means I can't be objective, so I should leave the story to you. But my fiancé—okay, former—was murdered, and you're not allowed to write the story. How many letters to the editor have we received about this? I haven't had the chance to check."

"More than sixty. Most of them end with some version of 'Cancel my subscription, you hacks.' Dan, Adam, Brian, and I were reading the best ones out loud yesterday. Busted a gut."

"Right, so if we don't cover the murder of one of our own reporters, how do we even pretend to be more than a coupon-delivery system? As the adage goes, 'Comfort the afflicted, and afflict the comfortable.' Matt was afflicted, and Greg Wurt and Ed Colapinto are comfortable, especially Ed. That they happen to be my bosses shouldn't be relevant."

"Go get 'em."

"Thanks."

"Take care of yourself, Hadley. Seriously, your cheek really doesn't look good."

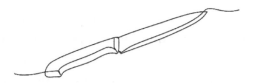

Chapter 12

Bias

After I entered the story about Matt into the content management system at 9 p.m., I walked to the other side of the newsroom, where the designers sat. Jake Smith was on that night, as I knew he would be.

"Hey, Jake."

"Hadley! Oh, my God! What happened?"

I must have looked as awful as I felt. Jake worked the late shift, and obviously no one had told him about the *Paducah Chronicle* Interrogation Incident.

"I fought the law, and the law won."

"Seriously, are you okay?"

"I'm fine, but I'm not joking. Officer Williams beat me up."

"Is that the idiot with the mustache?"

"Yes."

"He pulled me over because I have one of those COEXIST bumper stickers made up of various religious symbols on my car."

"Oh, come on. He didn't admit that."

"When I asked him why he pulled me over, he said I made an illegal right turn. I was on MLK and hadn't turned the whole way, and I'd turned left to get on it, so I knew something was up. It was night, so I don't see how he could've known I'm Black."

"Infuriating. How'd the bumper sticker factor in?"

"He appeared to be wondering whether to write me up. Out of nowhere he said, 'I see you don't support our troops.' I said, 'What?'

He said, 'The peace sign on your bumper.' It's the O in COEXIST. I laughed so hard I thought he might slug me. I finally said, 'For me to support our troops you think I have to be pro-war?' He said, 'You have to believe in our mission, in America, in spreading democracy.' I said, 'To you, spreading democracy means pulling people over for expressing their opinions, opinions that argue for keeping American troops and everyone else alive?'"

"Good for you. How much was the ticket?"

"Two hundred fifty-four dollars, but I fought it. He didn't show up, so it got kicked."

"A win for the law-abiders. Hooray!"

"I was lucky he didn't pull me out of the car. Based on your face, my fear was justified."

"Yeah, the guy's got problems. But I came over here to let you know I just filed a fifteen-inch story on Matt's murder."

"Okay. And I'm sorry about that, Hadley. I can't imagine the pain you're in. I was wondering why nothing ran."

"I don't know, and you don't know, so we have plausible deniability."

He laughed. "Do we need it?"

"Greg told Bill not to write the story but not *why* he couldn't. I wasn't in the newsroom then, so I can't possibly know—wink, wink—that Matt's story was ruled null and void. So, let's say I came back to the newsroom, saw this gaping hole in our news coverage, then rushed to fill our readers in."

"You mean, do what newspapers do."

"True, if you want to look at things rationally."

"I find it's easiest to do my job—and live my life—when I do."

"That makes two of us," I said. "I'm asking if you're cool with putting the story on A1, or even running it at all, now that you know the backstory."

"You could've just let me know the story was in, and I would've run it."

"Yeah, but that's not how I treat people. If you could get blowback, it's only fair I warn you."

"Thanks. Of course, I'll put it on one. I'm working on two now, but it won't be tough to find room."

"Thanks, Jake."

The story I wrote, without a byline, read:

Reporter murdered but no arrests yet

PADUCAH—The body of a local journalist was found by a Paducah resident early on April 9, submerged in the Ohio River under the city's transient boat dock.

Paducah Police Department determined the death to be a homicide. The death of Paducah resident Matt Ackerman, 40, was caused by blunt-force trauma, according to McCracken County Coroner John Mann. No arrests have been made, according to Paducah Police Department public information officer Jane Galliski.

Ackerman had worked for the Paducah Chronicle for seven years, most recently as the arts and entertainment reporter. Mann said Ackerman's body had been in the water for up to four hours.

"At this point in time, Paducah Police Department is working diligently, logging overtime, in fact, while pursuing all leads," said a PPD press release issued April 14. "We are not at liberty to discuss the direction of this case, but PPD will inform the public immediately when an arrest is made," the press release read.

Ackerman's cause of death, blunt-force trauma, has led members of the public to speculate about what kind of weapon the murderer or murderers used.

According to an employee of WKYC who was not at liberty to speak freely to the media without fear of retribution, the station had received more than one hundred calls about Ackerman's death.

The employee said, "Many of the callers have some of the weirdest theories I've ever heard. I mean, I guess any hard object could cause blunt-force trauma, but one guy swore the weapon must've been his wife's hard head. One guy said it was the frying pan his mother-in-law gave him for no reason last Christmas, another said the sledgehammer that went missing from his garage. One guy said a five-iron was most likely, probably a Titleist, and another said he'd use a log, then let it float away. Another said a bowling pin, and some kook swore Ackerman must have brained himself with his conscience after writing all those awful stories. It's all really nuts. I mean, a man was murdered, but half the calls seemed to be grinding axes or making jokes."

The responses to Ackerman's death varied significantly among local residents. "It's shocking when anyone is murdered, especially in Paducah," said Karen Peroni of Lone Oak. "But when the victim is someone whose stories I read, someone who was widely known in our region, it's unfathomable and devastating."

David Tarpley, a poker dealer at Harrah's Metropolis in Metropolis, Illinois, was friendly with Ackerman. "Whenever he joined a game, he made a point of making eye contact with everyone at the table, shaking hands with people near him," Tarpley said. "He was weird but in an interesting way, not a creepy-stalker kind of way. I liked him most of the time. He could be moody, but we all go through stuff. If you caught him on the right day, he was a lot of laughs. I mean, the monocle? Classic. I can't believe he'll never sit at my table again. I really hope they catch the guy who did this."

For more than three years, in addition to writing other articles weekly, Ackerman wrote stories for HeART of Paducah, the arts section that appears every Thursday in the Chronicle.

Referring to Ackerman, William Honey of Paducah said, "It's always the first section I turn to on Thursdays so I can plan my weekend, and now I'm going to miss seeing his byline and reading his stories."

Paducah resident Donna Ackerman, mother of the deceased, said, "I'm devastated. Any parent would be. There's a giant hole in my chest and in my life. Matty was a tremendous son—smart, funny, kind—and a very good reporter. He got wound up easy, went off on crusades, but being a reporter requires passion, and Matty was passionate. Some people thought he could be a jackass. True, but he was my jackass!"

Matt Ackerman's story about local quilter Missy Wendland, his last HeART of Paducah story, ran the day after his body was found.

"I'm not a fan of the Chronicle, or the media in general, but come on, a guy gets clubbed to death and the newspaper he works for doesn't cover it?" asked Chris Prabhu of Paducah. "I mean, that's bad even for the Comical," he said, referring to the name some members of the public use instead of the Chronicle.

Jim Knutsen of Lone Oak said, "I'm a law-abiding citizen and have great respect for law enforcement in general, but what does it say about Paducah PD and KSP (Kentucky State Police) if a semi-celebrity, or at least a guy a whole lot of people in the area knew by name, gets killed, but the police have made no progress on the case? Doesn't bode well for any of us, does it?"

Funeral services for Ackerman were held April 14 at St. Francis de Sales Catholic Church.

Would my story win any awards? No. Did I care? No. Was I glad I wrote the story and managed to get it on the front page alongside Matt's employee photo, the one taken seven years earlier when he'd joined the staff? Definitely.

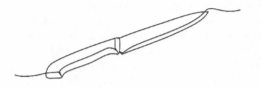

Chapter 13
Finger Pressing

As I suspected it would, my cell rang early the next morning at 6:15. Caller I.D. said Greg Wurt, as I'd guessed it would. I let the call go to voicemail, then listened to Greg's message: "Call me," it said.

If, as Polonius said in Shakespeare's *Hamlet*, "brevity is the soul of wit," then Greg was witty because his message was certainly brief. Therefore, Polonius was wrong because Greg was as witty as a rutabaga.

I didn't return his call. I needed to stop by the river, then do some investigating before I headed to the office. I took a short jog with Trapunto, showered, got ready for work, then headed to the river.

Had the murderer or murderers thrown Matt into the river from the dock? The assumption seemed reasonable because the dock jutted far enough into the river that the current would take his body downstream, at least theoretically. And the murderer—I decided to go singular for the sake of simplicity—wouldn't have to negotiate the muddy bank or risk slipping on the mossy river bottom while trying to get the body into the current.

But if I'd needed to dispose of a body in the Ohio, I'd have dropped it from one of the bridges so the current could take it, and I wouldn't leave any clues on the banks in the process. Of course, that would take careful timing so I wouldn't be seen by oncoming cars. But in the middle of the night, if I *had* to dump a body in the Ohio, I'd have chosen the rickety blue bridge that connects Paducah to Brookport.

But I had these thoughts while I stood on the dock, directly above where I'd found Matt. If I'd just killed someone, would I have been rational enough to make sound decisions? Probably not. Murders by blunt-force trauma usually signify a crime of passion, or at least spontaneity. A murderer isn't likely to plan a killing that involves a frying pan, whether or not his mother-in-law gave it to him. Someone upsets him, he grabs a heavy object within reach or nearby, then lashes out. Because it didn't appear that Matt's murder had been planned for months, including how to dispose of the body and which escape route to take, I wondered if the murderer panicked.

My gut said yes. I decided to trust my gut and to investigate Matt's crime accordingly.

Which left me standing above where I'd found Matt, wondering why someone would throw a body from the dock, then would leave without being sure the current had taken the body. Even if the killer panicked, I didn't believe anyone would be that haphazard, not to say that stupid. That meant someone threw Matt in upriver, he floated down, then got stuck on the dock.

I walked up the ramp, then, instead of driving to the boat launch at the base of Broadway, I walked the thousand yards or so southeast. I tried not to think about currents or the huge wakes shot shoreward by the extremely long barges hauling gravel or dry goods up or down river, or the tow boats and speedboats that ply that waterway at all hours. I tried not to think of these because the theory that was forming required that Matt had been jostled, maybe rammed, after death. I knew that shouldn't matter, but it did.

I walked down the ridged concrete ramp that runs from Paducah's famous, muralled sea wall to the river. A mother and her two children were eating a snack on the far side of the built-in cement bleachers, and a red Chevy Silverado was parked right at the water's edge, facing upstream, parallel to the water. The driver's window was down, the engine running.

If I'd been panicking and was trying to dump a body in a hurry, and I didn't have the presence of mind to dump it from the Irvin S. Cobb

Bridge between Paducah and Brookport, I'd consider parking where that truck sat. Then I'd open the door, maneuver the body out, carefully wade into the water, then let it go. Or I might have loaded the body in the truck bed, backed into the river far enough to float the body—but not far enough to get the truck stuck—then shoved the body out.

While speculating, I had to think of Matt as an entity, as an unfamiliar body or a crash dummy—not as my ex-fiancé. It was difficult to do because I couldn't disconnect the pain from the puzzle I was trying to solve.

The shore curves in a wide, gentle arc into the river downstream from the boat launch, so an object floating downstream could run into the bank. Or, it might get near the bank, then shoot into the main channel. And if it did, I guessed that only wakes from boats and barges could cause the object to drift into the main channel on the far side of the point, then make a left so it could get stuck on the dock that was sheltered by that point.

If my theory was correct, wouldn't the same right-left zig-zag occur to a shoe, one that slipped off a murderer's foot while he was trying to get Matt's lifeless, 190-pound body into the current?

I decided my theory was solid. I wasn't sure every detail mattered, but enough elements of it made sense to enable me to proceed with a tiny bit of confidence: a spontaneous murder with an available weapon; a panicked murderer, strong enough to move Matt's heavy body alone, trying to get it out into the current; a murderer who probably would have successfully made Matt's body disappear if a ship, boat, or barge hadn't pushed Matt toward shore; and a murderer who lost a left shoe while trying to dispose of the body.

But why was I trying so hard not to admit that a body thrown from a boat, barge, or ship wouldn't have to take a left turn and would simply be pushed toward shore by the wake?

Matt had sought and received the financial records of N&S Shipping, owned by Nick Stoddard. If the balance sheet I'd found contained enough information to get Nick arrested, would he be willing to kill to keep it quiet? And where had the missing sheets gone? Had Matt lost them, simply failed to return them to the drawer after sending copies to the district attorney? Or had someone stolen them? If they'd contained evidence of embezzlement or tax evasion, could someone have killed Matt because he'd seen them, then destroyed those sheets, not knowing that Matt had already sent them to Suzanne Bigelow?

I didn't know where Matt had been thrown into the water, or why, but the weapon that had hit Matt was probably in the river, either on the bottom, covered in mud, or in the Mississippi, working its way to the Gulf of Mexico, having made the left at Cairo, Illinois, where the Ohio flows into the Mississippi.

I really didn't want to go to work, where Greg would yell at me (or quietly issue words of rebuke, which, for him, was an out-of-control tantrum). Before driving to the office, I made a phone call to a friend from high school: Lisa Bannducci.

"What do you want this time, Hadley?"

"Remember when I covered for you in second period, Lisa?"

"Really, you're still going there? I've paid you back at least eight times for that."

"But it was pretty noble of me, falling on my sword for you."

"Yeah, you're a saint. I get it. What's the number?"

Lisa worked for the Department of Motor Vehicles, located in the basement of the McCracken County Courthouse.

"332 EYW"

"We left the favor zone a while ago."

"Are you soliciting a bribe, Lisa? I am shocked, shocked to find that gambling is going on here."

"What are you talking about? Just get me two tickets to the symphony. Better seats this time."

"But I was going to do that for you just because we're old school chums. Bribery has nothing to do with it."

"You always were weird. I'll get to it when I can."

"Sounds good, but there's one more."

Click.

That Lisa was a fan of the Paducah Symphony surprised me because more than once when we were teens, I saw her dry her armpits with her long, black ponytail. I'm not saying teens don't grow out of disgusting habits, and I'm not saying there's a direct correlation between cleanliness and culture, but I am saying: *Gross!*

Her grooming habits were beside the point when I needed her help, which I'd needed perhaps five times over the years (she might say ten, but how can you trust someone that gross?).

I'd decided to start at the top of the list of anomalies I'd found in Matt's two notebooks. The plate number I'd given Lisa might lead nowhere, but it was a place to start.

As I pulled into the *Chronicle* parking lot, my cell rang. I parked, then looked at the screen. Unknown Caller. Thinking it must be Lisa, I answered.

"You and Matt got what was comin'."

My stomach flipped, and my heart raced. It was Officer Williams. I started to respond, then tried to hang up, but I couldn't move. I could hear him breathing heavily, as if he'd just exercised. I wanted to scream for help, to tell him to drop dead, but all I got out was "Williams." Not angry or threatening—just the feeble whimper of a mouse in a cat's clutches. But I'd stopped being a mouse when I was ten. I'd worked hard not to be a victim. Who had I become? I took a deep breath, thought of my sister, Jenny, then felt the real me clawing her way up from the depths of sadness.

"Wanna get together, sweety? I'm gonna break your other cheek."

"You can try, but I'll set that thing you call a mustache on fire. Without it, how will anyone know you're a man?"

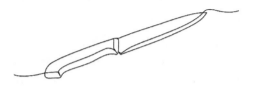

Chapter 14
Crazy Quilt

"Yes, my mother was. She practically bathed in Jim Beam."

"How do you think that affected you?"

I sat on the couch in the midtown office of Elaine Bourget, the psychiatrist Dakota had seen after she broke up with Freddie DiSalvo. Dakota said Elaine had been a big help. So, after Williams threatened me, I called Elaine, hoping she could squeeze me in sometime next week. But her receptionist said Elaine had a cancellation, and if I didn't mind hustling and getting a shortened session, I was welcome to the slot. Her office was only a few minutes away, so I sat down across from Elaine, with forty minutes of my first session of analysis ahead of me.

Her office was homey. The décor made me wonder if the effect she was going for was "grandmother's living room." It worked, but I'd never met either of my grandmothers, so I didn't know what their living rooms looked like. My guess would be a lot less homey than Elaine's office.

"I don't know how it affected me. Isn't that why I'm here, for you to tell me?"

"That's not how therapy works. We have a discussion about your life and the world and your hopes and dreams, and together, we figure out how big the gap is between who you are and who you *think* you are. Then we try to make that gap smaller. It's a collaborative process."

"Okay, then I guess her drinking affected me negatively. I mean, kids aren't supposed to take care of their mothers, right?"

"How did you take care of her?"

"At first, I kept a tally in my diary, just a checkmark, of all the times I had to clean up her vomit or take her contacts out after she passed out or get her inside when she passed out in her car or had to tell lies to hide her drinking from my teachers and other families. Jenny couldn't deal with it."

"Who's Jenny?"

"My sister. Younger by two years. She just bailed. First, by running to our room and slamming the door, leaving me to deal with the mess that was Mom. Then, later, by becoming a drunk like Mom, then marrying four times, with four divorces, at eighteen, twenty-five, twenty-eight, and thirty-five, I think. Since the last one ended, after six months, she's connected with so many men, I stopped trying to remember their names. I just say, 'How's your man doing?' when we talk on the phone."

"Where does she live?"

"Bell, California."

"What's that like?"

"Imagine a giant balloon full of smog surrounded by a freight-train hub, a chemical plant, and a fertilizer factory, then inject the balloon with ignorance and despair."

She laughed, then said, "You're funny."

"I'm funny how? I mean funny, like I'm a clown? I amuse you?"

"And a film buff. Nice. I love *Goodfellas*."

"Because Mom wasn't around or wasn't upright, Jenny and I watched a lot of movies we checked out from the library, most of which we shouldn't have been allowed to watch, but no one told us we couldn't."

"Where was your father?"

"I don't know. Never met him, or I don't remember meeting him, if I did. Mom said he left while she was on the delivery table with Jenny.

Jenny and I don't look alike, have totally different personalities, and I'm six inches taller, so I think that's just another of Mom's lies. I give her credit for inventiveness, though."

"As lies go, that one's truly toxic. It makes her the victim, absolves her of responsibility, and burdens her daughters with an unhealthy and unfair picture of men."

"I subconsciously pushed Matt away because of my lousy childhood?"

"No, Hadley. I definitely didn't say that. We don't know why Matt left, which means we can't speculate about cause and effect. If Matt had left a note that said he had left you because, let's say, you didn't listen to him, we still wouldn't have enough information to blame you for the breakup. That note would only tell us how *he* felt, or how he *said* he felt. What were his motives for writing the note? Did he want to hurt you more by blaming you? Was he dodging responsibility, not owning up to the real reason he was leaving? Was he projecting? Was it he who didn't listen to you?"

Despite her basically telling me that I was an idiot, I thought Elaine had a soothing voice and an expressive face that seemed to reflect my emotions. She nodded at my interpretations of events and seemed to agree with me, generally. She was what I imagined a maternal figure was supposed to be, except she was probably eight years younger than I was.

I said, "I think I get it. By telling you how I've screwed up, how I've disappointed myself, haven't been there for Jenny, wasn't able to save my mom, wasn't enough for Matt, I learn about myself, and, with luck, hard work, and perseverance, I learn to put things in perspective."

"The part about keeping aspects of your life in perspective is correct. But you are far too hard on yourself. You had no responsibility for your mom. She made every decision she made without consulting you or Jenny, even though many of her decisions, it seems, were unhealthy for the two of you. It was not your job to raise your sister, who is only two years younger. You couldn't have prevented her from becoming an alcoholic or from perpetually seeking validation—and perceived safety—in the arms of men.

"And Matt was an adult. We all have issues, so I'm sure he had his. Whatever those were, they might have been what caused him to do what he did. Or something else. We may never know, and as difficult as that is to accept, especially so soon—you should try to make peace with not knowing. If you don't find peace, your uncertainty about your relationship with him could adversely affect your future relationships. When uncertainty like that is combined with the grief we experience after a breakup and the grief we experience after the death of a loved one, the combination can be truly destructive."

"Okay, I'll do my best."

"If you don't mind, let's circle back to the threat by Williams." I nodded. "You told me how you felt about his words, and that was essential, but why do you think he made it?"

"Intimidation, probably. Trying to frighten me not to take legal action. Well, that's not going to work. He may kill me, but he's not going to bully me. I will not cower. I know what living in fear is like, and I saw how broken Matt was from the torture that Williams put him through. I have countless flaws—a few of which I only discovered in the last two weeks—but being spineless isn't one of them."

"I see that. But I'm wondering if you considered Williams' threat to be a confession."

"Meaning, was he referring to murder and not to bullying? Gee, Doc, thanks for helping me put my troubles in perspective."

She smiled, glanced at the clock on the wall, then nodded. "It's time. Take care of yourself."

I said, "I will. As I'm sure you're aware, reporters, especially reporters at the *Chronicle*, don't make much money, so when I heard your hourly rate, I thought, No way. But you're worth every penny. Thank you."

When I arrived at my desk, a Post-it that said "See me" was sitting on my keyboard. Greg was consistent in his brevity, and he knew I'd know who left the note. So, I set my purse down, then walked across the newsroom.

I stepped inside the door to his large office, which had huge pictures of clowns all over its walls. Not paintings or drawings, which would've been creepy enough, but actual pictures of men and women who'd dolloped makeup on their faces in grotesque pantomimes of human features. These painted examples of a hobby poorly chosen expected onlookers to laugh at their japes and hijinks, instead of being frightened or appalled.

As much as the clowns freaked me out, I was bothered more by the fact that not a single picture in his office was of his wife of thirty-five years, Wendy, or of his two grown children or of their five children. Who knows how crowded his walls would have been if any of them had slathered themselves in greasepaint?

Adding creepiness to bad taste, Greg had photographed each clown himself—maneuvering each red nose and seltzer bottle into position, adjusting each absurdly large shoe just so. A plaque identifying the photographer who created what I guessed Greg considered to be art hung above the door, so that as people exited Greg's Hall of Grotesqueries, they knew where the blame should fall.

Greg wore a cabled Aran jumper in light green, and it broke no hard-and-fast rules of fashion. It would've looked better had it been forest green, but, as difficult as it was for me to admit, his sweater was stylish. From behind his desk (on which sat a honk-able red nose), he asked, "Why on Earth would you write that story? It isn't your beat, and I told Bill not to cover it."

Not a word about my black eye or the huge contusion that was the right side of my face. Greg hadn't seen me since Adam, the photographer, had gently led me out of the police station (where cooler heads prevailed), then had driven me to the emergency room.

"The real question is why the editor of a newspaper would tell his cops reporter not to cover the murder of one of the paper's reporters."

"I'm the editor. You've just returned, at a significant increase in salary, no less, and here, on your third day, you're causing trouble again."

"Let me stop you there, Greg. To which past trouble are you referring? The time I was sexually assaulted at a company function, or two days ago when a police officer beat me up in the office while you, the rest of the staff, and the security guard did nothing?"

He stared at me.

"Which trouble did I previously cause, Greg?"

Anger replaced the sense of victory I'd felt for having done right by Matt by getting the story in the paper. Had I disobeyed a direct order from my boss? No. He'd rehired me because I was tenacious, resourceful, and didn't take no for an answer. The latter was apparently a great trait for a reporter to have—but only if the reporter took no for an answer.

"The issue at hand is the article you wrote without my permission."

"Permission? You don't assign ninety-nine percent of the stories that run, and the others violate the rule against running stories about our families, friends, and associates, just to stroke their egos or to curry favor."

The muscles in his neck were straining, which put them in line with his ears. Someone must've told him to increase the size of his neck, which might've been good advice if he'd learned how to increase the size of his head.

"You wrote a story outside your beat, Hadley."

"I wrote three others yesterday that weren't A&E stories, as I've done throughout my career, wherever I've been a reporter. Why aren't you concerned about those transgressions?"

"Because this story is different."

"Exactly. This story is about a murder, and the victim used to sit at the desk I currently occupy."

"Not for long, if this insubordination keeps up."

"Wow," I said, then shook my head. "We all consider you to be the worst editor we've worked for, but when we're in the bullpen commiserating over the latest inexplicable editing choice you've made, none of us has said you're stupid. That always seemed too harsh. But now?"

I stopped to let him respond, to defend himself, to berate me, but he said nothing.

So, I continued. "When we're in court and my attorney asks you why you fired me, and you respond, 'Because she wrote a story for the *Paducah Chronicle*, the newspaper I'm the editor of, about the murder of one of our employees,' how do you think that will play?"

"Are you threatening me?"

"You just threatened to fire me for insubordination, an offense I apparently committed by being a reporter. What do you think an editor would have to do to get fired? Consistently misspell words in headlines? Bully his employees? Not cover the local news? These aren't rhetorical questions, Greg. What do you think should get an editor fired?"

He stood, put both fists on his desk, then leaned forward over the red clown's nose—but still said nothing.

"Cover something up? Be complicit in whatever the publisher was covering up?"

"QuiltWeek is coming, Hadley. Thousands of flights have been booked, rooms reserved, seminars enrolled in. The whole city benefits, to the tune of millions of dollars, every year, when they all arrive. This paper is no exception. In fact, we make more on the special preview edition than we do with the Black Friday edition and the after-Christmas edition. More than those two combined, actually. If word gets out that people are being murdered, especially people in the arts community, quilters could start canceling. And, more importantly, at least to us, advertisers could pull out in droves. The paper's finances are none of your business, but let's just say the *Chronicle* has not been immune to the negative effects of the internet and social media—or from the attacks on the free press. As for your dereliction of duty, the damage has been done. The story has run. I'll consider disciplinary measures."

His face took on a satisfied look, and then he sat down as though he'd just cured cancer.

"If you want to fire me for insubordination, knock yourself out. In the meantime, I'm going to do my best to let our readers know what's happening in and around Paducah."

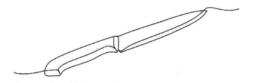

Chapter 15
Template

I was stunned because if I added up all of the words Greg had said to me in the four years that I'd worked for him, they wouldn't have added up to the number of words in whatever that was he'd just delivered— a screed, tirade, explanation, excuse, or alibi.

I turned, left the office, then saw Adam, Bill, Dan, and Brian standing outside Greg's door. They'd been listening, out of sight. Adam gave me an elaborate tip of his imaginary hat, followed by a deep bow. Bill gave me a thumbs-up. Dan clapped very quietly, and Brian, whom I had only met two days before, stepped over to me and gave me a hug. Maybe he was just a hugger, or maybe I should watch myself around him. I wasn't sure, but I accepted the hug and returned it, operating under the first assumption.

We walked to the other side of the office, past one of the two entrances into the bullpen in which we all worked.

"I'm proud of you, Hadley. You've got guts," Bill said.

"Thank you."

"Fighting the good fight," Adam said.

"Thank you."

"I couldn't hear every word," Brian, the education reporter, said, "but his reasons sounded weak for killing the story."

"He didn't kill it. He told me not to write it," Bill said.

"Afraid advertisers would pull out," I said, "if word got out that people in the arts community are being murdered. But I'm almost certain Matt was only one person."

"Correct," Adam said. "But there was that woman a while ago who got stabbed."

"Thought that was a robbery," Dan said.

"It was," Adam said. "But I don't think a woman stabbed and a reporter clubbed mean a serial killer's on the loose."

"Advertisers, most of them corporations, wouldn't even be aware of those," Bill said. "Local advertisers wouldn't give the killings a second thought. Seems paranoid of Greg."

"He said the paper's in financial trouble," I said. "That shouldn't surprise anyone, considering that his editorial philosophy appears to be based on attrition and retreat. But if the finances are more dire than he's letting on, maybe he doesn't want us poking around because of what we'll find. A murder of an employee wouldn't require management to open the books, I wouldn't think, but what if Matt's mom, Donna, decides to file a civil suit? Discovery would be required, and if Greg or someone else is cooking the books, skimming or something, he or they or everyone would be sunk."

"That's a great point," Bill said. "Not to mention we'd all be out of work. I'm not saying Greg had anything to do with Matt's death, but what if he knew something about it and hoped that by blocking the story, or at least delaying it as long as he could, he'd provide cover for the killer or prevent scrutiny of the paper? It's one thing to be a laughingstock but another to be subjected to discovery."

We were sitting at our desks by then, but we'd swiveled our chairs to face each other across the twenty-by-thirty-foot room.

"Matt and Greg certainly had more than their share of disagreements," I said. "Matt could be prickly, and he believed what he believed very strongly. I'm usually a fan of that. Can't stand wishy-washy. It means the person isn't intellectually strong enough to arrive at a conclusion. But Matt couldn't compromise, not with anyone but me, and then only after throwing a tantrum, and after I decimated him with my unassailable logic."

"I hope the ER ran an MRI," Bill said, "because, in addition to your cheek, your brain appears to be broken."

"Don't you have a Pulitzer to polish?"

"Is that supposed to be an insult?" Bill asked. "Oh, gosh, you sucker punched me in my proudest moment. Look, Matt could be irritating, but he wasn't a bad person, not even close. Half of his irritating habits were just cries for attention."

"The other half were him entertaining himself," I said. "He didn't find life amusing enough, so he helped it along. You guys didn't see that part of him, but Matt was really funny. When most of us would hesitate because something would make us look stupid or silly, or we'd feel embarrassed, he jumped right in. We were together a long time, but instead of taking our relationship for granted or falling into a rut, he kept coming up with new ways to make me laugh, to make me love him more."

I shouldn't have said the last part because my emotions kicked in. I'd always made it through toe-to-toe combat fine, but if a puppy romped through grass, or a little kid laughed, or love was thrown into the mix, I crumbled.

I turned away for a few seconds, then realized how pointless it was to try to hide my tears. The whole right side of my face looked like an eggplant that had been hit with a sledgehammer, so I turned back toward them.

"Any chance Greg could've lost his cool, then clobbered Matt with something?" Brian asked. "He's short, but he's solid muscle. He could've moved Matt if he had to."

"The guy barely speaks loud enough to be heard," Adam said.

"But I just heard him say more than he's said during the last four years," I said, "and he was far angrier than I've seen him."

"He knew the body on the dock was Matt before it was officially identified," Bill said, "which means a cop on the scene that morning has him on speed dial for some reason, Greg did it, or he knows who did. And that person told Greg, who told me to back away."

"Any of you know if Greg has any association with Officer Williams?" I asked.

"No, why?" Dan asked.

"I don't," Adam said.

"Not that I know of," Bill said.

"Wait, I just remembered," Adam said. "I saw Greg spotting Williams once at the gym."

"Officer Williams just threatened me on the phone," I said. "Matt and I both got what we deserved, he said. The guy's a punk, and he was on the scene first. He could have called or texted Greg to let him know Matt had been found, or that I had found him. I don't know. The net around me feels like it's closing. We know that Greg and Nick Stoddard have known each other for years."

"And Greg has no understanding of the traditional journalistic firewall between editorial and advertising," Bill said, "but what's Stoddard have to do with this?"

"Maybe nothing," I said, "but Matt filed an Open Records request against N&S Shipping, one of Stoddard's companies, and Matt was dumped in the river, which would be easy to do from a boat or barge."

"Wow. Sounds like our boy Matty couldn't leave the cops beat behind," Bill said. "Good for him. The whole Stoddard family deserves federal prison, at best. Are you thinking Matt's investigation caused Stoddard to retaliate?"

"It's possible, so I have to consider it."

"Smart girl," said Brian, the one I didn't know but had hugged me a few minutes before.

"Smart woman," I said, "but the adjective seems inaccurate lately."

"My apologies," Brian said.

"Not having anywhere better to start, I'll check my email," I said. "I'm sure the article generated a lot of responses. Maybe someone knows something."

It took me more than an hour and a half to carefully read all of the ninety-three relevant emails that the paper had received. I hadn't put a byline on the story, so the emails were all sent to the news desk, which meant we all received them. The process was a pain because we'd all have to wade through as many as 250 emails a day, then delete the ones that didn't pertain to our beats, meaning about 235 of them.

A high percentage of the emails that day, maybe forty percent, commented on how horrible it was that Matt had been murdered. About twenty-five percent said some variation of the following: Matt was a reporter, so he deserved what he got, and all of the rest of the reporters should be killed soon, too. About twenty-five percent expressed an opinion that included some of the following: Paducah was too good, too kind, too devout for anyone to have been murdered here; the fact that the newspaper took so long to report the story proved that it was fake news; the editor and reporters needed time to get their stories straight; and the paper had been setting this up for years by publishing stories using the byline Matt Ackerman, stories that were obviously written by someone else because Matt Ackerman didn't exist and never had. His picture in the Tilghman High School yearbook only proved someone was really good with Photoshop, even way back then. All of the people who claim to have gone to school with Matt or knew him from somewhere else were crisis actors, paid by the newspaper and probably by George Soros, who, as everyone knows, wasn't even a Christian.

About five percent mentioned Matt's murder only as a platform to complain that their papers weren't arriving three days a week, and the last five percent criticized Matt for having written such a tremendously inaccurate assessment of Wendland's horrendous quilts.

One email, sent from the email address iknowall@gmail.com, read as follows: "Missy is having an affair."

I looked at the header to see if I could learn anything about the sender, but the Internet Protocol only told me that the email had been sent from the downtown McCracken County Public Library.

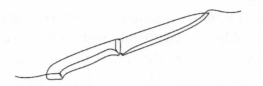

Chapter 16

Seam Allowance

I had to go with the assumption that ninety-two of those emails contained no information that would help me but that the one about Missy having an affair was relevant. I was only hoping that assumption was correct, but sometimes hope is all we have, so I embraced it.

Of course, Missy could've been involved with anybody, but if just anybody was involved, why would someone send an anonymous email about the affair to the *Chronicle*? Why would anyone at the newspaper care? I started to mull over the possibilities: Ed Colapinto, the paper's publisher, seemed like the most logical choice, assuming that Missy's paramour had some association with the paper. I only knew him from our occasional exchanges in the office hallway or in the lunchroom and from our interactions at company functions. But I was guessing that a man who could casually suggest at a company Christmas party a threesome that involved a game of naked Twister would not rule out a tryst with an older woman, no matter how poorly she quilted.

I started to bat around the possibility that Nick Stoddard, the paper's primary advertiser who had Jim Beam breath, roving hands, and felonious predilections, could be involved with Missy. I couldn't completely rule out that Stoddard wasn't the mastermind behind the $100 million Antwerp diamond heist or the Dunbar armored truck heist in Los Angeles, so nothing was outside the realm of immoral or criminal possibility with Nick.

As I moved on to consider Susan Loudon, the *Chronicle*'s ad director, my cell rang.

"Got a pen?" Lisa from the DMV asked by way of hello.

"Always."

"332 EYW belongs to a rental car belonging to Your Way Motors on 62 in Reidland." She gave me the address.

I wrote as she spoke, then said, "Thank you very much, Lisa. I have one more—"

"Best seats in the house this time." Click.

During my more than two decades as a journalist, I'd had much better luck getting people to cooperate face-to-face than over the phone. I grabbed my purse, notebook, and recorders, then headed to Reidland, about twelve minutes southeast of Paducah, along the Tennessee River, before it flows into the Ohio.

Your Way Motors appeared to cater to people who had to rent cars with cash, if its dilapidated building and junkyard-worthy cars were an accurate indication of its clientele. Eight cars, three of which appeared to be losers in a demolition derby, littered the dirt lot on the east side of US-62. The cars that weren't jalopies were still old and rusted. A gray Cutlass Supreme that listed slightly to the left sported the 332 EYW license plate.

"Hello," I said to the teenaged male whose pronounced acne made me wince on his behalf. He wore a Garth Brooks T-shirt that had likely been torn and tattered a decade before. The small office smelled of french fries and body odor, as though he'd been working out at a Burger King. He looked up from the comic book he was reading when he heard me enter. He nodded slightly at my hello, but that was all.

"I'm Hadley Carroll, a reporter for the *Paducah Chronicle*, and—"

"Can't help you."

"I'm sorry? You don't know what I'm going to ask."

"Don't matter. Don't like the media."

"Been treated unfairly by the press, have you?"

"What?"

"Never mind. I'm guessing you guys do a lot of business in cash. People have their reasons for not wanting to go on record, especially businesses that don't report their actual earnings to the IRS. So, here's the thing: I have no interest in writing an expose about tax evasion in small businesses in the area, although our readers probably would like to know which businesses aren't contributing their share to roads, schools, and law enforcement. Not to mention that I'd score points with my boss, and I could afford to burnish my image with the guy."

"What's burnish?"

"Sorry. Polish. So, here's what I propose: You tell me who rented that Cutlass Supreme over the last month or so, and I won't investigate this business further."

"One, we don't keep records of who rents what. That's the whole point. Guy needs to cheat on their wife, he rents a car he can park at a motel without being spotted. Guy needs to pull off something not legal but don't know how to steal a car, we're here for him. Second, what you're doing is blackmail."

"No, it's not. I'm simply saying that I will gladly let you run your tip-top, above-board business, catering to upstanding citizens of every stripe, without interference from me if you tell me who rented the Cutlass, then let me look inside it. I'm guessing you don't have the cars detailed between rentals."

"I should call my boss. He might could tell you who rented it."

"You work here full time?"

"Yup."

"Then you could probably tell me, too."

"Look, I just want you outta here. I'm not involved in anything. Just a guy who shoulda stayed in school. A dude—bald, fat, ugly—rented that car for two weeks, cash up front, hundred dollars more than what he shoulda paid. Left his ride right there. A pretty new Camry. Blue. Thought it was weird. He drives up in a better ride than he's paying too much to rent, leaves his car. But I just work here. Almost pocketed the extra. Think that's what he wanted me to do, but I ain't a crook. I don't *know* why people rent from us. Could just not have credit cards. I mean, our rates are like, stupid high. People who can rent somewhere else, do. Like, it's just a paycheck for me here, really."

"I'm going to take a shot in the dark," I said. I pulled out my notebook, flipped to the right page. "Any chance the Camry's plates were 555 WWE?"

"Man, how'd you know? It sat there all that time, and I kept thinking how it woulda been cool if it had been 555 WWW, you know, like all the same."

"Yes. Not every member of the media is incompetent. Some of them excel, or excelled, at their jobs, at least within certain beats. He could be a dingbat, but he was my dingbat."

"Don't know what you're talking about."

"That's okay. I'm notoriously clumsy, a real klutz. I'm going to take a look in the Cutlass, and I'll probably drop a twenty along the way. It's been known to happen. Be a shame if just anyone found it."

He nodded more vigorously this time, and as I headed for the door, I pulled a twenty from my wallet, then set it in the chair by the door.

Two decades of disappointment had been sprinkled on the floor of the Cutlass, based on the smell. It was somewhere between a slaughterhouse and a men's locker room, like a rotting carcass sprinkled with aftershave. I didn't know what I was looking for, but I thought I'd know it if I saw it. I didn't find anything worth finding, however, other than inexplicable stickiness, receipts from burger joints, a 1984 penny, a paper clip, and what appeared to be a ringlet of fur from what I guessed was a poodle, based on its curliness. Because poodles don't shed, I was wondering if someone had intentionally cut the ringlet off, or if it had been stepped on. I was about to end my search but decided—despite the disgusting factor— to reach under the driver's seat into who-knew-what. I felt a piece of paper, about the size of U.S. currency, then managed on my second attempt to grab it and pull it out. It was a win ticket for $1.40 from Harrah's Metropolis, where Matt regularly played poker. The date on the ticket said March 21, a Friday. Someone who rented the car had won the money on a slot machine but hadn't bothered to cash out, perhaps deciding that the payout wasn't worth the effort. Or maybe he or she was pulled away before getting the chance to cash it.

I closed the car door, waved to the kid, who didn't bother to nod, then sat in my truck, thinking. The Garth Brooks kid had told me why people rented cars from Your Way Motors—for tawdry trysts or to commit crimes. But renting a car for two weeks up front, meaning the renter knew he had a long-term plan, meant either the renter intended to take a long trip and didn't want to put a lot of miles on his Camry, or he didn't want anyone he was following to tie the plates on his Camry to him. And if this supposition was correct, then I had to bribe . . . I mean, convince . . . Lisa to run 555 WWE.

Or I could go on the assumption that a bald, fat, ugly guy rented the Cutlass to tail Matt. If I couldn't find out who he was or why he followed Matt, I could guess who hired him.

Who would overpay to rent a car on the assumption that the bribe would keep an employee of Your Way Motors quiet? Once again, my mind jumped to Nick Stoddard. Then to Ed Colapinto. Neither of them would blink at paying too much. They probably would just to show off, to show how inconsequential money was to them. But an extra hundred bucks certainly wouldn't bust Greg, either. And cops make much more than the average small-town journalist makes, so Williams could afford to spend an extra hundred so he could hire someone to tail Matt.

I had to get back to work because I prided myself in keeping my word, especially to myself. I had vowed at the beginning of my high school journalism career that I would never miss a deadline. I had honored that vow while at my college newspaper and at the three papers I'd worked for before returning to Paducah to take the job at the *Chronicle*. So, I didn't want to ruin a perfect record. But I had ho-hum stories to write about a book signing by a local writer of romance novels and about a local, private, for-profit theater troupe's production of

"Annie." When I compared those to the importance of finding Matt's killer, I . . . decided to head to the office because just about all I had left that morning was my word. I would bang out my stories, then pursue Matt's killer.

I nodded to the other reporters and to Adam, turned on my computer and tried, but failed, to tune out the conversation they were quietly having.

"Losing half your net worth has been reason enough for thousands of spouses to kill their husband or wife," Brian said.

"Of course, it is," Dan said. "That's what I'm saying. We're actually agreeing, if you'd listen for a second. If spouses are willing to kill so they don't have to lose half their wealth, they'd first try to cover up the affair."

"Right," Adam said. "Killing a story is obviously far easier, not to mention more legal, than killing your wife."

I wanted to start making calls so I could write about the romance writer, but instead, I turned and asked, "You're saying what I think you're saying, right? That Greg is having an affair with Missy, and to keep that quiet, he stopped Bill from writing the story."

"Bingo," Bill said. "We're thinking that while Matt was working on his Missy story, he learned that Missy and Greg were together, or sleeping with each other, or . . . doesn't matter. But let's say Matt goes to Missy's to interview her and sees Greg there, in a compromising position, or maybe he just acts guilty. Or maybe he had suggested that Matt cover Missy, and Matt thought that was garbage because even Matt could tell Missy is a truly awful quilter. So, maybe Matt is suspicious from the jump. One, because Greg almost never assigns stories, and, two, because he assigns one about Missy. Matt, being Matt—a guy who charitably could be said to bristle at authority— pokes around. He suspects Greg of having an affair, finds proof of it, goes to Wendy, or threatens to."

Greg's wife, Wendy, was a lovely, kind woman who took care of herself. She watched her weight, dressed well, and was skillful with her makeup. I'd spoken briefly with her a few times over the years, and she seemed friendly and genuine. How the Wurts interacted privately, however, I had no idea.

"Not impossible," I said.

"I'm not saying Greg killed Matt," Bill said, "but he certainly had motive. The affair would explain why we got the anonymous email, but I'm not saying the sender knew anything more than that."

"Y'all have fleshed out a lot," I said, "or let your imaginations run wild. Time will tell. I really have to write, but I poked around, and I'm pretty sure, or as sure as I am of anything lately, that Matt was being followed."

"Seriously?" Brian asked.

"Hard proof?" Adam asked.

"Hard-headed, probably," I said. "Let me bang out this dreck . . . I mean, these carefully crafted examples of meaningful journalism, and then I'll try to firm up my proof."

But, even with everything else hanging over me, I could almost feel the rumble of 30,000 people marching into town for QuiltWeek, which was less than a week away.

QuiltWeek, which occurs each April, is an overwhelming juggernaut that transforms much of Paducah. An army of quilters, most pulling wheeled sewing boxes, toting satchels, or wearing backpacks full of supplies, invades various venues around town, including the Julian M. Carroll Convention Center, where the attendees overdose on technique and minutia while taking classes taught by quilting luminaries or listening to lectures given by their quilting idols. They're my kind of people: a creative, fabric-obsessed, stitch-happy contingent.

Numerous entities take advantage of the enthusiasm that all of those quilters bring with them (and by enthusiasm, I mean money), so quilts hang in businesses that don't otherwise celebrate fabrics. The event is so significant and pervasive that I thought it was odd that the city hadn't declared at least one day of QuiltWeek to be a city holiday, considering that Paducah's nickname is Quilt City. I couldn't think of a better way to generate civic pride, but such a designation was beyond my powers because I wasn't on the City Commission, and I wasn't the mayor. Yet.

Paducah's inundation by more quilting enthusiasts than the city had residents had kind of begun because the Yeiser Art Center's *Fantastic Fibers* show was up and running. It wasn't technically part of QuiltWeek, but it contributed to the overall quiltiness each April. When QuiltWeek was in full-swing, visiting Hancock's of Paducah was like negotiating the overfilled space under the Twin Spires of Churchill Downs during the Kentucky Derby—but with fewer hats.

Many residents of Paducah and McCracken County flee during QuiltWeek, not so much because they'll be bothered by the aficionados of applique, but because they can make serious money by renting their homes to the quilters who make their annual pilgrimages to the Quilt Capital of the World for the planet's most prestigious quilt show.

After I filed the two stories that were due that day, I called Lisa, she of the DMV job and the Paducah Symphony tastes.

"Tired of this, Little Miss Hadley. You always thought you were better than me. Still do, but when you need—"

"Better than you? I barely existed in high school. Kept my head down, did what I was told. Why would you say I thought I was better than you?"

"You were the teacher's pet in every darn class. Couldn't let anyone else get the best grade."

"I'm sorry, Lisa. It bothers me that you took my striving personally, as an affront."

"See, there you go. Affront. Why can't you just talk like the rest of us? Like I said, better than us."

"My striving for perfection isn't a positive trait. The world is far from perfect, so trying to be perfect and expecting others to be is a character flaw. Really. A therapist I started seeing noted how I cling to proper grammar, trying to control the uncontrollable, trying to force order out of chaos, which is what children of alcoholics—"

"Don't care. Unless you got a thousand for me, I'm done doing your dirty work." Click.

I was stunned. Was Lisa's anger toward me justified? Had I done something I shouldn't have to her and to other Tilghman students while I became valedictorian? I don't believe I was among the smartest in my graduating class, but I'd worked harder than anyone else had, and I was really good at taking tests. My hard work got me scholarships to college, scholarships I needed. Without them, I would likely have worked at. . . .

The DMV.

Or in a restaurant—which I did in college.

But my striving for better had nothing to do with Lisa or the other students. I never lorded my grades over anyone, never gloated about my scholarships. We make choices, and those choices determine where we land. I wanted the approval of exactly one person: the alcoholic waitress who gave birth to Jenny and me.

Even asking for acknowledgement can be a character flaw—but asking for approval was idiotic.

I decided to go with the assumption that the bald, fat, ugly dude who'd tailed Matt wouldn't tell me who had hired him, even if I tracked him down and asked politely. Whether he'd been a private investigator, an employee of one of Stoddard's companies, or someone else didn't matter. Matt had evidently spotted the tail and written down the license plate of both the guy's Camry and of the rental car.

I guessed that either Stoddard or Williams had put the tail on Matt. I could believe that Greg didn't want Bill investigating Matt's murder because Bill would learn of Greg's affair, probably by interviewing Missy, whom Matt had recently interviewed. But I didn't believe Greg had it in him to kill, even in a fit of rage. If Greg had snapped when Matt threatened to tell Wendy about Greg's affair, then bludgeoned Matt, I think Greg would have collapsed in a puddle of his own tears, blubbering. He didn't have it in him to spontaneously figure out a way to dispose of Matt's body, to think on his feet. He could barely think sitting at his desk, in his top-of-the-line chair with lumbar support.

I wasn't sure it mattered anymore, but I called Edgar Wendland, Missy's husband. No answer. I called their son, Jimmy. After introducing myself, I said, "My fellow reporters and I are looking into the murder of Matt Ackerman, and your mother's name was passed along to us."

"Yup."

"This is difficult to ask, but do you know if your mom is, um . . ."

"Sleeping with that editor? Yeah. My parents are fighting about it now. Want me to put them on?"

"Wow. No, thank you. That's not necessary. We're just trying to confirm—"

"You've confirmed. Bye."

I stared at the picture of Matt and me on my desk.

Suddenly, Matt's atrocious, embarrassing HeART of Paducah story about Missy made sense. Greg had insisted that Matt write about Missy, and he'd almost certainly told Matt to heap praise upon her and her work. Matt, as I mentioned, liked to "stick it to the Man" whenever he could, and there's no way he would've taken that directive from Greg as anything but the Man trying to keep him down.

Matt didn't have the political capital I'd banked after Stoddard grabbed my butt and Williams beat me, so Matt couldn't simply say no to Greg. He could, however, mock Greg and Missy and the *Chronicle* and stick it to the Man all at once by making a mockery of the HeART of Paducah, whose name was self-mocking.

I thought and thought, took a break, drank some water, walked the halls, ate an apple, and thought and thought. I stretched, sat back down, then turned to check if anyone was in the newsroom. Bill sat behind me on the far side of the office. The other reporters and Adam were home for the evening or out on assignments, so only he and I were in the bullpen.

"Bill, I have answers."

He turned to me and raised his right eyebrow. I told him about Jimmy confirming his mother's affair with Greg, then told him why I thought Matt had written the story about Missy the way he had.

"I thought it was unfortunate that it was among Matt's last articles," Bill said, "because he deserves to be remembered as being better than that. We both know he wasn't in his element in A&E. He'd been much better on cops. I went back and read his stuff. But he was nowhere near as bad as that story made him look."

"I know. That was his way of sticking it to Greg, who must've insisted Matt write the puffiest of puff pieces in a section profuse with puff pieces."

"Alliterate much?"

"Daily. Keeps me sharp. Although Greg has motive, and his actions following Matt's murder were suspicious, my gut tells me he doesn't have murder in him."

"I know. He'd risk ruining a sweater, not to mention mussing his hair."

"Can't imagine he wouldn't leave a strand or two at a crime scene."

Bill's cell phone rang. He answered, listened for ten seconds, then picked up a pen and a notebook. He hung up, closed his laptop, put it in his palm vertically, turned to me, and said, "There's been another murder. This one's weird."

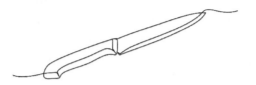

Chapter 17

Quilt as You Go

It had been dark for more than two hours by the time Bill and I arrived at the crime scene—the gazebo in the middle of Noble Park lake. Because very large, powerful lights now illuminated the area—run by a noisy generator—we could see six police officers, two EMTs, and the coroner on the bridge that leads to the gazebo in the middle of the lake or under the gazebo itself. The cops had strung yellow crime-scene tape across the entrances to the bridges that lead to the gazebo from either side of the lake. A crowd of about twenty people, a few of them young children, stood on the bank near the shortest of the two bridges so they were as close as they could get to the crime scene.

Photographer Adam Kerns had called Bill. Because Bill and I had been discussing the latest developments in Matt's murder, we hadn't heard this alert on the police scanner. The scanner was old, and it malfunctioned frequently, filling the newsroom with squawks, pops, and buzzing, so a lot of the time reporters on deadline turned the volume way down, or turned it off. Nearly all of the crime or legal stories Bill wrote began with an emailed press release sent by PPD or the district attorney's office, not by an alert over the scanner.

A large satellite truck from WKYC was parked on the grass as near as it could get to the water. A pretty, twenty-something brunette in a short, black skirt, white blouse, and maroon blazer appeared to be giving a live feed, which probably meant the TV station had broken into its regular programming with a breaking-news update.

Adam approached Bill and me, then said, "I heard on my phone scanner app someone call in a suspicious object in the gazebo. While I drove here, the scanner said someone called 911 to report a body in the gazebo. I got here when the cops did, so I ran to get an unimpeded shot of what had been reported, then got some solid shots of them figuring out what they'd found."

"Which was?" I asked.

"A dead woman wrapped in fabric, white fabric, from head to toe. Well, more than that. The reason the first caller didn't know it was a body was because she could've been anything. She was wrapped up like . . . I don't know . . . narrow on one end, then bigger in the middle, then narrow again on the other end, probably about eight feet in length. Here, look." He turned his digital Canon 5D on, then scrolled through about three-dozen photos he'd taken of the bundle and the officials surrounding it. After about the twenty-fifth shot, he said, "Look at these. You can barely see it, but when they unraveled her, there was blood every rotation, see, where it seeped out beneath her. Not a lot, but it's there. Can't see what else it would be but blood. And it looked like the cops pulled a purse out of there. See that sparkly thing at the edge of the frame?"

"Yes. Looks like a purse, so they'll likely have no trouble identifying her," Bill said.

"If it was *her* purse," I said.

"True. This is weird," Bill said.

"Did the blood look like it was in the middle of her body?" I asked.

"Yes. Why?" Adam asked.

"I was wondering if she'd been hit on the head as Matt had been."

"I can't say for sure, but I'd guess no," Adam said, "because the blood on the fabric wasn't near one of the ends, you know, the way it'd be if she had a head wound. It was more toward the middle of the . . ."

"Burrito?" Bill asked.

"Yeah, but maybe bundle or roll or something would be more appropriate," Adam said.

"Probably," I said.

"A couple more things," Adam said. "Don't know if it means anything, but the cops put an identifying marker next to it, number three, so they at least think it could be something. Here." He scrolled through a few photos, then said, "I think it's a scarf." A multi-colored piece of fabric, probably silk, lay on the platform, next to a white, plastic inverted V that had a black three on it.

"That's what I'd guess," Bill said at the same time I said, "Looks like one."

"They kept standing in the way of me getting a shot of number two," Adam said, "but, finally . . . the perspective's bad because it's flat, but if I had to choose one way or the other, here it is, I'd say that's a knife." He showed us the best photo of what was next to the number two placard, and Bill and I agreed that the glint we barely saw could be from light bouncing off of a blade.

Bill and I then tried to gather information so he could bang out the story for the next day's edition. But authorities act methodically at crime scenes, so whatever we would learn, we would learn slowly. And it was already late, so we would probably have to push the deadline, which wouldn't go over well with the powers that be, such as they were.

No one in the crowd had seen anything, or they wouldn't admit to reporters that they had.

I got the attention of four cops, one after another, then waved my reporter's notebook from outside the lighted area at each of them, indicating I'd either like to be allowed to duck under the crime-scene tape or would appreciate it if they'd approach me.

The first three individually approached as I stood at the crime-scene tape, but when the first two recognized who I was (I'm guessing from my smashed-up face and whichever lies Williams had told them about how my face got that way), they turned away. The third one approached, recognized me, said, "Bitch," then left.

Because I'm a resilient person and a tenacious reporter, I gestured the same way to a fourth officer. He nodded, then approached me. He was shaped like a well-muscled V, about six-two, with dark, wavy hair. I couldn't see the color of his eyes or even make out his features well because he was backlighted, which meant I was squinting at him because I was facing the lights. He stood about a yard from me but didn't turn away when he saw who I was.

Instead, he stuck out his right hand and said, "Officer Brandon Green."

"Hadley Carroll."

"I'm sorry for your loss, Hadley, and I'm sorry for what that moron Williams did to you."

I couldn't find words for a few seconds. A wound from my childhood caused me momentarily to become defensive, wondering what his angle was, how he would hurt me, or at least disappoint me. But a healthier part of me felt as though someone believed my side of the story.

"Thank you. Thank you very much, Officer Green. I didn't expect that. The other officers just walked away when they recognized me, except for the one who called me a bitch."

"I apologize for all of them. They stick together, almost like they share one brain."

"How'd y'all recognize me?"

"Williams took a screen grab of you from your Facebook page, then he . . . didn't do right by you."

"What does that mean, Officer Green?"

"Brandon."

"Okay. What does that mean, Brandon?"

"I'd rather not tell you. It's unpleasant."

"I'm not a princess. My fiancé was murdered, and Williams just busted my face, so, Officer Green, how did he do me wrong this time?"

"I'm sorry. You don't need me to protect you. Force of habit. Four younger sisters."

"I hope your house had more than one bathroom."

"Nope. I am, therefore, a patient man."

"That's good to know, but I'm not all that patient, unless I'm quilting. So, are you going to tell me, or do I have to make an Open Records request?"

"I'm pretty sure they don't apply to sophomoric locker room behavior."

"They do if there's documentation, and—"

"Okay, you win. Williams blew up your picture to eight by ten, taped copies up throughout the squad, then scrawled the worst words he could think of across your face. They were only up until I got there, but I'd guess most of the squad saw them. If he'd been around, I might've stuffed those photos down his throat."

"So, he hasn't been arrested?"

"No. The wheels of justice turn slowly. Word in the squad is he's being railroaded. What a shame—another good cop wrongly accused. They're saying you deserved what you got because you made him feel inadequate." He looked over his left shoulder toward the crime scene, and the light caught his face. I could see that his last comment made him smirk.

"Bet I'm not the first woman to make him feel that way."

He laughed, then said, "Look, I should get back. I just wanted to apologize to you."

"But I waved you over for a reason."

"Which was?"

"Can you give me details about what you've found? Anonymous, off the record, encoded. Whichever you prefer."

"The PIO is writing the press release now. You'll get it soon, so I'm not violating a thin-blue-line code by telling you."

"Telling me what?"

"You won't use my name?"

"No, but you're the only cop who's talked to either me or the other reporter here, so if you think your cohorts aren't smart enough to figure out who blabbed, then the citizens of Paducah should be very afraid."

He laughed, then said, "You're not normal, are you?"

"If you mean I am not average, then I'll take that as a compliment. If, however, you're suggesting we should aspire to be normal, well, Officer Green, shame on you."

"No, ma'am. Not saying that."

I looked to my left, and Bill tapped his wrist to let me know I was keeping him. We'd driven to Noble in my truck, and he had to get back to bang out his story under extreme deadline pressure. He might've started to write the story on his laptop.

I raised my hand and gave him the universal sign for one minute.

"I've got to go, too, Brandon. Last chance. If you want to step over that thin blue line, go for it."

"Natalie Loose, sixty-six, according to her driver's license. Lives in West Paducah."

"Thank you, Brandon. I hope you don't get beaten up or fired for your cooperation."

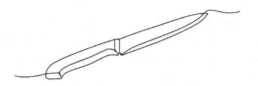

Chapter 18
Welt & Wale

When we got back to the office, I noticed that the red lights on all of the reporters' phones were blinking, meaning people had left messages. Because I'd never seen them all blink at the same time, I guessed the same person had called all of the phone numbers listed for the staff on the *Chronicle*'s website.

Bill continued to pound out his story on his laptop, and I picked up my cell to call Greg to tell him we were going to have to push the deadline. It was 10:45 p.m., and we usually shipped at 11. As I dialed, I heard Bill's desk phone ring, and he picked up and said, "Hello, newsroom."

"Sorry to wake you, Greg," I said into my cell, "but there's been another murder. According to a reliable source, Natalie Loose, sixty-six, is the victim, and she was left, wrapped like a mummy in white fabric, in the gazebo in the middle of Noble Park lake."

"Oh," Greg said, drawing from his well of eloquence.

"Bill's writing the story now. I'll see if I can pull together a sidebar about Natalie. Not sure I'll get much this late, but if not, we can run it as a follow-up."

"Okay," he said, accomplishing a stunning linguistic feat by doubling the number of syllables in his last response.

"We're going to have to push the deadline, probably a half hour."

"Why? That'll cost us money."

"So will losing readers and advertisers when we fail to cover a second high-profile murder in a timely fashion."

"Yeah, okay. Can you take care of it?"

Taking care of it required telling the design desk we needed to push the deadline a half hour, then calling the press guys to tell them the same thing. Those two tasks appeared to be beyond the scope of Greg's abilities, although not beyond the scope of his job duties.

Or was this his passive-aggressive way of showing me he was still the boss? He had lost the argument we'd had that morning. The story I'd written about Matt's murder had run, and his affair with Missy was no longer just between the two of them. He probably felt defeated and ineffectual, so he was asserting what little authority he could—having me do his job to show me he was still in charge.

I hung up and started to walk toward the far side of the office, where Jake and the other designers sat, when I heard Bill say into the phone, "Of course we can't hold it, Mildred. That's ridiculous."

I stopped walking to listen. Okay, eavesdrop. He must've been talking to Mildred Hoffman, the head of the Paducah Area Chamber of Commerce. I now knew why all of the phone lights were blinking.

"I understand, but QuiltWeek attendance isn't my concern," Bill said, "nor is it my job. My job is to report on crime in McCracken and the surrounding counties. A body dumped in Noble Park certainly qualifies as crime, so I'm writing the story. Goodnight." He looked up at me, and his expression asked, "Why was I born?"

"Let me guess. You're going to scare off hordes of quilters if they learn a killer is roaming Paducah, looking for other victims."

"Yup, and I should hold the story until after QuiltWeek, because . . . go ahead, guess."

"Because we held the story about Matt's murder for a week, so what's the difference?"

"Yup. Journalism at its finest, yet Greg's still in charge, wielding his decades of editorial wisdom like a sack of manure."

"I'll go tell Jake and the press guys we'll need about a half hour. Will that do it?"

"Sure," he said, then raced his fingers across the keyboard as Rachmaninov used to do.

After extending the deadline, I tried to find out as much as I could about Natalie Loose quickly. Even if I found the phone numbers of relatives and friends, I wouldn't have felt comfortable calling them then—not because I might wake them but because they likely hadn't heard the horrible news, and a reporter shouldn't be the one to break news like that, especially if Officer Green had looked at Natalie's driver's license in the purse but hadn't compared the photo to her body.

The last thing I'd want to do—other than vote for Mitch McConnell, obviously—would be to let family members know their loved one is dead, only for that loved one to stroll in the next morning, likely inducing at least one heart attack.

I gathered what I could, intending to email the info to Bill, who'd fold it into his story because my story would be too thin to stand alone, even as a sidebar. I'd be able to write a substantive story for Friday's paper if I had time on Thursday to write it.

I did the usual searches on social media, of social clubs, civic organizations, non-profits, and schools. What I learned was that Natalie Loose had graduated umpteen years ago from Tilghman and had married her high-school sweetheart (Gary Loose, who'd died five years earlier of lung cancer). They didn't have children. Natalie volunteered at Paducah Cooperative Ministries and the Oscar Cross Boys & Girls Club of Paducah, attended Twelve Oaks Baptist Church, had a lovely singing voice, and belonged to two quilting groups.

I compiled the information I thought Bill was most likely to drop into the end of his story, then emailed it to him. Just after I sent it, the newsroom's email address received the press release from the Paducah Police Department's public information officer. The press release confirmed the identity of the deceased.

I stuck around until Bill finished writing the article. I proofed it, and then he filed it.

We walked to the parking lot together.

"Great job, Bill. That was impressive work under the gun."

"Thank you, but, considering what's going on, maybe we should hold off on violent metaphors."

"Is using the word 'deadline' okay?"

He smiled. "Goodnight, Hadley. Thanks for your help. See you tomorrow for another day of *From Here to Absurdity!*"

I laughed, then drove home. I walked Trapunto, drew a bath, climbed in the tub carefully, keeping my tablet dry, then tried to read the latest edition of *Runner's World*. Then *Time*, then *Vanity Fair*, then *Yoga Journal*, but I couldn't concentrate on any of them.

Matt and Natalie Loose were killed in different ways, or at least appeared to have been, based on the blood we'd seen in the midsection of the fabric that had been wrapped around Natalie, as well as what might have been a knife. Could she have been hit over the head first, then stabbed or sliced? Yes. We'd have to wait for the coroner's report.

As the bathwater cooled and I debated whether to add hot water or to get out, then toss and turn while trying to sleep, I decided to focus on Matt's murder and let Bill and the police deal with Natalie's.

I got out of the tub, dried off, put on my pajamas—the blue pair with the sewing machine on them—got into bed, then tossed and turned, with Trapunto atop the quilt near my feet. After about two hours of running scenarios that led nowhere through my head, I finally fell asleep, only to have a long, creepy nightmare about clowns.

The next morning, after downing one more tumbler of coffee than I usually drank, and after walking Trapunto, I texted Bill to let him know I'd be in late, after I chased down a story.

"Anything scintillating?" he texted in response. "Doilies in the shape of Abe Lincoln?"

My response said, "Tell Justine she's married to a jackass."

While searching for stories, I'd learned that Harrah's Metropolis casino and hotel across the river would hold a big poker tournament as counterprogramming to QuiltWeek. While quilters took seminars, learned new techniques, hobnobbed with their quilting idols, and loaded their vehicles with a vulgar number of bolts (or shipped them home), their non-quilting partners who were either foolish enough to tag along—or who were blackmailed into doing so—could try their luck at Texas Hold'em in the casino.

The story wouldn't make an excellent HeART of Paducah piece, but excellence and the *Chronicle* had parted ways when Greg arrived four years before. I was a few days early pursuing that story because it wasn't due until Tuesday, and it was only Thursday. The tournament would be underway when the story ran, but I didn't see that as a problem. Someone else might have seen it as one, namely Editor von Sweater, but he'd probably be busy trying to hold his marriage together or searching for a divorce lawyer.

I figured I better pin down the story because HeART of Paducah couldn't be moved or delayed. Ads were sold against that regular feature as soon as the advertising department saw that week's subject in the budget. Or at least the ad department was supposed to try to sell ads against those stories. A corporate casino and hotel should be worth a half-page ad, but that assumed competence on the part of the ad department that was not in evidence.

Matt had played poker in the casino as often as he could afford to, which wasn't often because he earned hardly anything at the paper and because he rarely won. But he and his mom, Donna, went there together occasionally, despite her being borderline destitute. Her job at T.J. Maxx paid peanuts. Or was she borderline destitute because she went there more frequently than any of us realized?

I told myself as I crossed the river on I-24 that I was pursuing my HeART of Paducah story, and that was true, as far as it went. I knew something else was eating at me, but I didn't know what it was. I'd had an itch while tossing and turning, so I'd jumped out of bed, then looked at my notebook, the one I'd written the notes in that had stood out in Matt's notebook. I had run a line through the ones I'd resolved.

332 EYW
~~Being followed?~~
555 WWE
Payback time
Pat DeLott?
~~Really, Greg? Does Hadley know?~~

Yes, Matt, you were being followed, as you figured out because you tracked down the car that belonged to the follower. Did you have a suspicion who was following you? Did you write it down elsewhere? Did you confront whomever it was?

I'll figure it out, Matt. I promise you. I said those sentences out loud. Neither Trapunto nor I knew why.

Payback time for whom? Someone paying you back, as in getting even for something you'd done to him? Did you suspect you were in danger? Or was it time for you to pay someone else back? Williams, for the torture he put you through? Stoddard, for assaulting me at the Christmas party? Greg, for not standing up for me and letting me get kicked out of the newsroom? Or, did you intend to pay back someone else?

Was "payback time" part of why someone was following you, or was that unrelated?

Next on the list was Pat DeLott. I'd decided last night to look her up in the morning because I feared I could start researching, might fall down a rabbit hole, then would come out when I was eighty-three, if at all.

Yes, Matt, I now know that Greg is having an affair with Missy.

Or were you referring to something else?

Oh, Matt, why was all of this happening?

I had more questions than the SAT.

I parked in the huge lot at Harrah's Metropolis, in Illinois, intending to find at least a few answers. I conducted my interviews in the casino, which was neither as over-the-top extravagant as the Las Vegas casinos I'd seen in movies nor as downtrodden as the riverboat casino I'd seen in the Netflix show *Ozark*. I spoke with the casino's general manager, the manager of the poker room, and five players who said they intended to participate in the big Showdown on the River Tournament, which would be the second annual.

Peter Yett, the manager of the poker room, said, "Let's face it; fabric is huge in this region. Millions of dollars ride on the acquisition and the manipulation of fabric in Paducah and elsewhere. But there's one kind of fabric that money is especially drawn to, and that's felt. We'll have five to ten times our normal number of tables, depending on the number of players, and the green felt on our tables will sizzle with money, chips, and cards. You're probably aware of the $20,000 Best of Show prize QuiltWeek offers. Impressive, right? And, let's be honest, QuiltWeek is misnamed. The event is four days long, plus the opening awards ceremony. Well, Showdown on the River this year will be six days, Tuesday through Sunday, with daily tournaments in addition to the main one, and we'll deliver $40,000 to the player who wins the whole thing. So, you tell me—where would you rather be?"

As interviews go, his was excellent—filled with polished patter that got his points across while enticing people who were fond of Hold'em to test their skills and to try their luck. Although I'd joined Matt a few times at the poker table, basically throwing our money away, I thought that time spent gambling was time better spent quilting, so I knew where I'd rather be during QuiltWeek.

While mulling over all of those questions the night before, I'd wondered if I'd let my penchant for (or was it my obsession with?) neatness diminish the likelihood that I'd find Matt's killer. Had I thrown away receipts I'd found in his desk that could have helped me? I'd struggled to remember what I'd thrown away. The receipts that I could remember were one for two burgers from Fresh Country Kitchen, inside the casino, a dry-cleaning receipt from a store on Kentucky Avenue (although I hadn't noticed which cleaner or which item or items it was for), and a receipt for an oil change. I knew I was forgetting something else, but I hoped it would come to me. I kicked myself for throwing out the receipts, then prayed I wouldn't need them.

I pulled out the winning ticket for $1.40, then looked at the date. March 21, at 10:52 p.m. I'd taken that Friday off of work to fly to Los Angeles to help Jenny, my sister, through her latest crisis. She'd been dumped by that week's boyfriend, and she said she was afraid she'd hurt herself. I'd stayed on the phone with her most of the night until it was nearly time to pitch newspapers in the river. But instead of heroically saving readers from that day's crimes against journalism, I called in sick, then headed for Nashville so I could be charged an obscene amount of money for a flight to LAX in an attempt to save my sister's life. I'd succeeded, but I didn't know how long my words of solace and encouragement would last. Probably only until the next guy dumped her.

Did the winning ticket belong to the bald, fat, ugly guy who had followed Matt, or to someone else who'd rented the Cutlass? I went with the first assumption. Was it a large leap to assume that Mr. BFU had been following Matt that night? Probably, but, if so, had he placed bets while trying to blend in? I made that large leap anyway, then thought I could determine whether I was about to go splat or whether I would land gracefully.

I went back to the poker room, which wasn't open yet because it was still early in the day. The four kidney-shaped poker tables were empty. I asked Peter Yett, "You must have a master schedule that shows which dealers work which shifts, right?"

"Right."

"Any chance you can tell me who was working the evening of March 21?"

"Sure, there's a good chance, but why?"

"I'm trying to determine if my ex-fiancé, Matt Ackerman, was here—"

"Oh, I'm sorry. Really, really sorry. Didn't know you were together. I can't imagine."

"I hope you never have to."

"Whatever you need to know."

"I'm trying to figure out who killed him, and I think he was being followed. Maybe Matt was here that night. I found a small, uncashed win ticket dated March 21. It could mean nothing, but nothing's all I have right now."

"So, you're clinging to it. I get it. March 21. That was a Friday. I was off that night. Saw a movie I wish I hadn't."

"It happens."

"Too often, you ask me. Give me your number. I'll get in touch with the dealers who worked that night, see if we can tell you if Matt was here. Place has security cameras, but almost certain they're erased after so much time if nothing looks off. But I could check."

"Thank you. Anything will help. Or at least won't make things worse."

"Let's hope not."

I winced, then gave him a puzzled look.

"No, no, didn't mean anything by it. Not saying Matt was up to anything he shouldn't've been. I knew him to say hello, not much more. Nice enough guy. A little odd, lousy card player, but plenty of those around. No great failing. Again, I'm sorry for your loss."

I gave him a business card that had my office and cell numbers on it.

I should have gone back to work because I had stories to write, but I was already out, so I decided to try to pursue another lead—this one not piggybacking on a newspaper assignment. I drove across the river to Paducah, then stopped at both dry cleaners on Kentucky Avenue. I knew that playing the journalist card would be useless, so I played the grieving widow, a role that wasn't legally accurate but one whose emotions I didn't have to fake.

"Hello, I'm Hadley Carroll, and my former fiancé, Matt Ackerman, was killed a while ago. I'm checking to see if he had garments here that he didn't get the chance to pick up."

The cute young woman of about eighteen, with skin luminous enough to make me feel like a raisin, said, "Yeah, the reporter. Heard about that. I'm very sorry. Let me check." She typed his name on the keyboard, looked at the monitor, then said, "No, nothing here."

"Is he in your system, meaning has he ever left clothes here?"

"No, sorry. Unless I'm spelling it wrong." She spelled Matt's name for me.

"That's correct. Thank you. Sorry to bother you."

But the second shop, Out Damned Spot, just west of Joe Clifton Drive, had a record of Matt doing business there. I gave the matronly sixty-ish woman wearing a stunning bee-themed scarf she said she bought online the same spiel, and she said, "He picked up his last order on March 26. Left it the twenty-third." Matt had said goodbye to me on April 2 and was murdered on April 9.

"Do you mind telling me what it was?" I asked.

"Normally, I *would* mind. Privacy laws and whatnot. But, you being his ex, and seeing he's no longer with us, it was a woman's polyester blouse, floral print, size 2XL." She hesitated for a couple of seconds, then dropped her eyes before saying, "I take it the blouse wasn't yours."

No, it wasn't, for a few reasons. I wore a medium, I didn't wear polyester, and I wasn't likely to wear a floral print blouse, although I had a floral-print dress I really liked. I had never asked Matt to run an errand like that for me. I'd taken a pair of pants of Matt's to the cleaner one time when I mentioned I was going, but that was to Sparkling Clean on Park, which was closer to both of our houses. Why had he taken someone's XL blouse to Out Damned Spot?

"Do you mind if I ask if there were any special instructions?"

She'd anticipated my question and didn't have to look at the screen again. "You're not going to like this, honey, and I'm certain you don't need more bad news."

"I appreciate your concern, really, but I'm trying to find a killer, so sugar-coating whatever you have to tell me won't help."

"Blood stains. Not just a few drops."

The news hit me hard. What was Matt up to? No one deserves to be clubbed to death, then dumped in a river, but had Matt been courting trouble, or covering something up?

"Where was the blood?"

"On the chest."

I had to get to work, but how was I supposed to concentrate after learning that?

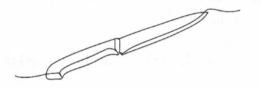

Chapter 19
Wonky

Back in the office, I dutifully slogged through three rewrites of press releases, then promoted a fundraiser that would be held on Saturday for the McCracken County Humane Society. The other reporters conducted phone interviews, wrote stories, and coordinated their schedules with Adam, who usually took the photos that appeared in the paper. Most of the reporters' photos were junk.

I filed my last story, walked around the office twice, made about two minutes of small talk with Brian, drank a cup of what someone in the lunchroom had mistakenly labeled coffee, then sat at my desk again, ready for the rest of my day.

I still had to write a follow-up about Natalie Loose. No one seemed any closer to solving either of the recent atypical murders. I wanted all of the typical murders—drug deals gone bad, guns interacting with alcohol, morons out-moroning other morons—to be solved, too, but my gut told me these atypical ones were related, even though they appeared to have nothing in common except that they were homicides. And, of course, Matt's murder was far more than a crime statistic to me.

I made calls to pull together the story about Natalie. I got quotes about how special she'd been and about how sad her friends and family were to have lost her, especially in such a horrible manner. Luckily, all of the people I called knew about Natalie's murder, so I didn't have to break the news to any of them. After eating the pasta salad I'd brought for lunch, I proofed my story a second time, then filed it.

I stood, stretched, walked two laps around the newsroom, filled my water bottle at the water fountain, returned to my desk, then said to Bill, across the room, "Mine's in. How's yours going?"

"Blah-blah-nothing. No one knows anything. Despite Natalie being dumped in Noble, there are no witnesses, or none has come forward, which means there are no witnesses. The cops have no suspects, but Galliski all but commanded me not to mention the scarf at the scene. Apparently, she hadn't read the story that mentioned it. They're at the top of their game over there. The coroner, off the record, told me Natalie had been stabbed two times in each lung.

"Based on the relatively small amount of blood on the scene—on the fabric—she was killed elsewhere, wrapped up, then transported to Noble. Hasselquist, again off the record, said the knife was an unserrated butcher's knife, J.A. Henckels, high quality, relatively expensive but available at Macy's and other fine retailers, as the ad slogan goes. No prints on the purse or its contents. Everything had been wiped clean. As I said, blah-blah-nothing."

"You are aware that your job is to report on the murders, not to solve them, right?"

"Oh, right. Sometimes I mistake journalism school for the police academy. Pffeeew. Thanks for setting me straight."

"My pleasure. It's why I'm here."

"Figured there had to be a reason."

"Touché! I deserved that. I can add to your frustration, if you'd like."

"Please. My doctor said I'm not hypertensive enough."

"Then this should help. Matt *was* being followed. In his notes, I found license plate numbers. Through an acquaintance at the DMV, I tracked one of them to a rental agency, where the car with the other plate number Matt recorded had sat for two weeks while the bald, fat, ugly guy who rented the Cutlass Supreme with the first plates tailed Matt."

"Great work, but why would someone follow him? And how do you know the guy was bald, fat, and ugly?"

"The clerk told me what the guy looked like. My guess is Nick Stoddard hired him."

"Probably. That Open Records could be motive. If Matt was onto something, Nick could have killed Matt, or had him killed."

"Or Matt could have confronted the guy tailing him but got the worst of the confrontation."

"Matt was big and strong, so—"

"But he was hit from behind. Anyone could kill anyone else with a hard blow to the head from behind. Look, Bill, I'm not saying I have a clue what happened. All I do, other than bang out mediocre blurbs and dreck filled with adjectives, is think about the possibilities."

"First, your copy hasn't suffered. I just read your piece on Natalie, and it's everything a piece like that should be. And, second, you've made significant progress. Finding out Matt was being followed is enormous. Wait a sec: Why didn't you run the second plate?"

"My contact at the DMV told me to get lost."

"Why?"

"She said I think I'm better than she is."

"Almost certainly are. You're exceptional in a lot of ways. Sure, you're messed up in a lot of others, but—"

"Don't go into counseling. She wants a thousand bucks as a bribe, although she might have just thrown that number out to send me away. I don't have anywhere near that kind of money, not after Jenny cost me what little I had saved when I flew to L.A. for the weekend."

"You're not the only one with a friend at the DMV. Give me the plate number, and I'll call my guy."

"555 WWE."

"After I file this story, I'll see what I can come up with. By the way, I called Suzanne Bigelow to see what was happening with Officer Williams, and she said, off the record, quote, 'Something's in the works that should please fans of justice and accountability. But if you print anything, the DA's office will never work with the *Chronicle* again.'"

"That's great. But good luck finding jurors here who will convict an officer."

"Ye of little faith. One step at a time. If my DMV guy doesn't come through, maybe we can create a GoFundMe page."

"Yeah, that would be great. 'Journalist needs to bribe public official. Please contribute.' And I don't like asking for help."

"You're grieving and in mourning and stressed out. Asking for help isn't a sign of weakness. It's what humans do. We're social creatures. You're doing everything you can to solve this case, more than the entities whose job that is, it seems. According to PPD, two detectives are working Matt's and Natalie's murders, one per case."

"Not exactly a task force," I said. "If public perception links what appear to be two unrelated murders, or if another body is found in the next few days before QuiltWeek, Paducah could suffer a catastrophic economic hit."

"Which would seem like the worst-case scenario to everyone but the next victim."

I needed to stretch my legs, to take a nap, to eat a mountain of chocolate, and to erase the last fifteen days of my life, or some combination thereof. But instead of doing these, I turned toward my computer, then typed Pat DeLott into the *Chronicle*'s content-management system.

A horrible mistake—and the best thing I've ever done.

Paducah resident Pat DeLott had been a fifty-six-year-old real estate agent for Century 21, according to the story Bill had written about her, which ran in the paper on Tuesday, March 25. DeLott had been the victim of a push-in robbery that turned deadly late Sunday or early Monday, according to PPD. She'd been stabbed in the stomach, then collapsed in her foyer, where she died. When police arrived the next morning after a neighbor walking his dog saw DeLott's door open and found her body, the officers discovered that the house had been ransacked, with the perpetrators stealing nearly everything of value, according to PPD.

The meth and opioid problems in Paducah were as bad as they were nearly everywhere else, so it didn't seem unlikely that an addict or addicts needing money would steal valuable items from a house so they could sell them for a fraction of their worth to buy drugs.

Whether the killer or killers knew Pat would be at home and killed her as part of their plan, or whether her presence there was a surprise didn't seem to matter. She was dead, and her valuables were gone, sold in half a dozen different ways to who knows how many people.

The two follow-up stories that had run the week after Pat was murdered didn't add much, except to say that she was an avid quilter, a member of the Rotary Club of Paducah, and a volunteer at Paducah Cooperative Ministry. Cherie DeLott, Pat's daughter, provided Bill with a list of the valuables that she thought were missing, including a large flatscreen TV and an expensive sewing machine.

Why would Matt have written her name in his notebook? Maybe she was an exceptionally great quilter whom he was considering writing about for HeART of Paducah. But a Google search and a scouring of social media didn't seem to indicate that Pat was more than a hobbyist. She didn't appear to be aspiring to quilting fame nor have the creative vision nor technical knowhow, based on the competent quilts she'd featured on her Facebook page. So, there had to be another reason why Matt had written her name.

But Pat was a quilter who'd been stabbed to death. Matt couldn't have known that Natalie Loose, another quilter, would be stabbed to death, but did he know something that could have predicted Natalie's murder? Or prevented it?

One of the many adages I'd heard in the various newsrooms I'd worked in was this: "When in doubt, pick up the phone." So, I called Cherie DeLott, Pat's daughter.

After I introduced myself and told her why I was calling, she said, "I'm not sure I have much to say. Your paper ran stories after it happened, and two different reporters followed up, but I had nothing to add, and the police don't seem any closer to catching who did this than they were right after it happened."

"One of those reporters was Bill Lang, our cops and courts reporter. Do you remember who the second one was?"

"He didn't want to say his name, but I insisted, considering what had happened and that the killers haven't been caught. When he was killed, I thought he must've rubbed someone else the wrong way, too."

"Matt Ackerman."

"Yes."

"Did he say why he was calling?"

"He wanted to know what was taken and what kind of fabric my mom used."

"Wow, that's weird. What kind did she use?"

"I told him to hold on, then went to check. My mom's fabric stash was probably worth as much as the other stuff taken, but they didn't touch it, or didn't appear to. She had a lot of different kinds of fabric, mostly quality stuff. She did very well in real estate, so she didn't have to buy junk. I just gave him a few names. He asked about one specifically, a funny name, but I don't remember it. She didn't have any of it that I could see."

"Okay, that's great information. Bill's story said it was a push-in robbery. As I understand the term, that means your mom opened the door to the perpetrator or perpetrators, rather than the door being kicked in or the glass in it being smashed. Is that correct?"

"That's how I understand it. The door wasn't damaged, so the push-in part seems right."

"Was your mom the type who would open her door to strangers at night?"

"Absolutely not. She was very gregarious, which helped her a lot in real estate, but she was cautious. The doors to the outside had two locks on them, and she slept with a .22 on her nightstand. That was stolen, of course."

"It sounds like you feel confident your mom must've known her attacker, otherwise she wouldn't have opened the door."

"Yes. She would've sooner called 911 than open the door late at night to a stranger."

"Okay. One last question. What were some of the items that were stolen?"

"Her television was almost brand new, a huge fifty-six-incher. Most of her jewelry wasn't worth much, but she had a few heirloom pieces, stuff her Italian grandmother had passed down. She had a bunch of collectible plates that were probably worth something, and a few expensive tablecloths that also came from her grandmother in Italy. Let me see. A camera, a Mac laptop, a sewing machine she paid a lot for, a second TV in her bedroom, the gun, a mink coat, which I told her long ago to get rid of because they're so evil, but she could be stubborn. I guess that's it. I can't remember anything else."

"You remembered a lot. Do you think your mom's neighbors would know anything about that night?"

"The police talked to all of them, and nobody heard anything. Mr. Glass, an elderly neighbor a couple houses away, saw her open door early the next morning when he was walking his dog and thought that was weird, so he walked up the driveway and saw her from a distance. He said he went back to the street as fast as he could, then called 911. He never went near my mom, and he didn't hear anything that night, either."

"Again, I'm sorry for your loss. Is there anything else you'd like to add?"

"No. Oh, wait. When the police were done with the scene and returned my mom's effects, they included a necklace that I don't think belonged to my mom. A broken necklace."

"I'd bet mistakes like that happen a lot. Broken how?"

"The clasp was broken. They said it was probably torn off during the attack. They found it under her, and that *could* make sense, but I'm almost certain it wasn't my mom's necklace."

"Why do you say that?"

"Not her style at all. She had pretty conservative tastes. Diamonds, pearls, nothing out there. And this was something an artisan would make and sell at a farmers' market or a craft fair. Pretty silver swirls. I liked it, but I don't think my mom would have."

"Forgive me for asking if this is a delicate subject, but is there any chance your mother could have been seeing someone who could have purchased the necklace for her as a gift? We can learn to like a present if it's given by the right person."

"Yes, I agree. But, no, it's not a sensitive subject. I kept telling my mom she had to move on, that Dad would have wanted her to, to live her life, to find happiness again. She got offended every time I mentioned it, like I was insulting my father. So, I hadn't considered that possibility. I really hope you're right. Maybe she had a little hope in her life for a while." She started to cry.

"Thank you for your time, and I'm sorry I upset you, Cherie."

"No, you didn't. Really. You let me at least consider that Mom was moving on. I have one request to make."

"Sure. What is it?"

"Catch the monsters who did this!"

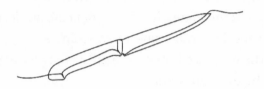

Chapter 20
Raw Edge

I was hoping for an uneventful, borderline-boring day on Friday, but thoughts were pinging and ponging around my head like popcorn in a pressure cooker, so peace and calm didn't make it onto that day's agenda. Usually, I ate my bag-lunch in the lunchroom, but the antsy feeling creeping through my head had invaded the rest of my body, so I decided to walk to Kirchhoff's downtown to buy a sandwich. I'd eat the salad I'd brought for lunch later.

When I got outside, I was surprised to find it wasn't raining because rain was probably Paducah's most-defining feature behind quilting. More than half of my morning runs could have been called puddle-jumps. Trapunto loved to splash his way through town, but I preferred my expensive running shoes not to look like wallowing bison after I wore them once.

In Kirchhoff's, I ate three bites of my delicious portabella sandwich and drank half a cup of coffee, and I'd almost managed to eliminate the panic that had coursed through my system for more than two weeks. But then Nick Stoddard walked in with a leggy, gorgeous blond I'd never seen before. He wore what I guessed was a very-expensive black suit, which was at least one size too small, struggling to hold back his Jim Beam weight. She wore next to nothing. His silk rep tie was probably older than she was. She could have been his granddaughter because he was in the neighborhood of sixty. But I really hoped they weren't related because his right hand caressed her right hip in a manner that didn't shout "friendly and platonic."

They stood at the bakery counter, considering their order. I turned away from them, but he must have seen me because ten seconds later, I heard, "Well, if it isn't the troublemaker."

I set my sandwich down slowly, finished chewing, took a swig of coffee, then took my sweet time turning his way. He stood close to me, crowding my chair. I looked up and smiled the most fake smile I'd ever smiled, hoping he would recognize it as phony. His tan was as bogus as my smile. He was bating me, hoping I'd bite, and I really wanted to bite in the form of a scathing reply. I tried to count to ten before speaking, as I'd read that people are supposed to do when faced with a verbal confrontation. I made it to two, then said, "Well, if it isn't Nicky Corruption, evader of taxes and all-around jackass."

His eyes got huge for an instant, then became slits as he squinched his face and glared at me. In my peripheral vision, I thought I saw his right hand form a fist, but I wasn't about to take my eyes off his face. I did, however, move my left hand on top of the fork I intended to use to eat my coleslaw. His lunch date was not in my vision. Probably off playing with blocks.

"You been snooping," he said. "Small town. Things get around. People get hurt, dead sometimes. But you know all that."

I'd left my purse in the office, having only taken some cash with me. If I'd had my purse, I would have had my recorder, which I would have pulled out as soon as I saw Stoddard enter. Grabbing my recorder had served me well in the office when Officer Williams had said from behind me, "Miss Carroll." If I hadn't caught on tape the beating that he gave me, I probably wouldn't have had a winnable case against him.

In Kirchhoff's, I didn't want to look away from the human garbage stuffed into an Italian suit in front of me, but I hoped other customers were sitting near enough to hear him. I didn't have much hope for that, however, because he leaned down and whispered in my ear. "You know nothing. You can prove nothing. Your boy Matt thought he could prove something, but he ain't with us no more, is he?"

My left hand closed around the fork, and in a split second, I calculated the odds that I could drive its tines into his hand. But in the next split second, I dismissed that possibility because the fork was plastic, and humiliating myself while causing him very little physical pain solved nothing. Had the fork been metal, I'd like to believe I would have made the same decision, but, luckily, I didn't have to test that supposition.

Instead, I stood up quickly, accidentally catching his chin with my shoulder, hard enough that he had to shake it off. His expression indicated he'd bitten his tongue. When he'd grabbed me at the Christmas party, followed by me decking him, I must have realized that he was two inches shorter than I am because my punch hadn't lost any oomph by having to punch upward. While he stood above me in Kirchhoff's, I'd felt overmatched and threatened. But on my feet, I saw once again that I was every bit his physical equal, maybe his superior. He outweighed me by a lot, but it was booze and pretzels weight—not the muscle that athletes have. Not the kind Matt had. The squinting glare Stoddard had tried to intimidate me with a minute ago now looked like the grimace of a scared bully, hoping I wouldn't call his bluff.

I called his bluff.

"If you had anything to do with Matt's murder, I *will* prove it, and then I'll throw a party when you're locked up. If you're an embezzling tax cheat, the D.A. will do her best to convict you. And if you're only a philandering scumbag, maybe I'll let Sandy know about the high-schooler you're with who forgot to get dressed this morning."

"You fight dirty. I like that. Don't mean you'll win, but I respect fighters." He laughed loudly, then turned and walked toward the bakery counter and his gorgeous dalliance. He put his left arm around her, then pointed his right index finger at me, with his thumb up, as if shooting a pistol. He fired, then blew invisible smoke from his finger barrel.

I was supposed to meet Dakota that night at Mellow Mushroom, the huge, thriving pizza joint in the converted Coca-Cola Bottling Plant in Midtown. The pizza there is the best I've eaten, including the slices at Five Points Pizza East in Nashville.

But, as much as I loved Dakota, my exchange with Stoddard had bothered me, and I wasn't up for one person after another approaching me to ask how I was doing. They'd think they were being polite, but, if they'd ever endured a stretch as devastating as the one I was experiencing, they'd know that talking about the devastation makes it worse.

Isolating myself was not what I was supposed to do while depressed, but I thought quilting for a few hours would be more therapeutic and relaxing than socializing would be.

I settled into my chair in The Stash Hash, then lost myself in "Labyrinth," a pattern from Jacqueline de Jonge's traditional collection that I had been chipping away at for about two months. The pattern was inspired by an antique floor. It used batiks and required me to be better at paper-piecing than I was. Despite getting frustrated with myself and the universe, I added about half as much to the quilt that night as I'd produced in the previous two months.

Plus, I kept thoughts of the non-quilting world out of my head.

For short periods. Okay, for a few minutes at a time, but I managed to do that numerous times, so I had at least eleven murder-free minutes.

When I looked at my phone to check the time, I was surprised to learn I'd spent nine uninterrupted hours quilting, and it was 3 a.m. Trapunto woke up when I decided it was time to surrender. I stood, then turned out the light. He went to the bedroom, jumped onto the bed, curled up on the quilt at the foot of it, then was snoring again before I'd finished brushing my teeth.

Late Saturday morning (meaning 11:50 a.m.), I bounded out of bed like a woman with a quilt to work on. I hadn't planned to spend my weekend hunched over inside, especially because—for reasons unexplained by meteorology—no rain was forecast for TWO STRAIGHT DAYS.

After having felt a sense of accomplishment while quilting, I thought I'd dive back into "Labyrinth." But as I was washing my coffee mug, adorned with a picture of a quilter's brain on it, a question popped into my head. Which fabric had Natalie Loose been wrapped in?

For the sake of argument, I speculated. Of the four categories of textiles—plant, animal, mineral, and synthetic—I chose plant, then went with the subset cotton. Brand? How about Northcott. Because Natalie was wrapped in white, I went with Toscana Picket Fence.

Then, if I miraculously came up with the correct brand name and style, from the—I don't know, 10,000 choices?—what would that tell me about Natalie's killer? Or about Natalie? The only thing it would determine, it seemed, was that I was a great guesser.

Toscana Picket Fence by Northcott was sold in countless venues. If Northcott supplied a list of all of the venues that sold Toscana Picket Fence, I wouldn't be able to call every one of them worldwide, and even if I could, they wouldn't divulge the names of the customers who'd purchased that fabric.

That left everyone who'd paid cash at any of those venues, anyone who'd purchased Toscana Picket Fence from a swap meet, an eBay seller, or some other third party, and every venue that refused to play along with the absurd invasion of privacy the above scenario required.

And all of this falderol depended upon the accuracy of my impossible guess. Plant, cotton, Northcott, and Toscana Picket Fence, as opposed to Groucho, Harpo, Chico, Zeppo, and Gummo.

In other (and many fewer) words, it didn't matter which fabric Natalie Loose had been wrapped in. This conclusion was reasonable, rational, and based in reality. Fabric makers would not have to break laws to provide me with their customers' names, and I wouldn't spend the rest of my life looking for a fabric that likely would never lead us to Natalie's killer and definitely wouldn't identify Matt's killer.

But what if it did?

I called Bill, who answered like this: "It's Saturday, Hadley. You're the A&E reporter. I'm the cops reporter, but I'm spending my Saturday the way Saturdays should be spent—not working."

"Is that what won you the Pulitzer?"

"Maintaining boundaries played a small part, but talent and good looks brought it home."

"Then you must be *really* talented."

"Touché, right back at you. What do you need?"

"Don't tell me I'm insane. The voices in my head do that in harmony. I need to know if you know anyone who'd let me see the fabric Natalie was wrapped in. Don't ask why."

"Why?"

"Because it might matter."

"How?"

"I don't know."

"But you want me to call in a favor no one owes me so you can look at the fabric to determine if it will reveal something about the killer?"

"Correct."

"Do you want to slide down a rainbow, too?"

"If you can arrange it."

In the background, I heard Justine say, "Come on, Billy. It's your shot."

"Where are you?"

"Paxton Golf Course."

"Didn't know you played."

"I play badly enough not to admit I play."

"I bowl the same way."

"Look, I have to assume the fabric is in an evidence locker, and I'm pretty sure a court order would be required for a member of the press to see it. I met one of the officers who checks in the evidence when he was watching a trial just for fun, but I don't remember his name, and he doesn't owe me a favor, definitely not one that could cost him his job."

"So, you're saying you'll find a way to get me in there to see the fabric, right?"

"Goodbye, Hadley."

"Thanks. Keep your head down and make some birdies."

"I didn't know you played."

"Bought clubs and paid for lessons, but I'm not good enough yet to let people know I play. If I did, they may ask me to fill out their foursome, and that could be dangerous. I don't agree with Twain that golf is a good walk spoiled, but the state of my game proves he had a point."

"I'm about to hit one in the lake, so I gotta go."

"With positive self-talk like that, how could you go wrong?"

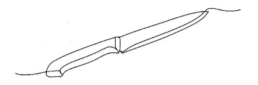

Chapter 21
Variegated Thread

I hopped on my thrift-store Cannondale road bike, rode two blocks to Noble Park, then pedaled the Greenway Trail until it ended downtown, along the river. I rode farther than I would've if I'd just ridden down Jefferson, but it was a rain-free day, and I had nothing against exercise. I rode up Jefferson to Sixteenth, cut across to Broadway, took a left, then locked my bike to a tree near the police station at 1400 Broadway.

I clipped my bright-orange Lazer bike helmet to my top tube. Then I entered the station wearing my bright-orange cycling cap, an orange cycling jersey, burnt-orange capris (can you guess the color of my bike?), and blue Tretorn sneakers. I hoped no one thought I was on fire.

As I approached the desk, I pressed the "record" button on my recorder. A Black officer with a shaved head asked, without looking up, "May I help you?" His nametag said Officer Armstrong. When he looked up and saw who I was, his bored "May I help you?" expression changed to one of disgust.

"I hope so. I'm wondering if Officer Green is working today."

He hesitated, then said, "No, he's not." He scowled.

"Are you sure?"

"I am."

"Would you mind double checking, please?"

"I would."

"Would you double check anyway, please?"

"No."

"Okay, then would I be violating any laws if I were to sit on that bench until he arrives?"

"No, but he might not be in until second-shift tomorrow."

"Or he could be working now."

I walked to the bench, about twenty feet away, sat down, turned off the recorder, deleted the file, folded my left leg over my right, leaned my head back against the wall, then closed my eyes. About fifteen minutes later, I heard, "Hello, Hadley."

"Hello, Officer Green. How are you today?" I uncrossed my legs, stood, then shook his hand.

"I'm doing well. It sounds like you are, too, if making another enemy of an officer of the law can be considered doing well."

"Not my objective, but I do seem to have a flair for it." I smiled. "How did he declare my enemy-combatant status?"

"The B-word. Three times in two sentences."

"Impressive."

"How may I help you?"

"You probably can't, but I figured I'd try. Natalie Loose was wrapped in fabric. I assume that the fabric is in an evidence locker. I also assume there's no way I can look at it."

"You assume correctly on both counts."

"I don't know what I'm looking for. I don't even know if I were to find what I'm looking for that it would help me find Matt's killer."

"You know that's our job, right?"

"I don't mean to be disrespectful, Officer Green, but how much progress has the department made on his case?"

"It's reasonable for you to be disrespectful because one of our officers assaulted you under color of law in the course of the investigation. But I can't talk about our progress."

"So, you understand why I'm using my investigative skills to see what I can turn up?"

"Yes."

"Journalists get bad raps—"

"Just like cops."

"I don't agree. A lot of cops get a lot of unwarranted criticism from angry, disgruntled people, many of them criminals, and many of those cops are doing great work and honoring their departments. So, as I said, that criticism is unwarranted. But, more than a few cops are behaving horribly—beating people, raping women, killing people, then planting guns to cover their tracks. But I've never heard anyone denigrate law enforcement as an institution, declare all cops to be evil or corrupt, or that police forces shouldn't exist. Police officers and sheriff's deputies are admired, respected, and even revered. When was the last time you heard any of those words used to describe journalists, the ones who inform the public about the bad cops, the unscrupulous corporations, and the corrupt politicians?"

"You're an excellent writer, Hadley, even when speaking. I agree with everything you just said. But I can't do anything to influence the public's view of the media, or a lot of the public, anyway. Explain to me again why you'd like to see the fabric."

"When you investigate crimes, do you ever play a hunch despite not knowing why?"

"Often."

"Okay, then maybe you'll understand. I don't know why I need to see the fabric. My gut is telling me to try to make sense of something I can't verbalize. I'm not here to get you in trouble. I understand you owe me nothing, and I understand I won't be allowed to see the fabric, but could you take a look at it, if doing so doesn't put you in a bind?"

"Maybe. I'll check with the evidence clerk. What would I be looking for?"

"You're not going to see a label or a hidden watermark. I don't know if you are looking at Matt's murder and Natalie's murder as being connected—"

"No. Different MOs."

"I understand, but I think they're connected, and they could even be connected to Pat DeLott's murder. My gut thinks they're related, even though I'm just a helpless, ditzy girl who only writes silly A&E stories."

He laughed. "So, I'd be looking for what?"

"See if you can tell the quality of the fabric. I'm guessing you're not a quilter or a fashion connoisseur—"

"I own two Brooks Brothers suits, so don't dismiss me just because—"

"Sorry, my mistake. If you can, please tell me if the fabric is rough and cheap, smooth and expensive, a high- or low-thread count, intentionally shiny or just a cheap sheen, something Princess Di would have had a dress made from or something Roseanne Barr would wrap her dog in."

He smiled, then said, "I'll see what I can do." He walked away.

I closed my eyes, said a prayer, then rested my head against the wall again. After about five minutes, I heard his footsteps coming toward me. I opened my eyes.

He sat down next to me. "Rough and cheap, just a sheen, low thread count, and Roseanne's dog."

"Excellent. Thank you."

"Do you think that info tells you something?"

"Definitely. I just don't know what that something is." He laughed, and I smiled.

"Enjoy the rest of your day, Hadley."

"You, too, Brandon. Thanks for your help."

As I walked away, I glanced back at Officer Armstrong. He was glaring at Officer Green and me.

Before I put on my helmet, I called Dakota and asked if she wanted to kick off QuiltWeek early by visiting the *Fantastic Fibers* show at the Yeiser. She said yes, so I told her I'd meet her there in a half hour.

I rode to Roof Brothers Wine & Spirits on Park and bought a bottle of dry white wine from Fancy Farm Vineyard called Harvest Gold. I slipped the bottle into the middle pocket on the back of my cycling jersey, then rode the mile to Donna Ackerman's house. I wasn't up for—

and didn't have time for—a long, tearful discussion about the chasm of emptiness we were both falling through, so I set the bottle down out of the sun, next to the large ceramic, teal, and turquoise mushroom Donna had created about a decade ago. Harvest Gold was her favorite wine, and she'd know the bottle came from me because she, Matt, and I had discussed Fancy Farms wines a few months before.

Dakota and I hugged outside of the Yeiser, the small-but-substantive gallery in the heart of downtown. Within a block of the Yeiser were half a dozen restaurants, various artsy shops, Maiden Alley Cinema, and a few Market House Theatre venues. The area would be overrun in a couple days, but that afternoon, it only had the usual Saturday crowd—meaning hundreds of people, not thousands.

We entered the single-room gallery, which featured floating partitions that could be arranged to feature the works in a particular show to best advantage. Every year, *Fantastic Fibers* was among my favorite aspects of QuiltWeek, even though it wasn't overseen by the American Quilter's Society. Not only did *Fantastic Fibers* exist in an intimate space that featured many other media during its annual shows, but this curated show also featured extraordinary quilts that some of the other shows that piggybacked on QuiltWeek wouldn't likely receive. The quality of the Yeiser shows was always high.

That year was no exception, and Dakota and I thoroughly enjoyed admiring and studying the works as we moved slowly through the gallery with seven other patrons. After we visited for a few minutes, she asked, "How are you really doing?"

"Poorly enough that I took your advice and had my first session with Elaine, but well enough to admit the session helped a lot."

"I'm glad to hear that. You know I love you, and I'm here for you, at any hour, however I can help."

"I appreciate that, D. I really do. Are you going to Natalie's funeral?"

"Yes. It's all a bit much, isn't it? After attending Matt's, Veronica's, and Pat's, we're in a constant state of mourning."

"Wait, Veronica? Who's she?"

"Oh, right. You were in L.A. with Jenny. Veronica Yarnell won big on the dollar slots, in the neighborhood of six grand."

"That's a nice win."

"Normally, yes, it would be great. But someone followed her to her car and shoved her backward while robbing her. She hit her head on the side of the van her car was parked next to, then on the asphalt, and she never got up."

"Wow. Broken neck?"

"And head trauma. Very tragic. What made it worse is the van blocked the security camera in that far corner of the lot. The other cameras didn't show anyone identifiable walking to or from her car. All the money she'd just won was gone. Bill's article said all this."

"That's awful. When I got back, I was exhausted. Don't ever fly across the country on a Friday, deal with a suicidal sister, fly back Sunday, then try to be at work at 5 a.m. Monday. I'd almost stopped reading the papers back then, so I didn't read any of this."

"They think it was either a casino employee who saw a teller hand Veronica the cash, or it could have been the teller him- or herself. I'm sure a small bribe could get someone to erase any incriminating security footage, if the killer employee didn't know how to do it. There was speculation that low-rent thugs messed up their MO that night because a few other winners had been robbed in the last six months, but no one got hurt. The thugs just followed people they saw cashing out to their cars, then demanded their money. A security guard started patrolling the lot since Veronica was killed, so I'd guess the robberies have stopped."

"How did you know Veronica?"

"She, Natalie, and I volunteered at Paducah Cooperative Ministry. Pretty frightening that two volunteers there have been killed. Wait, do you think I should be worried?"

"You're asking the wrong woman. I worry about worrying, then worry whether I haven't worried enough."

"Sadly, I know what you mean. By the way, did you see Mike Weiss?"

"Yes, he's a wonder. Disproves the negative opinion of lawyers. Thanks for the recommendation. He says Williams is toast."

"Great to hear."

"Oh, I think I met the man for you."

"I'm listening."

"He's a cop but not a cop. Unlike any I've met. Tall, dark, and handsome. Well-spoken, well-groomed, well-built. No ring. Nothing like Williams."

"Hook me up."

"Officer Brandon Green at PPD. I've done the reconnaissance. Now go win the battle."

"I'd prefer a more romantic metaphor, but I appreciate you thinking of me, and I'll work my magic."

"Yikes, if you have magic, too, no man stands a chance."

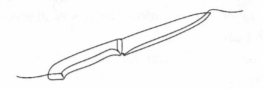

Chapter 22
HIPS

Because I knew I'd just spin my wheels at home, I decided to spend Saturday night at work, going through Matt's notebooks. I slipped my raincoat off, shook it hard under the awning above the door to the *Chronicle* building, then used my company fob to enter. As the newest reporter, Brian Cairns had to work on Saturday nights on the chance there was any breaking news. Technically, I was the newest reporter, but in my contract—the one I insisted on when I doubted Greg would make good on his promise of a raise—I specified that, short of an all-hands-on-deck emergency, I would not work Saturday nights.

Most of Sunday's paper had already been put to bed, so Brian would probably be watching YouTube videos or keeping up with the latest sports developments. The guys in the sports department down the hall put in real effort on Saturday nights, depending on the season and playoff runs. I had no editorial interactions with them and just made small talk in the lunchroom when we were in there together.

I draped my wet raincoat over the spare chair beside my desk and set my purse down on the avocado-green carpet that was campy in the Seventies. I said hello to Brian, sat down, then turned on my laptop. I preferred writing on it, then emailing the finished stories to my work address. I'd then enter them into the content management system on the desktop computer.

On the desk, between the stacks of Matt's notebooks and the picture of Matt and me, was a yellow Post-it note, on which was written, in Bill's handwriting: *Garrett Hunt. Bald, fat, ugly private investigator.* Followed by his phone number, which I put into my phone.

I called the number, got no answer, didn't leave a message, then grabbed the notebook on the top of the pile containing the most recent notebooks. I would work backward chronologically. I combed through that notebook as I'd done with the previous two, jotting down anything that didn't seem to go with the notes that surrounded it. Matt's penmanship did not qualify to be called such. Was slopmanship a word? Crapmanship? I struggled to decipher it but eventually came up with this:

- Veronica Yarnell
- EMR fabrics
- 555 WWE
- Cops withhold facts?

It seemed that Matt had seen Garrett Hunt following him, or at least had seen a blue Camry with the 555 WWE plates. Garrett must have figured out he'd been spotted, then rented the rust-bucket Cutlass Supreme, paying cash because he didn't want to leave a paper trail of the transaction. I put a line through the plate number, then wrote myself a Post-it reminding me to call Garrett Hunt again soon.

I went into the digital archives, then read Bill's story about Veronica Yarnell's murder. Dakota had done a good job describing what was included in the article. Veronica, fifty-eight, had cashed out for $6,015, after hitting two significant jackpots on two different dollar slot machines. The second win, for $5,000, happened at 10:26 p.m. on March 21, on a Cleopatra machine. At 11:02 p.m., Veronica cashed out at the main cashier, then headed to the restroom. Two minutes later, surveillance cameras saw her leave the restroom, walk through the casino, exit, then walk all the way across the nearly full parking lot to the northwest corner, where she was last seen stepping into the blind spot created by a white panel van. The driver of the van pulled out at 1:36 a.m., and his headlights illuminated Veronica's prone body. The van driver, Daniel Davis, checked for a pulse but found no signs of life. He called 911, then ran inside the casino to report the robbery and murder to the hotel security staff. Because Veronica's body was not discovered until early Saturday morning, the story about what law enforcement was calling her murder didn't appear in the *Chronicle* until Sunday morning.

What had Matt discovered that made him write the names of Pat DeLott and Veronica Yarnell in his notebooks? And why did EMR Fabrics sound familiar?

I Googled it to confirm or refute what I thought I knew: EMR Fabrics was a company that produced low-quality fabrics and employed a salesforce of independent contractors to sell its products—a multilevel marketing model similar to Amway, Avon, and Jafra. I probably heard about EMR Fabrics during a PQQ session.

I stuck the note with EMR on it next to the one with Garrett Hunt's name on it, then launched into my articles for the special QuiltWeek issue. I should have started writing those stories days before, if not a week, because I'd need to write at least four stories that covered various aspects of the huge annual event. An overview of this year's QuiltWeek and how it would differ from those in the past was first up. Thankfully, most of that information was on the American Quilter's Society website, and it was still early enough for me to call Jill Haynes, the CEO of AQS, to get a quote. I called her, and she gave me the kind of quote I knew she would.

"This year's QuiltWeek will fascinate, educate, and amaze in new and exciting ways. Even the most technically savvy quilters are certain to learn from this year's seminars, led by many of the biggest names in worldwide quilting. I don't even want to start naming them because your readers might not believe all of those quilting superstars will be gathered in Paducah at the same time. But, believe me, they'll all be here, as will more than 30,000 quilting connoisseurs, taking seminars, buying supplies and QuiltWeek merchandise, socializing, and, of course, frequenting the many area businesses that sponsor the world's largest and most prestigious quilting event, QuiltWeek Paducah.

"I hope to visit with as many participants this year as possible. My goal is to meet more than ten percent of the participants. So, if you spot me in the Julian M. Carroll Convention Center, the auxiliary tent, in Hancock's, at the Rotary Show, in the Yeiser Art Center, in a restaurant or even in one of the seminars, please come up and say hello. I'll be the one with the huge grin on my face. Well, come to think of it, there will probably be more than 30,000 of us. But I'll certainly be one of them, so just ask around. You'll find me."

I selected the best parts of her quote, filed the story, then thought about which one to write next. Had Greg been an actual editor, he would have assigned the stories for the special issue. And if he'd been a good editor (yeah, right), he'd have hassled me about not turning them in by now, or at least asked if I'd have them in early on Monday. I called Kris Vierra, one of the world's greatest quilters who would be giving a seminar, interviewed her, then tried to capture how amazing she is in a twenty-inch feature.

Next, I emailed Ian Berry, another seminar presenter. The hunky fabric artist created incredibly detailed cityscapes, celebrity portraits, and other seemingly impossible creations out of denim. I figured he was probably in transit from England, or soon would be, so he'd answer my emailed questions when he got the chance, which I hoped would be soon.

I made a few calls, visited half a dozen websites, then banged out a story about the various fabric shows that would not officially be part of QuiltWeek but would entice and entertain many members of that invading army of quilters at venues around town, notably the Yeiser and the Robert Cherry Civic Center.

Exhausted, hungry, and in need of a bath, I finally closed my laptop at 11:22 p.m. I thought about calling Garrett Hunt again but decided it was too late. I would call in the morning. I left the office, drove three miles home, parked the truck in the driveway, turned off the engine, leaned over to grab the backpack with my laptop in it, then tried to stop myself from having a heart attack when I turned toward my house and noticed someone sitting on my front steps.

Trapunto barked furiously. My porch light wasn't on, so I couldn't determine who was leaning against my door, but someone was. I started to turn the ignition key, but it stuck, as it had been doing frequently for the last two months. The key finally turned, the engine and the headlights kicked on, and I started to back out. The person on the steps jumped up when the engine caught, then bounded toward me as I backed out. Enough of the headlights shined on him for me to see that he was bald, fat, and ugly. Private eye Garrett Hunt. I continued to back into the street, and he kept coming, waving his arms back and forth, as if to say, "Relax. I'm here in peace," which is what a smart attacker would do.

In my peripheral vision to my right, I noticed a light go on in the house across the street. I hoped I now had at least one witness. I put the truck in drive, ready to floor it, when he shouted, "Hadley, I'm private investigator Garrett Hunt. You called me."

Those facts were consistent with reality as I knew it. I didn't want to take my eyes off him, but as I'd pulled out, I thought I'd noticed a car in front of my next-door neighbor's house that wasn't usually parked there. Was it a blue Camry?

"What do you want?" I shouted, without rolling down my window.

"Should I call the police?" my neighbor Diane Brandt yelled from across the street. I lowered my passenger window, then shouted, "Not yet, but stay there, please." She nodded.

My neighbor next door, Christine Clark, who didn't like me or Trapunto, shouted, "It's almost midnight. Shut up."

Hunt made a gesture to roll down the window, as though my truck had hand cranks. I pressed the button, then lowered my window an inch.

"I want to talk about Williams . . . and Matt," he said.

I wanted to tell him we could talk in the morning, but I wanted to hear what he had to say, so I said, "Give Diane across the street your business card so she knows who you are and what you look like."

"Fine, but I'm here to stop something from happening to you." He walked toward Diane, pulled a business card from his wallet, handed it to her, nodded, then walked back toward me. She waved at me, then closed her door but left her light on.

I pulled into the driveway, parked, and asked him to wait on my front step. He was about sixty-five, and the rental-car clerk had been right about him being bald and fat, but he'd been kind when he defined him as ugly. He looked like a Picasso portrait that had been pummeled with a mallet. He had scar tissue beneath both eyes, and his bulbous, bloodshot nose zigzagged down his face and ended in nostrils that weren't level. His lips looked permanently bee-stung, and his left cheek looked swollen. I felt sorry for him, after I stopped feeling afraid of him and my pulse slowed.

I went inside, calmed Trapunto, closed him in the bedroom, then let Garrett in. He wore a black leather jacket, a teal golf shirt that fit him the way it would a beer keg, faded black jeans, and black Nike running shoes. He sat on my couch and declined my offer of something to drink. I sat in the lounge chair across from him, near the open door.

"You have my attention, but I don't understand why you simply didn't return my call."

"First, my condolences. I know loss, and it's awful, so, I'm sorry. Second, I was at your house when you called me, so I figured I'd wait."

"*What?* Why?"

"Watching Williams. Well, I was watching your house when Williams arrived."

"Hold on. One step at a time. Why were you watching my house?"

"Because someone tried to hire me to follow you. I thought you might be home. You weren't. Nothing else to do but wait."

"You won't tell me who hired you."

"Technically, no one because I didn't take the case. The guy's scum."

"Nick Stoddard."

He smiled. Surprisingly, his teeth were excellent. Probably fake. My guess was he'd been a boxer.

"You were following me while not on a case. Explain."

"Guy stiffed me on my last job, following Matt. Got paid thirty percent of what he owed me. My professional ethics stop when the payments do, so I don't care even a little about violating that monster's trust. He told me, 'Guy got killed. You didn't find out what he knew, so blow.'"

"Okay, but why follow me?"

"Said you threatened him, said you might know something, and if you don't, he still owed you for slugging him, so I was supposed to find something against you."

"I buy far too much fabric, I'm not the shy, retiring type, and I've been known to jump to conclusions, but you're not going to find anything else, not that he can use against me."

"I'll take your word for it, but I'm not really following you, not in that way. It's personal now between Stoddard and me. I got my reasons, so I figured I'd do a little pro bono surveillance. Got nothing else going on." He stretched his arms above his head, interlaced his fingers, then rolled his neck in a circle. "Been out there a while," he said. "Got stiff."

"Sorry. Was working."

"Not your fault. Just part of the job."

"But why blow your cover? You could have watched me from your car."

"Told you—Williams showed up. Didn't recognize him at first because he arrived at 11:04 in the dark, wearing black from head to ankle. The guy's an idiot because he's got on shiny white running shoes with orange on the back. Don't know if he thought you were home or not. You coulda parked in the garage. He walks up the drive, opens the gate, then disappears into the backyard. As soon as I see him walk up the drive, I slip outta the car, then follow him quietly. When I round the house, he's working on your backdoor with lockpicks. Sure, I want to know what he's up to, but I'm watching a guy commit B&E. I don't know it's Williams yet, but I figure he's a burglar, about to empty your place out. Bunch a robberies lately. People work hard for what they got. I coulda yelled, 'Stop,' but he'd a taken off, and I ain't running down no one no more. Think about pulling my piece but figure I can take him by surprise. And he's not near my size, so I take a few quiet steps and tackle him.

"His head hits the metal rail on the stairs hard, stuns him. I got probably a hundred pounds on him. I wrap him up and get a good look. Recognize the scum. He's upset half this town. Got at least one screw loose. Had a run in with the idiot more than once. I think I'll make a citizen's arrest, maybe get him off the street for about four seconds, but he kicks me where it hurts, slugs me in the face, jumps over the rail, and disappears."

"Oh, wow. I'm so sorry. Are you okay?"

"Fine. Had much worse. Used to be a fighter, if you couldn't tell by my face. That guy couldn't fight flyweight, his punch was so weak. But, yeah, when he got away, thought maybe I shoulda pulled the piece. But he coulda had his, and I coulda been dead, or I coulda shot him, and what chance does a schmo with a P.I. license have against a police officer in court? I'd do it the same way next time."

"Why do you think he was breaking in? My lawyer has the same paperwork about my civil suit I do, so what good would taking mine do?"

"Think he was gonna plant something. Drugs, a stolen gun, something else hot. He wasn't carrying anything obvious, so my guess is drugs. Small, portable, and guaranteed jail time with a Class One narcotic."

"Okay, I get it, but he'd do that just to discredit me? Blame the victim?"

"Yes. Cops get the benefit of the doubt almost always. You're a reporter. Lotta people hate the media. All juries are made up of people, so who knows what happens in a trial? He probably heard charges were about to come down. Thought he better stack the deck."

"You sure I can't get you something? Water, orange juice, beer?"

"Sure, after tonight, wouldn't mind a beer."

I went to the refrigerator, poured a Budweiser in a glass, then brought it to him. I went back to the kitchen and drank some water. I returned and sat.

"Stoddard suspects I know something about him and his business, probably the same something that Matt made the Open Record request about. Whatever it was could have gotten Matt killed. Do you think Stoddard killed Matt? Were you following him that night?"

"No. I'd followed him for about two weeks, starting maybe a week, ten days after he filed the request. Stoddard wanted to find dirt he could use on Matt, so Matt wouldn't go public with whatever he found."

"Which means Stoddard knows he's dirty and there was something for Matt to find."

"My guess is every big company cuts corners somewhere, and, let's face it, Nick's scum. The worst kind."

"Please ignore me if this is too personal, but you seem angrier at Stoddard than getting stiffed should warrant."

"Told you, it's personal between us. He was seeing someone, and she's dead. Now he's seeing my granddaughter. He's nearly my age. It disgusts me."

"Is she blond and very pretty?"

"Yes. Rachelle. Kind, sweet but naïve and trusting, the wrong combination for this world."

"That's rough. While following Matt, did you find anything Stoddard could use?"

"No, the kid was clean. Visited his mom, went bowling, collected junk on the side of the road, lifted weights, jogged, rode his bike, went to work, conducted interviews, stayed at your place. He tried once to ask questions of N&S employees when they left work, but security ran him off. Assumed he nosed around online, trying to land a knockout punch on Stoddard. But nothing outta the ordinary I could see."

"Did you follow him to Harrah's?"

"A couple times."

"Any chance you were there on March 21?"

"I was. Veronica Yarnell got killed that night. Heard about it on the scanner next morning."

"What did Matt do that night?"

"Played poker. Talked with a woman I took to be his mother. Saw her kiss his cheek before he bought in at the table and she headed for the slots. After that, I did my best to watch them both. Not hard because he was just sitting there with his back to me. She got in an argument with someone I couldn't see, but I heard her. A woman. She was behind a row of slots, Matt's mom at the end of them.

"Didn't see nothing violent but heard shouts mostly from his mom. She yelled, 'Thought I was your friend,' then stormed off. Matt saw and heard his mom say that much, 'cause by then he was looking her way. I kept looking back and forth. He got up to see what was happening, went over there. They exchanged a few words, not kind and gentle, then Matt went back to his table, obviously upset. He played one hand, then shoved away from the table, no chips left. She was still there."

"Thank you. That's good info. I was dealing with a family crisis that weekend. I'm guessing you weren't watching Matt when he was killed, early on the morning of April 9."

"Nope. Dealing with my own family crisis. What are families for except to cause us sleepless nights. Am I right?" He smiled again. Those dazzling teeth in the middle of his beaten-up face were disconcerting, but I understood his perspective all too well, so I smiled and nodded. "That's why I got canned," he said. "Wasn't there when I was supposed to be, Stoddard said. But I thought it was convenient I tell him I need the night off, and Matt gets killed that night. Then suddenly, I'm not needed anymore, then get stiffed. But if he hadn't stiffed me, maybe I'm not here right now, and who knows where you'd be with Williams? Every once in a while, I think someone above rearranges things just so, you know what I mean? So evil sometimes doesn't win. Doesn't happen often, you look around at all the killing, cheating, stealing, but sometimes."

I nodded. "I think I have something that belongs to you." He raised his eyebrows. I picked up my purse, fished through it, then handed him the win ticket for $1.40. He looked at it and laughed.

"In the Cutlass? Yeah, I didn't wanna lose him, so I didn't cash out when he headed for the exit. Thought he'd go to the cashier, which woulda given me time to cash out, but I didn't count on him tapping out."

"He wasn't a good poker player."

"But seemed like a good investigator. He spotted my tail on the second day. That never happens, and it seems like he had something on Stoddard. But part of me thinks he mighta been rattling Stoddard's chain, messing with him."

"Why do you think that?"

"Because why hassle workers in the company parking lot if you're trying to be subtle, and Stoddard told me the reason he hired me, or one of 'em, was 'cause Matt walked up to him in Pipers while Stoddard was drinking a cappuccino and said, 'It's payback time, chump,' then walked away. Why let someone know you're trying to take them down, if letting them know gives them a chance to get rid of evidence?"

"Or kill you."

"Yeah, there's that." We stared at each other for a few seconds.

"If I want to hire you, what would it cost me?" I asked.

"Four hundred a day, minimum, plus expenses." I must have winced, because he said, "Hold on. But for you, considering what you been through, we might work out a better price. What do you need me to look into?"

"I don't think I'd feel comfortable getting a pity price, but I barely make a fourth of that a day, and money's been so tight lately it's about to snap, so maybe I have to do it myself. I guess that's what credit cards are for, though."

"Didn't answer the question."

"I *need* to know why Matt left me and who killed him. Need as in not sleeping. Need as in feeling unmoored. Need as in being pulled into darkness."

"I'll see what I can find out in my free time. Won't turn down a paying gig, but I watched all I need to watch on Netflix for now, so if I fill my time by helping you, maybe I'll score some points with the man upstairs."

"Bless you. You're in my prayers, and I'll find a way to pay you a rate we'll both feel miserable about. Isn't that the definition of compromise?"

"What I heard."

"But why are you really doing this for me?"

"Rachelle, mostly. I talked to her, warned her about the scum, but she's young and responds to shiny objects. He can shower her with jewelry. Me telling her he's a bad man doesn't compare. I wouldn't mind seeing him get hurt. Also, I know what it feels like to lose someone, and I've lost two someones."

"I'm so sorry, Mr. Hunt."

"Garrett, please. I know grief. It wasn't only boxing made me look like this."

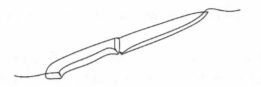

Chapter 23
Motif

After struggling to pay attention in church, I dusted, vacuumed, watered my indoor plants, mowed the lawn, wrestled with Trapunto on the newly mowed and still-wet lawn, then listened to Billie Holiday (who once lived in Paducah) sing *Gloomy Sunday, Good Morning Heartache, I'll Be Seeing You,* and other gut-rending songs. I dusted the sculpture I had never liked that Matt gave to me a few years before on Christmas. He made it from stuff he'd found around Paducah, scraps of metal and wood he'd fashioned into a sculpture he called *Tomorrow.* I never let him know I didn't like it, but now I would never get rid of it.

As I made peanut-butter cookies, I wondered if I'd be able to distract myself from the tumult in my head with Paducah Quilters Quorum. It was my turn to host that week. I had missed last week's session because I'd been, let's say, indisposed—which sounds more civil but is less accurate than the phrase "I was cuddled up in a depressed stupor."

About a half-dozen sessions of the Paducah Quilters Quorum had been cancelled over the years when Christmas fell on Sunday, or when more than one quilter planned to be out of town. Of course, we didn't hold a session on Easter, but that didn't mean we didn't quilt on our own.

Each week, the host provided dessert, and the others coordinated which items they'd bring to the potluck, so we'd have a complete meal.

I set up the large folding table and chairs in my main room, which qualified as main only in relation to my other smaller rooms. My house and Donna's house were the smallest of the homes of the seven regular members. Their homes were three-, four-, or five times the size of our modest homes in the Glendale section of town.

When 2 o'clock arrived and my doorbell rang, I expected the usual array of gossip, laughter, quilting, and calories to follow. But I didn't expect Dakota to be standing on my doorstep with a perplexed look on her face.

"What's wrong, D?"

"I don't think wrong is the right word. Maybe odd."

She stepped inside, walked past the table we would all be quilting on, then set a large pizza box from Mellow Mushroom on the kitchen counter. She wore white pants that seemed to be perfectly tailored to her lithe build, and a navy silk blouse that probably made other blouses jealous. Her strappy sandals had a splash of her requisite orange on them.

"You're worrying me. What is it?"

"No, no, please, Hads, I didn't mean to worry you. Nothing else horrible has happened." She sat down in the tan reclining chair, and I sat on the tan couch, which I'd had to push about five feet to the left of where it usually sat to make room for the table and chairs.

"You mentioned Officer Green yesterday, so, because I'm lonely and . . . and it's time for me to find a true partner, I called a friend who might know how to reach him, Suzanne Bigelow."

"Makes great lemon bars."

"I know, right? She didn't mind giving me Brandon's number, so I called him, and we had a pleasant chat. He said to forgive the short notice, but, considering he didn't know I existed until half an hour before, he couldn't very well have asked me out earlier, which he then did. 'It's Saturday night, we're single. What do you say?' I said yes, of course, so I met him at 9 at Doe's. I don't think you described his looks as well as you could have, Hads. He's really handsome, and he's a great listener."

"He grew up with four younger sisters. Must've helped."

"Yes, he mentioned them. So, we had a nice meal, and I thought the conversation went very well. A good combination of substance and whimsy. Compared to the more than a dozen lousy first dates I've been on recently, this one was fantastic. Brandon's a gentleman without being stuffy, funny without needing to dominate the conversation, and he made me feel like what I said mattered to him."

"That all sounds awful. No wonder you're upset."

"Hush. So, he walked me to my car, and—after all those guys from all those bad dates trying to put a move on me despite our total lack of chemistry—I expected him to give me at least a peck on the cheek. But he stepped in, gave me a routine hug, then said, 'I had a nice time, Dakota. Thank you. Drive safely.'"

"And you think he was giving you the brush-off?"

Vivian Franey and Janet Loy walked in carrying their prepared meals. Janet also had our quilt draped over her shoulder. Based on the size of the Pyrex she was carrying, Vivian had made a casserole, and Janet had made a side dish—her roasted potatoes, I hoped. Janet wore her usual outfit: a navy-blue Murray State sweatshirt and seen-better-days jeans. Vivian wore a yellow cable-knit sweater that Greg Wurt would have envied and seen-better-days jeans. They both wore white sneakers.

They started to say hello, saw the look on Dakota's face, then waved instead, while on their way to the kitchen.

"Well, he did give me the brush-off, didn't he? I understand not going for a kiss on the first date, but wouldn't he have said something like, 'Let's do this again,' if he liked me?"

"I don't know. He probably does like you, so maybe he'll call you tonight or tomorrow to ask for a second date. He could've gotten tongue-tied in the moment. No one knows how to handle those situations, especially if a guy's trying to impress you. Even a self-assured guy could be intimidated or insecure while trying not to blow his chance for a second date with you."

Janet and Vivian reentered the room, then sat at the long table.

"Crisis?" Janet asked.

"No, nothing like that," I said.

"I had a first date last night with a really nice, considerate man, and I don't think he liked me."

Justine Lang, reporter Bill Lang's wife, walked in, carrying two bottles of wine. We all said hello, then she asked, "What'd I miss?" as she headed to the kitchen. She was wearing black pants with black boots and an off-white blouse that highlighted her nice figure.

I said, "Dakota's forty-four years old, and she just experienced for the first time what the rest of us did at fifteen or sixteen: A stupid boy rejected her."

"*Possibly* rejected me."

"Wow," Justine said.

"Oh, honey, it hurts no matter what age we are," Vivian said.

"Maybe even more when you're our age," Janet said, "because we know we might only have a few chances left. I'm fifty-six, and a man who made me laugh a lot on our first date actually said at the end of it, 'You're too fat for me, and I want someone younger.' I felt like he'd hit me in the stomach. And this was an extremely heavy, unemployed bald man. He insisted we go Dutch."

"Count your blessings, Janet," said Donna, who stood in the doorway holding a loaf of Kirchhoff's bread. She walked in, and all of us stood up, then gave her a hug when it was our turn. She wore the same bland, brown K-Mart dress she usually wore to PQQ, the one she'd purchased long ago, when the local K-Mart still existed.

"Thank you for the wine, Hads," she said quietly while we were hugging. "Probably shouldn't have downed it all in one sitting, but . . ."

"No one's judging. If there's any upside to all this, and I'm not saying there is, it's that people are willing to cut us some slack." Then I asked more loudly, "How are you today?"

"I wasn't going to come. I just wanted to mindlessly watch QVC, but then I thought that could lead me to never getting off the couch."

"Well," said Dakota, "we're all very glad you made it."

"Will Cindy be here?" Vivian asked.

"She better be. She's bringing her candied yams," Justine said.

We sat around the table. I'd set out everything we'd need to continue to make progress on the highly complex modern take on the traditional double wedding ring quilt we'd been working on. We'd all contributed our opinions about values and color combinations, made the arc templates, and were in the process of hand-sewing the blocks. Whichever one of us would host the next PQQ took the quilt we were working on home at the end of our sessions. Because I hadn't attended last week's session, Janet had called me to see if I was up for hosting, then said she'd bring the quilt with her this week. She set it down on the table, unfolded it, then straightened it out.

Cindy arrived, apologized for being late, although she wasn't, and we all said hello. She wore what looked like new jeans, nice flats, and a navy Murray State sweatshirt. She and Janet smiled at each other because they were wearing the same sweatshirt, then both said, "Go, Racers!" at the same time. We all laughed, then Cindy asked Donna to stand so they could hug.

Although we were free to sit anywhere, we almost always ended up seated in the same positions as we had been seated in the week before so we could continue to work on whichever sections we'd been working on previously.

"Y'all were talking about dating," Donna said.

"Yes," Dakota said. "I had a great date last night that ended with a splat, and that's never happened to me."

"Are you sure he wasn't blind?" asked Cindy. We laughed.

"Had to be. Either that or gay," Vivian said. "I mean, look at you."

"I try not to look at Dakota," Janet said, "because it hurts that much more when I get home and look in the mirror."

"Different strokes," Justine said. "Some people have class; others don't."

Our routine was to quilt for exactly one hour, then eat, then quilt for another two or three hours, depending on whether any of us had other obligations. As ways to pass a Sunday afternoon went, I couldn't think of a lot that were better.

For the most part, our session went smoothly. Donna teared up once after Cindy mentioned her dead father. Janet berated her ex with such intensity that I think we all felt scared, and Justine said her husband was "cheaper than a hobo," which led to the others mentioning the various faults of the partners they'd had over the years. Then they talked about the degrees of discomfort their ailments were causing them and which medications they were taking to diminish that discomfort or simply to help them stay alive: Janet, Chloroquine for rheumatoid arthritis; Donna, Plavix for heart disease and Lipitor for high cholesterol; Vivian, Tramadol for lumbago; Cindy, Crestor for high cholesterol. As the youngest members of PQQ, in descending order, Justine, Dakota, and I didn't contribute to that part of the conversation, except to express sympathy and, in my case, feel anxious about my future.

Janet mentioned how awful the murder of Natalie Loose was, and everyone else chimed in about how weird it was.

"It seems like a ritual," Donna said. "Wrapping her body in fabric like that."

"Creepy, that's for sure," Dakota said.

"Puts things in perspective," Justine said. "One day you're fine, and a few days later, you're being eulogized."

"Hope they send the ones done this to Eddyville," Janet said.

"Death's too good for them," Vivian said. "If they're dead, they don't suffer."

"I agree," Donna said. "Better they spend the rest of their days wrestling with their conscience, regretting their actions."

"In a certain light, being tortured by regret is worse than not existing," Dakota said.

"In my view," I said, "not existing is an absence of pain."

"Amen," Justine and Donna said simultaneously.

"I disagree," Janet said. "Give 'em the needle, and they'll be filled with regret from the moment they're sentenced to the moment it's lights out. In Kentucky, that could be until you die of natural causes, they're so stingy with the needle."

"Agree to disagree," Dakota said.

We finally transitioned to other subjects, but the mood that day was not as fun and frivolous as it usually was.

When Donna got up to refill her coffee cup, I went to the kitchen with her, then said, "An acquaintance told me that while you were at Harrah's the night Veronica was killed, he saw you arguing with someone. With whom did you argue?"

"Wait, Hads, you're not really asking what I think you are, are you?"

"I'm asking only what I asked, Donna."

"It's none of your business, really, but I'll tell you because we were almost family, and we're friends. I wouldn't call it an argument, though. I simply asked Justine why I wasn't invited to her birthday party."

"Wait, they were celebrating her birthday that night? I had to go to L.A., but I didn't get an invite either. Who was invited?"

"Looked like only Dakota, Veronica, Justine, and Bill. I don't know. Saw a handful of people from here that night, so I can't be sure who was part of the party and who was just there."

"Odd," I said, "but it's not a big deal, not to me. I don't like making a production out of my birthday. Celebrating it with Matt was enough."

"Yeah, well, you had Matt and the cultural events you attended together. My social life consists of PQQ and not much else. An occasional trip to Harrah's, sometimes with Matty." She started to tear up. "It didn't sit right, that's all, me not being invited."

Dakota entered the kitchen with dirty plates, which she stacked in the sink. "I'm not interrupting anything, I hope."

"Nope. Just two quilters reminiscing," Donna said. She left the kitchen.

"Is that so?" Dakota asked. "Talking about patterns from the Eighties?"

"No, about Justine's birthday at Harrah's."

"Ah, that unfortunate evening."

"You were there?"

"Yes. It was just supposed to be a few of us having dinner, nothing fancy, a quick, early bite at Max's. But Veronica suggested we head to Harrah's. I wasn't interested, and Bill didn't seem to want to go, but Veronica and the birthday girl wanted to try their luck, so we all drove in separate cars so we could leave when we wanted."

"Anything unusual happen? Other than Veronica getting killed, of course."

"The normal stuff that happens when alcohol, money, pettiness, games of chance, and women get together."

"Anything more specific?"

"I thought it was odd that in the middle of us throwing our money away we couldn't find Veronica for a while. I don't know how long, but I took three laps around the casino looking for her. I finally found her right where I started, and she said she'd been there the whole time. I just must've missed her, she said. I wasn't going to call her a liar, but she was lying, and it bothered me. I left a few minutes later."

"Did you see Donna argue with anyone?"

"No. Why?"

"She said she was hurt that Justine hadn't invited her to her party—"

"It wasn't a party. It was a small dinner—I picked up the tab when everyone else seemed to lose the use of their hands when the bill arrived—then we took a spontaneous trip to Harrah's."

"You'd believe Donna if she said she simply told Justine she was hurt by not being invited, and didn't have an argument?"

"I don't know Donna not to be truthful, so, yes, I'd believe her. But until that night, I would have said Veronica was truthful, too, so what do I know?"

We rejoined the group, then continued to quilt. I missed some of the gabbing because I thought I shouldn't be wasting time. I started to beat myself up for not spending every waking minute trying to solve Matt's murder. I didn't have the right to take a day off, to laugh and quilt and talk about boys. My boy was gone forever, and all I was doing to find his killer was helping to create another quilt.

"Hads," Dakota said. "You okay?"

Her words pulled me up from the hole I had slipped into, and I said, "Yes. Excuse me a second, please." Dakota looked concerned as I stood up. "I'm fine. Really."

I walked into my bedroom, then closed the door. I called Dr. Elaine Bourget on my cell. It went to voicemail.

"Hello, Dr. Bourget. Elaine. It's Hadley Carroll. I'm not doing so great, and I'm wondering if there's any chance I could move my appointment up from Tuesday morning to tomorrow morning. Any time would be fine. Thank you."

I rejoined the group, then made it through the rest of our session without heading into darkness. After we'd all said goodbye and Dakota helped me clean up, she gave me a long, tight hug, and said, "I love you, Hads. We all do. We know that, but we worry you don't know that."

"I do. And I'm sorry for making fun of you. That was the jealous me talking."

"Shhhh. I didn't take it as anything but my best friend teasing me. QuiltWeek starts Tuesday. When are we going?"

"I have to check which stories I need to write about it, then I'll let you know when I'm free."

"Sounds good. I have a question, and I'm looking for an honest answer, bestie to bestie."

"Of course."

"Am I absent minded?"

"Not even close. Probably the least absent-minded person I know, other than me. Why?"

"I wanted to wear the necklace you gave me on my date last night, but I couldn't find it. I can't think of a reason why it wouldn't be in my jewelry box, but it wasn't there."

"Weird. No chance you loaned it to someone and don't remember? Or maybe it fell behind something."

"I checked. I'd gladly loan anything I have, but I think I'd remember doing so. I'm concerned about my memory. Aunt Betsy died of Lewy body dementia, and that's hereditary."

"D, it's far too early to worry about something like that. It will turn up. You checked all of your purses and your gym bag and both cars?"

"Well, no. I was hustling to the date, but, you're right. I'll check everywhere before I diagnose myself with a deadly disease." She laughed, then we hugged.

After she left, I checked my phone. Elaine had texted me. The text read: "We're on for 8 tomorrow morning. It's okay not to be okay. That's why I'm here."

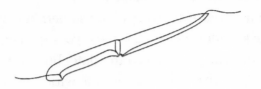

Chapter 24

Improvisational Quilt

I filled the prescription for Wellbutrin that Dr. Bourget prescribed at the Walmart on Hinkleville Road, then took my first pill. I knew there was zero chance the Wellbutrin would make me feel better quickly, but I felt better for having taken it.

I wanted to write meaningless drivel, instead of diving back into the murder investigation, but it wasn't an either/or proposition. After saying hello to Jake, Brian, Dan, and Adam, I banged out three crime rewrites, followed by the last story I needed to write for the QuiltWeek special edition, which would hit the streets the next day, the first official day of the event, with the awards ceremony kicking off the festivities that evening.

I filed that story, about a seminar on advanced applique techniques, and two sidebars at 2:33 p.m., after I'd eaten pasta salad for lunch. When I returned to my desk, I wondered if I'd been repressing an obvious possibility—had Matt been murdered because he was a journalist? My mind had kinda-sorta allowed for the possibility that his Open Records request could have brought about his murder because Stoddard, in my mind, could be capable of murder.

But what if someone else had killed Matt because of a story he'd written or was investigating? More than one maniac had walked into a newsroom, then gunned down the people working there. One murderer killed five people and injured others in a newsroom after he lost the defamation suit that he'd filed against the newspaper, which meant the journalists were murdered for printing a story about the gunman that was true—but one he hadn't liked. I did a Google search and learned that the Committee to Protect Journalists reported that at least thirty journalists had been killed worldwide in the last year.

The prospect of being killed for doing our jobs was too frightening to think about, and so I hadn't considered it when I thought about Matt's murder, which I did even while I slept.

If a maniac killed Matt because of a story he'd written, then that probably separated Matt's murder from Pat's and Natalie's. After all, Matt had been clubbed on the head, and the women had been stabbed, although their crime scenes were very different. If Matt was killed because of a story he'd written, then I had a lot more work to do than to go through every page of the remaining notebooks stacked on my desk: I had to read every one of Matt's stories. How many would that be, if I only counted ones that included his byline? Two thousand? Twice that? While reading them, I'd have to look for people mentioned in the stories who could've been upset by what he'd written, but I didn't know how to think like a maniac.

If printing the truth had set off the guy who killed five journalists, then how could I determine which facts might have upset someone so much that he had to kill Matt for including those facts in his story?

I realized I had come up with another task that was as impossible as finding Natalie's murderer by tracking down whomever had purchased the fabric in which she'd been wrapped. I decided to find the notes I'd taken about the ninety-three letters-to-the-editor we'd received about Matt's murder: About fifty percent of them said he got what he deserved because journalists deserved to be murdered, or they said the story about his death was fake news, or that he himself was fake news. In other words, about half of the readers who sent those emails believed that killing the messenger was warranted or that the messages the messengers sent were part of a conspiracy, although they didn't specify what the objectives of the conspiracy were.

If I had to go with the assumption that anyone who'd ever been upset by anything Matt had written in the *Chronicle* could be his killer, then I might as well start counting the grains of sand on the beaches of California. One, two, 345 trillion.

Instead of launching into that futile search, I continued my march through what appeared to be extraneous notes in Matt's notebooks. He had written Veronica Yarnell, so I poked around, found a phone number, then called Sarah Gonzalez, the adult daughter of Veronica, the woman who had been killed in the Harrah's parking lot in Metropolis, Illinois.

"Hello, I'm Hadley Carroll, a reporter for the *Chronicle*. I'm sorry for your loss."

"Thank you."

"I'm wondering what you can tell me about your mother's death."

"For a story? Two reporters already talked to me, and you already printed her obituary. I have it framed in my living room."

"Bill Lang, our cops and courts reporter, must have been one."

"Yes."

"Do you remember if the other was Matt Ackerman?"

"Yes, it was. Why?"

"He's been murdered. He happened to be my fiancé, up until the week before someone killed him."

"Oh, I'm so sorry. That's awful."

"Thank you. You and I are members of a club no one wants to belong to: people whose loved ones have been murdered." She didn't respond, so I continued. "Can you tell me anything about your mom's murder that wasn't in the paper?"

"I don't get the *Chronicle*, so I don't know what's supposed to be in a story like that. A friend told me the one about Mom was in there, so I bought it and read it. Nothing really jumped out at me except I didn't know a Paducah paper would cover news in Metropolis, and, I guess, maybe the story coulda said something about Mom not being a regular at the casino."

"Okay, so she didn't go there a lot. What does that tell you?"

"I don't know. Maybe something about the killer. I talked to a couple employees, the manager, and he said the robberies that happened, not a lot, but more than just my mom's, had been after people'd won bigger amounts, more than Mom won, and they bragged about the wins, waved their money around, that kind of thing. Then someone followed them. Mom woulda been happy as a clam to win, but she wasn't dirt poor. She was doing fine. Dad left her in good shape. She woulda been happy as could be. She won six grand, but it wouldn't'a changed her life much. Maybe take an extra cruise this year, upgrade her cabin. I guess I'm saying she wouldn't'a waved the money around or screamed, 'I won six grand,' or something stupid like that."

"That's what you told Bill and Matt when they called?"

"Pretty much, except Matt knew something I didn't."

"Which was?"

"To my surprise, he was right—Mom was seeing Nick Stoddard, that skeevy businessman."

"Really? Matt told you that?"

"He asked if there was any chance they could be seeing each other. After I said, 'Don't think so. Why?' he said, 'Because I saw them leave the casino together a little after 8 and return about 9:15. The casino has a hotel.' I was angry at him for a few seconds, but he didn't do anything. He just asked a question, and if I saw what he saw, I woulda asked the same question.

"I checked Mom's call history on her cell, and, yup, Matt was right. Stoddard and Mom had been having phone conversations for about four months, a lot late at night. She'd seemed happier than I'd seen her in years, but there's no way she would have told me she was sleeping with a married man. I woulda bet everything I have that wouldn't happen, but I woulda lost. I've heard about women being swept off their feet, throwing away whatever they believe in, for a man. I'm married, but I never felt that—that kind of stupid. Considering what happened to Mom, gotta be glad I was never swept off my feet.

"Now that I say that, it's not really a happy image is it? I mean, if you get swept off your feet, you fall, don't you? I guess it comes from being picked up and carried away, but he's gotta put you down sometime."

"Or drop you."

"Exactly. If she didn't win that night, she'd still be here. And who knows about the Stoddard stuff? I mighta given her grief about having an affair, but she was an adult, so, who knows? Maybe I woulda let her enjoy her happiness while it lasted. We all deserve love. Or at least happiness."

"Yes, we do. You've been very helpful. Please take care of yourself."

"You, too. And let's hope no one else joins our sad little club."

I'd made progress in the investigation, maybe for the first time. I learned something that, if I squinted and tilted my head just so, came close to being evidence.

My Nissan Frontier ran great, and I loved its storage room, but the key wouldn't turn in the ignition about forty percent of the time recently. Something was out of line with something else. The doohickey was now incompatible with the whatchamacallit, which, as everyone knows, made the thingamajig as useless as the thingamabob.

So, I sat there jiggling the key after I left the office, turning the key over, jiggling it again, turning it back over, until, after the right combination of curse words spoken in a specific order, I cracked the safe that was my truck's ignition, then drove home.

I put Trapunto's leash on, then we headed for the park. The air carried a little of the humidity that would soon turn the summer air into pudding. We crossed H.C. Mathis Drive and walked on the grass, among the pines and dogwoods, with Trapunto futilely trying to break free to chase squirrels. As we walked, I called Jenny.

"Hey, Sis," she answered, with joy in her voice.

"Hello, Jenny. How are you?"

Trapunto and I walked past a swing set that two young boys were swinging on.

"Better than usual. I got a job at Cracker Barrel."

"That's great, sweetie."

"Remember, that was our birthday treat?"

"Absolutely. Every year. Have you started?"

"Tomorrow. And my new man, Stephen, is really nice. He lost his job at Harbor Freight. His boss never liked him. How about you? Anything new?"

"Nope. Everything's fine. Plugging along. Really just checking in. Anything else new?" She told me about a dress she really wanted to buy and how she could use a car, now that she found work, because the buses were so unreliable. She said her latest favorite food was penne with butter and parmesan, which she called "sprinkle cheese." After she talked herself out, I said, "It's been great talking with you, Jenny-bean, and maybe you can come to visit sometime, when I come up with the money. Love you."

"Love you, too, Hadley Gladly." I liked that nickname as much as I liked curried snot, but she'd given it to me when she was six, so what could I do?

I poured water for my lovable mongrel from the aluminum bottle in my back pocket into the collapsible dog bowl clipped to Trapunto's leash. Then I sat down on a bench to watch the mothers and their children bounce on, scramble through, and swing above the colorful playground. I called Dakota to see if she could give me Brandon's cell number. She asked how I was doing, then gave me his number. I called him.

"Hello, Hadley. How're you?"

"Still breathing, so things could be worse."

"True, but the laws of probability say you're due for a break."

"We'll see. I hope you're right. How was your day?"

"No bizarre murders that I've heard of, so . . ."

"That's a pretty low standard. I'm wondering what's happening with Williams and Kramer."

"The wheels of justice grind slowly," he said. "Williams will be arrested any day now, maybe today, and the department's contemplating what kind of action to take against Kramer. If I were you, I'd pursue the matter in a civil case."

"I am, but if Williams isn't locked up soon, I may not be around to file the case. He tried to break into my house. A private eye watching my house—it's complicated—stopped him, tackled him, in fact."

"Did you call the police?"

"To tell them one of their own was no longer on the premises and left no evidence behind? No, Officer Green, I did not."

"Don't trust us, do you?"

"The 'us' part of that question throws me. You've obviously shown me I can trust you, but trust in my life has always been a precursor to disappointment, if not betrayal."

"That's sad, Hadley. It's no way to live."

"I know. I'm trying to change. Thought I had with Matt, but then . . ."

"I'm sorry. A lot in this world is outside our control. Adaptability is key, I've found. We have to seize opportunities when they're presented and bounce back when we fail or when we have the rug pulled out from under us. Why do you think Williams tried to break in?"

"To plant something illicit, according to the P.I. Garrett Hunt."

"I know him. Good man. Why would you assume Williams wanted to set you up rather than harm you?"

"Gee, thanks for that. I'd just thought he was trying to frame me."

"You suspect he could be involved with Matt's murder, right?"

"How did you know?"

"I didn't. That's why I asked."

"His attitude was bad from the jump. Well, bad from high school, according to Matt, who was tormented, if not tortured, by Williams. In one of Matt's notebooks, he wrote, 'Payback time,' which could mean he'd finally had enough—decades of pain, self-loathing, and feeling inadequate. He could have confronted Williams, but Matt wasn't a fighter. He probably convinced himself he was because he was great at mustering enthusiasm, mostly for Quixotic causes, then Williams clobbered him. But I have semi-sorta proof that Matt told Nick Stoddard it was payback time, so all I'm doing is speculating."

"Look, Hadley. Nothing you said is impossible, or even implausible. Being bullied, or brutalized, in Matt's case, can fester, and confronting the source of that brutalization can be cathartic, therapeutic. But we have no evidence that that's how Matt's murder played out."

"I'm not saying anyone can prove anything. I'm just saying that the guy who tortured Matt, beat me up, then tried to break into my house should be considered for Matt's murder. I thought he was going to frame me, but you suggested he might have been there to kill me. Based on that, perhaps your men and women in blue should put Williams under surveillance."

"Had you reported his attempted break-in, perhaps—"

"Okay, truce. I'm going to change the subject, and you'll change course with me because Paducah PD owes me at least that much."

"Yes, it does."

"A little birdy told me you didn't go on the world's best first date Saturday night."

A boy of about four, wearing a Superman shirt, sky-blue shorts, and shoes that lighted up with each step, approached Trapunto. His mother ran toward him to stop him from trying to pet a strange dog.

"It's okay. He won't bite. I promise," I said to the mother, who nodded to her son. He gleefully started to pet Trapunto's back as his mother scratched Trapunto's head. "Sorry. I have my dog with me in Noble," I said to Brandon.

"What kind of dog?"

"A mongrelly mutt."

"I prefer mutty mongrels."

"So, do I, but the Humane Society was fresh out."

"Tough break. I'll keep an eye out, see what I can find."

"Good to know, Officer Green, but you're deflecting."

"The date was fine. Dakota's an amazing woman."

"But you prefer women who are short, fat, ugly, mean, and stupid, huh?"

"How'd you know? Every guy has a type. You just described my dream woman."

"I'll scroll through my contacts, see who I know."

Trapunto and I took a longer route home so he could smell different scents and bark at different dogs than he had on our way to the park. We walked for two blocks on Park Avenue, and the uptick in traffic I'd noticed on my drive home had become a steady stream of cars, moving slowly toward downtown. The quilters were arriving for AQS QuiltWeek Paducah.

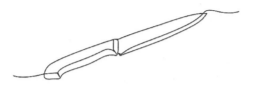

Chapter 25

Redwork

In my regular session with Elaine that Tuesday morning, I discussed the childhood traumas that our mother had inflicted on Jenny and me, including physical violence. My tears flowed throughout much of the session, and Elaine said that the drive, tenacity, and resilience I'd developed during my dysfunctional childhood would almost certainly get me through the loss of Matt. The only word of her statement that I focused on was "almost." Then she warned me that I could feel much worse before I started to feel better.

Although I could have lived without that last nugget, my therapy session had been cathartic, my key managed to turn on the first try, the first few notes of Miles Davis' "So What" filled the cab of my truck, and my cheek had healed significantly, so I was ready to have a good day. I actually had that thought while driving to work.

What a moron!

I don't believe in the power of curses or jinxes or hexes or spells or potions or even breakfast. If you want to buy into any of those, go ahead and do so with gusto, so long as you don't foist your ideologies or habits on me—or make me eat grits. Sand doesn't have any cholesterol, either, but we don't smother it in cheese and call it food.

But that morning, I might as well have eaten a giant bowl of cheese-laden sand because Paducah had to be cursed.

My cell emitted a text chime, so I pulled over before reading the text from Bill, which said: "another body fabric greenway wastewater."

Bill's text was self-explanatory, except to those who hadn't walked, run, or ridden a bike on the Greenway Trail past the Wastewater Treatment Plant. If you were to stroll or ride along that trail on an August afternoon, especially while a breeze is blowing toward the asphalt ribbon that snakes along the berm between the river and the city, you would inhale a cloud of airborne fecal particulates so gag-inducing that four breaths into this olfactory torture you'd hope the wind-blown waste is toxic enough to kill you before your fifth breath.

Okay, I admit I didn't really think Paducah was cursed because that would indicate a supernatural force—rather than a very sick homicidal maniac or maniacs—was responsible for the rash of murders. At least two of the killings appeared to be connected, if MOs meant anything. Were Veronica, Pat, and Matt's killings connected to each other, connected to the two victims wrapped in fabric, or were they stand-alone murders?

By eliminating the supernatural, I managed to summon up a dollop of relief because when Paducah's nightmare was resolved, we would be able to identify a cause, rather than say, "Who knows? Might happen again next month because we're cursed."

The trick, of course, was to still be alive when the murders were solved.

I passed the enormous, temporary, white, inflatable tent that would soon be filled with QuiltWeek quilters, then parked a block away from the scene. I scrambled at an angle up the grassy bank, then walked along the paved trail until I reached the yellow crime-scene tape, which I'd seen far too much of lately. The stench punched me in the nose, and for a second, I wondered whether I really had to be there. Of course, I did. But did I have time to go to a military-surplus store to buy a gas mask?

I approached the toxic cloud. Once again, cops swarmed the scene, and the young woman from WKYC was giving another remote broadcast from another crime scene in which another dead victim was wrapped in fabric. The reporter was outside the tape, standing near Adam and Bill.

When I got close, I heard her say, "There is simply no way around the fact the murder of Natalie Loose and this victim are related. From here, the methods appear to be similar, if not identical. Someone is murdering Paducahans and wrapping them up like mummies. How frightened should we be? And who's next? This is Brenda Barton for WKYC, Western Kentucky's reality."

She delivered her presentation well—clear enunciation, somber expression, and without vomiting from the stench—but her two questions veered far into the bounds of editorializing. I'd always hated the station's tagline, "Western Kentucky's reality." I agreed that the station was, in fact, real and was based in Western Kentucky, but when any entity starts declaring itself the only arbiter of reality, truth, justice, and the American way, my hackles go up, and I don't look good in hackles.

Because Brenda Barton had no idea why this victim or Natalie Loose had been killed (or even if this victim was from Paducah), she had no reason to instigate panic among the station's viewers by introducing fear into the broadcast, then implying that any of the viewers could be the next victim. For all we knew, Natalie and Heather Cain, sixty—whose identity I would learn later when the PPD public information officer sent out a press release—had been killed for entirely personal reasons, so everyone was not at risk. Sadly, I had known Heather, unlike Veronica, Pat, and Natalie. A few years before, we'd taken group guitar lessons together. She'd had more natural ability than I had.

As I pondered yet another loss, it occurred to me that I'd failed to ask Sarah Gonzalez, the daughter of Veronica Yarnell, an important question. I'd decided to consider Veronica the first victim, and she *was*, chronologically. She could have had nothing to do with the other killings, and her murder sure appeared to be unrelated, but I decided to consider her the first victim anyway. If doing so made me crazy, well, that ship had long since disappeared into the horizon, and I'd always wanted to go on a cruise.

A drone now flew high above the body, presumably taking photos, and I hoped one of the cops would shoot it down. The buzz of the drone, the incessant hum of the WKYC truck's generator, and the chatter of the cops and the onlookers, who were arriving by the minute, would've made talking on my phone while standing there difficult, especially because I was only getting one bar.

I jogged away from the noise, but I also wanted to stop punishing my nostrils. I jogged fifty yards farther than necessary to make the call without background noise. As I started to dial, looking back at the crime scene, I saw Freddie, Dakota's ex, run down the bank, make his way around the group of cops and onlookers, run back up the bank, then run toward me. He was wearing a gray Harvard sweatshirt and gray sweatpants. When he approached, he waved but didn't slow down. I turned to follow him with my eyes, and I would have sworn he was wearing new Adidas running shoes. I didn't know whether potential murderers were as brand-loyal as most of the rest of us are, but I wasn't willing to dismiss Freddie as a suspect just because he wasn't wearing Asics.

I called Sarah Gonzalez and asked her if her mom had been a quilter. Sarah said, "Yes, a bad one, but she liked getting together to gab and torture fabrics."

The murders of Natalie Loose and Heather Cain proved officially to be related when the Paducah Police Department press release confirmed that Heather had also been stabbed in her abdomen. Veronica Yarnell had been a quilter, and Pat DeLott had owned an expensive sewing machine. Was quilting a cause or just a coincidence?

The victims probably had a lot in common—they were women who likely all went to church, bought bread at Kirchhoff's, ate at Mellow Mushroom, attended plays at Market House Theatre, saw shows at the Carson Center, and celebrated birthdays or Valentine's Day at freight house, a fine-dining restaurant that was gaining a national reputation but didn't allow capital letters in its name.

Therefore, singling out quilting could be selective attention on my part—I saw what I understood, and I excluded other possibilities because of my biases. Even if I was not letting quilting color my perception, it seemed like a longshot that these four murders could be connected because they were committed by different methods. The last two were obviously connected, but the PPD press release didn't mention a knife being left at the scene of Heather's murder, unlike in Noble Park; nor did it mention a scarf.

Everyone who watches any of the forty-three CSI shows knows serial killers don't have multiple MOs. However, savvy murderers who don't kill to satisfy some twisted compulsion but who kill for some other reason could use different methods, perhaps to keep homicide detectives off balance.

But when I factored in Matt's method of death, blunt-force trauma, I figured I had to be grasping at straws. Matt thought quilting was something little old ladies did (he wasn't wrong)—so calling his death quilting-related seemed far-fetched because, to my knowledge, he'd never even threaded a needle. And three distinct killing methods—four if Pat's stabbing during a robbery was considered different than the other stabbings—probably meant more than one killer, and that was too troubling to wrap my head around.

I did my best to steel myself against the olfactory attack, then walked back to the crime scene. When I found Adam and Bill standing together, I said, "Let's get out of Paducah's toilet bowl," then pointed down the trail. They both nodded, and then we jogged to safety.

"I can't confirm there's blood because of the red fabric," Adam said, "but I'm pretty sure whoever's in there was stabbed, too."

"This is bad on so many levels," Bill said. "People are being killed, and the killer or killers are sending some kind of message. Is it aimed at QuiltWeek? Quilters in general?"

"I don't know, but I'm going to go way out on a limb and say that when they unwrap this victim, she'll be a woman," I said. "Is the message just age-old misogyny?"

"The cops have circled the wagons even tighter than they did in

Noble," Bill said. "We'll be lucky to get a press release, so we definitely won't get a quote, on- or off the record."

"I don't need their cooperation," Adam said, "so I'm gonna stick around to get the best shot. Nothing too gruesome, but maybe the vic being put in the van."

"There's close to a zero percent chance we'll find a witness over there," I said, "but we better hold our breath then ask questions in sign language."

"I only know one hand gesture," Bill said, "and it isn't likely to foster cooperation."

We wasted fifteen minutes on the edge of the crime scene tapping people on their shoulders, then getting no useful responses. Why people would want to see a bloody, dead body was beyond me.

As I walked back toward my car, I wondered if the killer or killers were trying to hide a clue by dumping the victim next to the Wastewater Treatment Plant. Did the fabric give off a particular scent, a scent overwhelmed by the toxic cloud the fabric was now steeping in? Or were the cops, coroner, and reporters being subjected to that stench so their unpleasant tasks would be more miserable? The gawkers could have been collateral damage, and they pretty much deserved any discomfort they were in.

The vast majority of the 30,000 QuiltWeek attendees were either on their way to Paducah or had already arrived and were frequenting its shops and restaurants while officials tended to—and ghouls gawked at—Heather Cain. The QuiltWeek attendees had paid for their seminars months earlier, then booked their rooms, packed their bags, and made their annual pilgrimage. QuiltWeek was almost certainly their favorite week of the year because they got to visit with quilters from around the world, learn from master quilters, study the amazing quilts that won awards each year, and step away from their day-to-day troubles. They hadn't yet heard about Heather Cain, so QuiltWeek that year would be nothing but fun.

Ignorance is bliss. And knowledge can be a pain in the butt. And yet, I'll take knowledge and pain every time.

Because I'd be covering the awards ceremony that kicked off QuiltWeek that night in the Carson Center, I decided—based mostly on exhaustion but also on feeling overwhelmed—that I'd work a split shift, instead of putting in another absurdly long day. So, I driveled words across my laptop's screen, mostly in complete sentences, some of which made sense, on subjects as diverse as an ice-cream social on Saturday and a shave-ice festival on Sunday.

I made a bet with myself that Greg would scrap the headlines I'd written for those stories. Later, during the panic gripping Paducah, I looked at the paper to check a fact and learned I'd won my bet: "Friendly flavors" had become "We all scream," and "Frozen festival" had become "A close shave," proving, for the 311th time, that Greg was allergic to words.

I decided to disprove my belief that I was allergic to sleep, and, to my amazement, I managed to take a two-hour nap with Trapunto near my feet. I awoke refreshed, made myself a spinach salad, paid some bills, then dressed more upscale than I usually did for work because I would interview the Best of Show winner that night. I always tried to be presentable whenever I was in public, without appearing to try hard, but trying hard wasn't sneered at while attending any event held in the Carson Center.

The venue is a civic miracle. It seems impossible that a city of only 25,000 people would be home to such a first-rate, 97,750-square-foot homage to the arts. Yet, using determination, force of will, and fundraising prowess never before utilized in Western Kentucky, the powers that be managed to create a gorgeous, well-run entity that houses the Paducah Symphony Orchestra and features traveling Broadway shows, rock stars, and a host of other forms of entertainment and educational programs.

That night, the Carson Center—officially known by the mouthful of a name, Luther F. Carson Four Rivers Center—would fill many of its 1,806 seats with quilters hoping to win one or more of the dozens of awards that would be presented.

Wearing my CeCe three-quarter sleeve moss crepe shift in royal blue, matching Nazima platform dress sandals, the royal-blue sapphire necklace that Matt had given me for my birthday four years ago, and carrying a navy clutch, I strolled in, waved to some people, hugged others, and avoided many more. Dakota and I visited for a few minutes, and I gave a long hug to Donna, asked how she was and whether she was up for holding Paducah Quilters Quorum at her house on Sunday. She said she was hanging in there, staying busy with quilting and work, and she would definitely host.

I walked from the lobby, which is graced on either side by a sweeping staircase, to the main hall. Although I looked good, I ruined the look by accessorizing with a notebook, two pens, and a recorder, but we do what we must.

I had escaped reality during my nap. While getting ready, I did my best to minimize the "What happened?" factor by concealing my less-purple-than-it-used-to-be cheek with cover-up. But when I settled in among the multitude of fellow quilters (ninety-nine percent of whom were women), reality sat down next to me. Was someone in this room the killer? Would someone here be the next victim?

Luckily, I couldn't worry about what-ifs because I had to fill about half of my reporter's notebook with the names of the winners, the names of the awards they won, the sponsors of those awards, and any other information I thought might help me race through my story later.

Only a few seconds after I took my seat, the band on stage kicked off an upbeat number that made we wish I were deaf. A twenty-ish, dangerously thin woman wearing a hot-pink mini dress and a white T-shirt that had apparently been run through a Cuisinart, began singing in a voice that, objectively, was okay. Her lyrics, however, made me wonder if she'd thrown sentences in the Cuisinart with her T-shirt and was now singing the words in the order they'd ended up.

She hadn't announced the title of the song, but I tried to come up with a title as she sang the chorus:

No, now, nowhere, new
Nothing anyone can do
One plus one is two plus two
No wonder I'm so blue, blue, blue.

I would've titled the song "Learn to Add" or "Silence Destroyed." The verses were as inane but musically more discordant, which, amazingly, left me wanting to hear the chorus again.

As she sang the chorus for the second time, I started to hum the melody and to sing the words silently, and it came as a shock to me that I'd lost my mind. Either the performers were insane, or I was, and there were five of them, so do the math—One plus one is two plus two.

And the next song was worse. If a four-car wreck on I-24 were recorded, then randomly combined with the sounds of a slaughterhouse, the resulting sonic atrocity would be sixteen percent as atrocious as "Underwear," a song about, you guessed it, tighty-whities.

I looked around the hall, and nearly all of the heads were nodding, and nearly every face smiling. How was that possible? I'd seen more than a few hearing aids in the lobby, but everyone in the room couldn't be having trouble hearing the Carson Center cacophony I was enduring.

Had the fumes of Paducah's poo pools ravaged my olfactory nerves, then moved on to my auditory canal? Which would go next, my sight or my taste buds?

Was I experiencing my first hot flash? Had one of the mushrooms in my salad been hallucinogenic? Was I just a sullen, angry, judgmental shrew?

I chose not to answer those questions and instead focused on getting through the third song without adding to Paducah's spate of recent murders. And that's when I realized why I was so out of sorts: I was sitting in an otherwise wonderful venue, experiencing an otherwise well-run event that celebrated and rewarded the best quilters in the world, heroes in the quilting pantheon. I had happily and enthusiastically inhabited that world for decades, but I'd gotten dolled up, given air-kisses or friendly waves to friends and acquaintances, and I was about to take notes for the story I would soon write, but to what end? All of it was meaningless, total garbage— every daub of concealer, every stroke of mascara, my dress, my shoes, my neckless, my career, all of it—because I had nothing.

Matt was dead, my mother was dead, my father never existed, and my sister granted not much more comfort or empathy than a stranger on a park bench would. I loved her, and I loved Trapunto, but these non-relationship relationships weren't much to show for a life. Yes, I had friends, but gathering on Sundays to quilt together and going for an occasional run or bike ride didn't give life meaning, didn't cause people to say on their deathbeds, "I've led a happy, fulfilling, productive life, so I'm now ready to go."

I realized, as the music gave way to a speech by Jill Haynes, the CEO of the American Quilter's Society, that the worsening depression that my therapist had warned me about had taken hold. The bottomless emptiness had slowly encircled me, and I was falling down an increasingly narrow well.

I sat there shaking, and I don't remember hearing any of Jill's words beyond, "Welcome, quilters."

But as my shaking subsided, I managed to do something that surprised me: I gave myself credit for recognizing my sudden, all-consuming negativity for what it was—acute, worsening depression. I hadn't downed a bottle of Maker's Mark, I hadn't weighted myself down, then jumped in the river, and I hadn't curled up on my couch and surrendered.

I'd managed to make myself presentable, then set out to do my job, despite the darkness I was falling through. In the overall scheme of human achievement, I knew my actions didn't compare favorably to moon landings or to Shakespeare's plays. But, later, after all of the other recipients had accepted their awards, I approached Amy Thorstead, the winner of Best of Show, in the lobby. As I did, I felt as though I'd hit rock bottom, managed to survive, then rebounded. And now I was heading up toward the distant spot of light. I had no way to know if I was correct, if I'd really hit bottom, but I suddenly knew, with complete clarity, that I needed to reach the light.

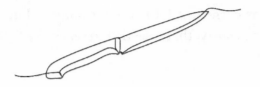

Chapter 26
Signature Quilt

Clusters of people—mostly groups of four or five—milled about the lobby. The families of many of the winners handed them roses, hugged them, or patted them on the back, full of pride. Autograph seekers tried to figure out how to butt-in politely, and other fans of quilting's royalty tried to soak up as much of the creative energy in the voluminous space as they could.

Because it took me a while to find the pen I'd dropped in the row I'd been sitting in, I was late getting to the lobby. I hoped to be the first to interview Amy Thorstead, but I saw the young, female reporter I'd seen at the last two crime scenes setting up near the door to interview her on camera. The cameraman was about the same age as the reporter, twenty-three or -four. He was dressed in a dirty and stained plaid, flannel shirt, jeans, and dirty hiking boots, and she was dressed in what I guessed had been an over-the-top bridesmaid's dress in 1987—magenta poofs pillowed atop plum flounces, set off by lilac ruffles. I don't know what happened to her between the time she did the remote broadcast that morning wearing a sharp blazer, crisp, white pants, and sensible black flats, but she appeared to have had liposuction that sucked the taste right out of her.

I approached the three of them—hoping the reporter's dress wasn't contagious—pulled out a pen, my notebook, and recorder, then nodded to the reporter, who was by then holding a microphone. She didn't return my nod, but she turned her ruffled rear to me, then stepped closer to Amy so I couldn't scoop her.

The cameraman gave her the nod, and she said, "This is reporter Brenda Barton from WKYC reporting from Paducah's own Carson Center, where I have an exclusive interview with the winner of the Best in Show Award at this year's American Quilter's Association's Spring QuiltWeek, Amy Thorstead. Of all the awards available in the quilt world to be won, this one is the most prestigious and carries the largest cash prize, $20,000. It must be quite a feeling, probably amazing, even unparalleled, to be recognized by the judges in such a prestigious event for being the best of the best."

Amy glanced at me, raised her right eyebrow, then said, "I didn't hear a question."

"Neither did I," I said, off camera.

Brenda snapped her head in my direction and said, "Hush! This is my interview!"

"Is that what that was? If you put that schmaltz to music, you could take it to Broadway."

Amy laughed and smiled at me.

Most of the countless quilters who lost out to Amy's impressionistic cityscape called *Teaneck, New Jersey* were older than Amy was. I guessed she was a well-preserved forty-five. She was dressed in a smart, blue pantsuit that flattered her athletic figure. The Michele Deco watch on her left wrist revealed that she or someone who loved her had expensive taste.

"I don't have to put up with this," Brenda said, actually putting her hands on her poofy, purple hips, still holding the mic in her right hand.

"I have to get to the Museum," Amy said, addressing Brenda. She was referring to the National Quilt Museum, where all of the winning quilts would be displayed. Amy said, "Do you have something you'd like to ask me?"

"Yes," Brenda said. "How does it feel to win Best in Show? Were you surprised by your victory? If so, how did that surprise make you feel?

Did part of you, even a very small part, really believe you'd win? Be honest. And what was your inspiration for *Teaneck, New Jersey*, and do you plan to keep the money and donate the quilt to the Museum?"

Amy became visibly irritated as she listened to Brenda's game of Twenty Questions. When Brenda finally stopped talking and tilted the mic toward the winning quilter, Amy turned to me and asked, "Do you have anything you'd like to ask?"

"Yes. Hello, Amy. I'm Hadley Carroll with the *Paducah Chronicle*. Nice to meet you."

"Likewise."

I didn't want to look at Brenda because I knew her fuming would make me laugh, but I took a quick peek, and she was huddled with the cameraman, planning a coup. I smiled but managed not to laugh.

I hit "record" and pushed the point down on my pen. I'd prepped my notebook earlier, listing the date, the subject, and a couple of questions I hoped to ask.

"First, congratulations. How does it feel to win Best of Show?"

"Fantastic, tremendous. I'm over the moon. I'm not sure I really believe I've won the big prize. I'm just so grateful to AQS. QuiltWeek is always the highlight of my year, and I've been attending this amazing event since the beginning. I've won a few prizes over the years, but only in my wildest dreams did I think I'd be in the running for the big prize."

She smiled brightly, and I understood why she had an endorsement deal with Moda Fabrics, one of the biggest players in the nearly $4 billion quilting industry. Amy was relatively young, pretty, articulate, and amazingly talented.

"And yet you have definitely won Best of Show. Please describe the genesis of your winning quilt."

"I'll try." She thought how best to express herself. I noticed that the cameraman was now filming my interview, keeping me out of the shot, of course, because he was smart enough to know that Amy was finished with Brenda, and he'd be fired if he returned to the office without footage of the woman who won the quilting world's biggest, most prestigious prize on quilting's biggest night.

"I took a while to gather my thoughts because I get emotional when I think of my father," Amy said, "and my father was in every stitch of this quilt, every thread. He was the beginning, middle, and end. He grew up in Teaneck, and he would talk about it like it was Paris and London and New York combined, even though he knew that I knew it wasn't anywhere near as nice, creative, or thriving as any of those cities. My dad, I called him Pops, was a storyteller. As he liked to say, he had the gift of gab. His proudest moments were when he listened to my brother, sister, or me tell a story well, captivating an audience. The truth was much less important to his stories than the yarn was, than making his listeners laugh.

"So, when I decided to dedicate a quilt to Pops, I was influenced by his exaggerated stories, his winking at his audience. The resulting quilt, which I started the day after his funeral two years ago, will be unrecognizable to anyone from Teaneck trying to find Teaneck landmarks. It's Teaneck as fable, as a story told by Pops. I think it's technically sound, but I think the reason I won is because the love I have for him comes through in every element. He was with me as I quilted it, guiding my hands, stopping me from overdoing something—from stepping on the punchline, as it were—so I look at the win as a win for both of us. We quilted it together."

"Wow, Amy. I'm going to stop pretending to be objective for a second and say that was an amazing answer. You've just written my story. Thank you."

"No, thank you. I hadn't really put those feelings into words. I appreciate you giving me the opportunity."

"Although I regret having to ask a question that my esteemed, purpled colleague has already asked, do you intend to accept the cash award and donate the quilt?"

"Of course. I can always come visit the quilt. Pops would not be happy if I turned down twenty grand."

"Anything else you'd like to add, Amy? Anything I should've asked but didn't?"

"I'd like to thank AQS, one of the best organizations in the world, and, of course, Jill Haynes, AQS's incredible leader. I'd like to thank the National Quilt Museum and the Carson Center, of course, but I also want to tell quilters out there who doubt themselves, who don't like how slowly they're progressing, that if they find a subject they're truly passionate about, something that inspires them more than they ever thought they could be inspired, they'll instantly become better quilters, and their technical limitations will seem far less significant. If you're an excellent technical quilter, but you don't quilt with passion, are you really even a quilter?"

"You're amazing, Amy. Thank you so much, and I can't wait to see *Teaneck, New Jersey* up close in the Museum. Congratulations again, and safe travels."

"Thank you, Hadley. It's been my pleasure. Good luck."

Amy smiled, ignored Brenda, who appeared to be internally combusting, then was approached by numerous quilters who'd been waiting for the interview to end so they could congratulate her or have her autograph their programs.

I hightailed it to the office, then wrote the easiest story I'd ever written. The winners, first- through fourth place, in each of sixteen categories received cash awards totaling $125,000. The winners came from thirty-three states and ten countries. I listed most of the big winners and wrote short bios of the four who won the most-significant awards. I included nearly all of Amy's quotes, mentioned that Jill Haynes spoke and the Earsplitters played (real name: Funsicle), proofread the story three times, then filed it.

I drove home feeling pretty good. I'd weathered my dark night of the soul, raged against the dying of the light, and felt lucky to have met a fellow quilter who'd managed to transform love and inspiration into such creativity and beauty. I walked Trapunto, drank a cup of Sleepytime herbal tea, read a chapter of a novel titled *Lady in the Lake* by Laura Lippman, then turned out the light and was asleep in minutes, which hadn't happened in years.

My ringing cellphone startled me from a dream about swimming with porpoises at a resort in Cancun, Mexico, where I'd never been. I knocked the phone to the carpet on my first attempt to grab it. The clock's red numbers read: 2:15. The caller I.D. said Bill Lang.

"Hello?"

"There's been another murder. Amy Thorstead."

"No, no, no. I can't believe it."

"Wrapped in blue fabric, which makes red, white, and blue now, but not in that order."

"Where'd they find her?"

"Leaning against the Native American child holding the American flag in the Lewis and Clark memorial on the Museum lawn."

"What? The killings are political now? Indicting westward expansion? Or are they some kind of perverted patriotism?"

"I don't know."

"What's your guess?"

"My guess is, the world is going to hear of Paducah tomorrow, and a swarm of media will arrive."

"Yeah, you're right. With QuiltWeek in town, every room from here to Nashville will be filled. Are you at the scene?"

"On my way. You coming?"

"Do I have a choice?"

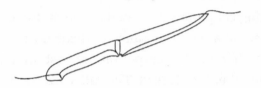

Chapter 27
Background Fabric

Did I have a choice? The question was worth asking. I didn't cover cops and courts, I was not a law enforcement officer, and I didn't work for the city, the National Quilt Museum, or for a fabric manufacturer. I had recently started seeing a psychiatrist and taking an antidepressant because life had knocked me down repeatedly in the last three weeks, and it hadn't picked me up a whole lot during the previous forty years. I lived only with a dog, meaning without a husband, fiancé, boyfriend, girlfriend, lover, partner, or significant other—and without children.

My man—Matthew Gerard Ackerman—could no longer share his wonders and flaws with me, and, therefore, I couldn't share mine with him. Death hadn't taken me, but it was closing in: Veronica, Pat, Matt, Natalie, Heather, and now Amy. I had literally discovered one dead body, had seen from a distance the bodies of Natalie and Heather, and had made a friend in Amy, only to have her be murdered hours later. Therefore, I think most people would forgive me if I didn't go to the latest crime scene, especially because while I'd been asleep, a thunderstorm had once again started to pummel Paducah with a vengeance.

Trapunto, who was too large to squeeze under the bed except when he believed he would soon explode, wedged himself under the bed. The rumblings, booms, and arhythmical kettledrums disturbing the night made me want to let the pros handle this murder so I could settle underneath the bed with Trapunto. I'd met and liked Amy, sure, but it wasn't as though we'd braided each other's hair during sleepovers—and it wasn't as though I could do anything for her now.

But I knew I was lying to myself because I still had a chance, however remote, to see something no one else had seen, to connect one piece to another that had stumped the pros. I started to dress for the rain, but by the time I'd slithered into layers, then pulled my rainboots on, I'd revised my plan: I wouldn't just hope to see something no one else had seen or hope to connect one piece to another that had stumped the pros—I would solve the murders.

The crime scene on the National Quilt Museum lawn swarmed with three times as many officers of the law and officials from the city and county as the one on Tuesday morning on the Greenway Trail. But the one in the early hours of Wednesday featured driving rain, gusts of wind, and powerful, portable lights. But that description doesn't capture the emotional toll.

Cops who often arrived first on the scenes of car wrecks in which people died appeared to be visibly shaken as they assessed the scene. The PPD photographer turned away from Amy's unwrapped, bloody body to wipe a tear from his eye. He was crouching to get a particular angle under the pop-up canopy that the department had put up to preserve the crime scene above Amy's body and the Native American girl holding an American flag.

I wasn't sure why hardened professionals who regularly dealt with violent deaths were shaken by this scene, but I suspected this murder confirmed they had a major problem on their hands, one that would resonate through the city, county, and beyond. The other murders had received limited publicity, but Amy Thorstead was from Los Angeles, so at the very least, the *Los Angeles Times* would cover the murder of the woman who just won QuiltWeek's Best of Show. National media would cover the murders, which would put Paducah in the national spotlight—for the wrong reasons.

Paducah PD only considered Natalie Loose, Heather Cain, and

Amy Thorstead to be linked because they had all been stabbed and wrapped in fabric, and those three victims were sensational enough to have FOX, CNN, MSNBC, NBC, ABC, and CBS send crews to Paducah. The networks' private planes were probably in the air as I stood, holding an umbrella, outside a perimeter made of crime-scene tape. Those crews would broadcast from the makeshift press area about thirty yards south of the statues by 6:30 that morning. Nationally, and maybe internationally, Paducah had gone from Quilt City to the home of the Quilt City Murders.

Photographer Adam Kerns held an umbrella over Bill Lang and himself at about 3:20 a.m., while Bill wrote in this notebook. Our umbrellas only deflected some of the rain because much of it hit us in gusts from the side.

"Who knows if the cops will give us any info on this one?" Bill said. "PPD not solving the first two murders in time to prevent the Best of Show winner from being killed doesn't make them look good and doesn't jibe with their demand for pay raises."

"Do we know if there's a knife in there?" I asked.

"Couldn't tell," Adam said. "So many people crowded around, I haven't gotten a usable shot yet. In this weather, I may not."

"A file photo or a publicity shot?" Bill asked. "Maybe a shot of her winning quilt?"

"Ugg," Adam said. "Not ideal."

"Not much has been lately," I said.

"That's my girl," Bill said. "Upbeat and positive."

"Hey, Mr. Ace Reporter, which solutions have your chipper attitude found?"

"Unlike you, I'm not operating under the delusion I'm a homicide detective."

"Sorry. Didn't mean anything by it. A couple minutes ago I wondered if that could've been me inside that blue fabric. I'm a quilter who wore blue from head-to-toe last night, then interviewed Amy, who also wore blue, and we got along well. She was impressive on so many levels, and the story in which she describes how she created the winning quilt will hit the streets in a couple of hours—and she'll be in the morgue."

Because Amy's body had been found after the paper had shipped, most print subscribers would read the story about her QuiltWeek Best of Show victory either after having learned about her murder from WKYC, from the radio, or from word of mouth. Or they would learn she was dead soon after reading the story, which would likely trigger a flood of emotions.

We stood there, being pummeled by sideways rain, knowing we would learn almost nothing from the scene, especially because a swarm of Kentucky State Police appeared to have wrested control of the scene from PPD. KSP was far less likely to cooperate with the media. When Matt was the cops reporter, he used to consider it a minor victory if a KSP officer said, "No comment" on the record.

I felt a tap on the shoulder, turned, then saw Officer Brandon Green in a rain slicker standing behind me. He took my umbrella from me, then held it over us. The floodlights facing our way cast just enough light for us to see each other's faces.

"Hello, Hadley. How are you?"

"Peachy, Officer Green. Nice evening for a stabbing, don't you think?"

"It seems more fitting than a sunny day, doesn't it?"

"Guess you're right."

"I know you're working, but—"

"Technically, Bill's working. I'm just displaying my desperation publicly."

"Well, I thought I'd let you know in case you hadn't heard—Williams has been arrested."

That was great news, and yet I didn't know how to process it. If I let a positive emotion creep in—satisfaction, relief, joy—would I only be setting myself up for disappointment, or worse? Especially when the charges were dropped or when a jury found him not guilty of all charges after deliberating for four seconds. But I risked suffering a future negative emotion by allowing myself to feel a momentary wisp of relief.

"Thank you. I'm going to do my best to keep a positive outlook about this."

"If I were in your shoes, I'd feel pretty great because word is, they're going to charge him with violating your civil rights, which is much more serious than an assault and battery charge."

"I think it will be a while before I feel great about anything, but I understand what you mean, and I appreciate you telling me the news. Thank you."

"You're welcome. Take care of yourself. The threat from Williams is gone, but I wouldn't put it past Kramer to retaliate against you. He's facing a significant suspension. He may try to do what Williams couldn't."

"Well, now you've brought me back to the land of fear and sorrow. Thanks for that." I smiled, and he returned the smile.

"Mr. Yin Yang, that's me."

"If you say so. Why are you out here? Do you work nights now?"

"No. It's all-hands-on-deck. Paducah is officially in the midst of a murder spree, so we'll all be pulling a lot of overtime."

"Almost gives cops an incentive to kill." I smiled. "Sorry, couldn't resist."

"You're something else."

"Last time you said I wasn't normal."

"Still aren't." He smiled. "Sorry, couldn't resist."

I went home, let Trapunto out, dried him, took a shower, got dressed, then went to work. I really needed to head to Barbados, then Tahiti, then Fiji, then to a quiet cocoon in which I could sleep dreamlessly for a year. But the *Chronicle* office would have to do.

"The story's yours if you want it, Hads," Bill said when we were back at our desks. He'd changed into the gym clothes he had in his truck, rather than making the hour round-trip drive to his house to change out of his wet clothes.

"I liked Amy, and I appreciate your offer, but I used nearly every quote she gave me in today's story, so I don't really have anything to add. If you want to step out of bounds a little by quoting me as one of the last people to speak to her—or at least as the last one to interview her, I'll give you something."

"Okay. It's really early. I should be able to get plenty, but I'll keep your offer in mind."

It was 6:50 a.m., so papers had been landing for a while on porches, in front yards, in rose bushes, and in wet gutters throughout McCracken and the surrounding counties.

I said, "Why don't you write the crime story, and I'll pull together short bios of Amy, Heather, and Natalie, then do a word-on-the-street story about how the murders are affecting citizens?"

"Sounds good, but maybe Dan should do the street story."

"Makes sense, but I was guessing he'd be busy writing about how the city government was handling all of this. What does Mayor Lewy have to say? Would there be a public announcement or a press conference? An increased police presence? Community patrols? The beats are blurred on this because obviously I have to write at least a sidebar, but probably a main for page one, about how the CEOs of AQS and the Museum are responding, if they're changing plans for the rest of the event, bolstering security. Should I ask Brian to do a word-on-the-street just with the quilters here for QuiltWeek?"

"That sounds about right," Bill said. "Despite this crisis, I don't see any reason to allow Greg to muck things up, do you?"

"It would be a shame not to let him take a crack at our headlines. Tomorrow's banner head will read *QuiltWeek kills quilters!*"

He laughed. "We obviously have a long day ahead, so we better put our heads down. And, yes, let's keep the man in charge out of the loop."

The day played out pretty much as we planned. None of the reporters outranked any of the others (in our minds, we all outranked Greg), but Bill and I had been working in newsrooms when Dan was learning to count his toes, and Brian had only a couple of years of journalism experience, after having changed careers from teaching. So, after Dan, Brian, and Adam arrived a little after 9 a.m., Bill and I laid out the plan for tomorrow's paper.

Pulling together the A1 story about how the American Quilter's Society and the National Quilt Museum were responding to the murders should have been easy because it would only require me to call Jill Haynes, CEO of the AQS, and Robby Golden, CEO of the NQM. They would then make reassuring comments about how they had everything under control, would say the quilters have nothing to be concerned about and that QuiltWeek was business-as-usual. But it was probably even more special this year than it usually was.

I didn't report on the quaver in Jill's voice or her very deliberate cadence, but I couldn't do anything to hide her word choices. I'd never changed a direct quote or deliberately used a quote out of context to make a speaker look bad, so I wasn't about to start then. On the other hand, it wasn't my job to make the people I interviewed look good, either, despite what most interviewees seemed to think, so I used this direct quote from Jill:

"It's very sad the poor women lost their lives, but they could've been killed on their way to QuiltWeek, and we certainly wouldn't change the program that has been in place for ten months if that occurred, so we won't change it now."

I couldn't reach Museum CEO Robby Golden. I called, texted, and emailed, but he didn't respond. Obviously, he was in the middle of the busiest time of the year. Having the national media on the property reporting about a murder, a few yards from where Amy's body had been found, didn't put answering a local reporter's questions at the top of his to-do list.

I called John Lenard, head of security for the National Quilt Museum.

"Since the dawn of civilization," he said, "people have been getting murdered. Not much we can do about it. We hope for the best, then move on. What more can we do?"

I said, "The winner of QuiltWeek's highest honor, whose winning quilt now hangs in your main gallery, was murdered last night, perhaps on NQM property. We know she was *found* on NQM property. I'm guessing the *Chronicle* readers, other Paducahans, and the 30,000 quilters in town for the show would feel relieved if you reassured them by saying NQM has taken or will take steps to ensure their safety. I'm not telling you to say that. I'm asking if you're taking any steps to bolster security."

"This is off the record. If I took steps to bolster security, I would be acknowledging we have a *need* to bolster security, and business could be adversely affected."

"You think if you don't acknowledge these murders, then the murders didn't happen?"

"Perception is reality. I didn't coin that truism."

"It's not a truism. It's a bumper sticker for superficial people in denial."

"Do you have anything you'd like to ask me that's unrelated to what you say happened early this morning?"

"No. You've said plenty by saying nothing."

Had I just burned a source on the A&E beat? Probably. Could I do my job if I didn't make people aware that I knew when they were treating me as their P.R. flack, asking me to lie in print for them because they thought that was my job? No, I couldn't. Well, maybe I could do my job, but doing it poorly wasn't an option.

I didn't know if John Lenard feared for the Museum's bottom line, or if he was trying to protect the Museum's reputation, Paducah's, the quilting world's, or his own. I did know that a large percentage of the Museum's admission-paying annual visitors made their pilgrimages during QuiltWeek to the galleries to admire the beyond-belief creations hanging within them.

As we wrote our stories, panic quickly spread through Paducah like a virus. Many of those 30,000 visitors were rethinking their plans, if not heading home. Downtown restaurants that relied on quilters to fill their tables were nearly vacant. Not only were the extra employees who were brought in to accommodate the larger crowds sent home, but the employees who usually worked those shifts also were.

While I pulled together my word-on-the-street story (they're usually called man-on-the-street stories, but I refused to adhere to this antiquated, patriarchal paradigm), a woman of about fifty outside of the Yeiser Art Center gave me the following statement: "It seems clear to me you dang reporters hate capitalism, and you're doing your best to hurt QuiltWeek and all of the small businesses that depend on it. Shame on all of you."

An eighty-year-old man, who refused to give his name, spoke to me as he waited in line to buy a sandwich at Midtown Market: "Stopped reading newspapers decades ago. What you people did to Nixon was criminal. He was our president, and those Jew reporters should've gone to jail."

A twenty-two-year-old woman sipping a latte in Pipers Tea & Coffee said, "I read on my friend's blog, like, you guys are killing people to sell papers. She said that's what William somebody did about a war, and it worked, so, like, reporters have been doing that ever since."

"What's the name of your friend's blog?" I asked, trying not to shout, "We're all doomed."

"IgnoreTheMedia.com."

"She's telling you to ignore her blog?"

"What do you mean?"

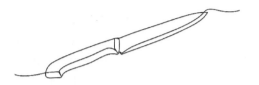

Chapter 28

Prewash

While I was driving around town gathering quotes, I saw evidence that the murders had shaken visiting quilters and Paducah residents. The QuiltWeek attendees, who in previous years had walked from their cars to the Convention Center singly or as pairs or trios, were gathering together, maneuvering down Park in groups as large as twenty. Around town, as they entered the Yeiser to see *Fantastic Fibers*, stepped off the shuttle at the Rotary Quilt Show at the Robert Cherry Civic Center, or shopped at Calico Country Sew & Vac or at Hancock's, the groups were significantly larger and more tightly bunched than they'd been in previous years.

This strength-in-numbers theme continued outside of City Hall, where about seventy-five protesters walked in an oval across the cement walkway and the grass in front of the building, perpendicular to the walkway, looping over and over again past the entrance. Many of them carried signs:

Why Can't You Keep Us Safe?
Mayor Lewy is Lousy
A Murder a Day Keeps Tourists Away
Who's Next?

I took photos with my phone in case Adam couldn't get to City Hall in time to take better ones. But he made it there in time, climbed a tree in Dolly McNutt Plaza across from City Hall, then took a great high-angle shot of the protesters with City Hall in the background. That photo ran on the front page the next day.

After I filed my story, I drove across the river to Metropolis, then tracked down Peter Yett, the poker-room manager. He apologized for not calling to tell me which dealers had worked on March 21. The Showdown on the River Tournament had begun the night before, and my HeART of Paducah story would run the next day. But it was early afternoon, and the tournament wouldn't start back up until 5 p.m., so he and I were the only ones in the poker room. Otherwise, the casino was busy, probably filled with the partners of quilters who had dragged them to QuiltWeek.

I said, "I understand corporate rules and how tight-lipped security forces in general are, let alone security forces at casinos, but I'd like to see security footage from that night."

"Not going to happen," he said, shaking his head.

"I understand, but you know my circumstances. The man I was supposed to marry dumped me, then was murdered."

"Didn't know the first part."

"He left me without explanation, then was dead a week later. I know you don't owe me anything, and I'm not asking for a favor as a reporter—"

"What do you want to know? You're not going to see the footage, but maybe I could look at it, or I could talk to Sammie, head of security, and she can scan it for you."

"Any chance you know who Donna Ackerman is, Matt's mom?"

"Sure. She came in with Matt sometimes, sometimes without him. More than once, I gave him the evil eye when she was bugging him for money during a live game. Not good for business, having a family squabble on the floor."

"Of course not. I want to know if the security cameras caught Donna arguing with anyone. She told me she just asked a question of a friend of ours; I have a source who said he saw a heated exchange, but he couldn't see with whom she was arguing."

"You want me or Sammie to let you know who that was, and, let me guess—you think it coulda been Veronica Yarnell."

"I hope I'm wrong, but I think it could have been. Not sure you need to know this, but you're being helpful, so I'll go with full disclosure. Matt dropped off a bloody blouse at a dry cleaner a couple days later. My guess is he stopped by her house, said he was heading to the dry cleaner or to a particular section of town, and she asked him to do her a favor. If she had an argument with Veronica, maybe asked her for money after Veronica's big win, maybe they got in a shoving match at Veronica's car, and maybe Veronica got a punch in, or maybe Donna fell, too."

"Lotta maybes, but it makes sense. I still got your number. I'll see what I can do. I give you my word this time. I'll call you either way, with a no-can-do or some info."

"Great. Thank you very much, and I hope your tournament goes great. The article will come out tomorrow."

I returned to the office in time to learn that Greg decided to hold an emergency editorial meeting at 3:30 p.m., long after all of us had filed stories for the next day's edition and were waist-deep in two others. He insisted we come in from the field, no matter which stories we were pursuing, to attend the meeting. He actually used the words "or else" in the group-text he sent.

"Thank you all for getting here on time," Greg said. "I know this is a difficult day, but isn't this why we all became journalists?"

Apparently, his question wasn't rhetorical because he looked at us as if awaiting a response. I wanted to say, "Yes, I've always wanted to live in a town being terrorized by a murderer. Isn't journalism great?" Instead, I said, "Why are we here?"

"Yes, let's get right to it," he said. "We're going to put out a special edition tomorrow that will include all of the stories about the murders."

"As opposed to the non-special edition that will include all of the same stories?" Bill asked.

"I don't appreciate your tone," Greg said.

"You mean we're gonna run a graphic saying tomorrow's paper is a special edition?" Adam asked.

"No. Like I said, we're going to run a stand-alone, special Panic in Paducah edition."

"And not put out the regular paper?" I asked.

"Of course not. We've printed a daily edition of this paper for well over one hundred years," Greg said, "so we're not going to stop now."

"If I understand you," Bill said, "we're going to run all the stories we've written or are working on or will write in a special edition."

"Correct," Greg said. His sweater that day was chartreuse.

"You're just going to fill the regular edition with AP stories?" Brian asked.

"No. That's ridiculous. We're first and foremost a local paper, and we always will be, so we'll feature numerous local non-murder stories in tomorrow's regular edition."

"Do you have a second staff we don't know about?" Bill asked.

"You're bringing in reporters from out of town?" Dan asked.

"Are you and your clowns going to write those stories?" I asked.

"Enough. I've told you what's going to happen. Ed, Susan, and I worked hard on this."

Bill said, "And by hard, you mean one of you said, 'Let's put out a special edition' and one of you said, 'Sounds good.'"

"I don't understand this pushback. I really don't," Greg said. "There's nothing unreasonable about what I've just said."

"Other than the fact it's 3:45, and I'm the only designer scheduled tonight because for reasons I don't understand, you let two of them take their vacation at the same time," Jake said.

"And other than the fact it's 3:45, and everything you said is not only unreasonable but also nonsensical," I said.

This hogwash went on for another twenty minutes, which seemed like a decade because we were trying to put out the most important edition in the history of the newspaper. Instead, we were bouncing around inside Greg's hollow skull. Or had he managed to build muscles in there?

Eventually, just after Greg threatened to fire all of us (as though the paper's unblemished streak of publishing daily editions for more than one hundred years wouldn't go poof as we exited), I stood, looked around the room, then said, "Gentlemen, and Greg, congratulations on another job well done. The world will certainly be better for our efforts, but we still have work to do. The Middle East Crisis remains unresolved, so let's hop to it."

Oddly, Greg wasn't as amused by my summation as the others were.

When the next day's edition hit the streets, a graphic featuring a lemon-yellow screen overlaid with words printed in blood-red, seventy-point Bookman Old Style italic ran above the name of the paper.

Special Edition: Panic in Paducah!

Mayor Richard Lewy gave a speech at 10 a.m. on Thursday in front of City Hall. He was flanked by three of the city commissioners, the city manager, National Quilt Museum CEO Robby Golden, American Quilter's Society CEO Jill Haynes, and Police Chief George Wilkins.

"I mean, he said what he's supposed to say, I guess," Dan told Bill and me when he returned from the press conference. "But, saying Paducahans are strong, and officials are working hard to solve the crimes, and people have nothing to worry about so they should go about their lives like normal makes no sense. He was holding a press conference in front of national news organizations because law enforcement hadn't solved the murders, so the event itself contradicted the content. Paducahans have plenty to worry about because no one even has a motive for the killings. Sure, you can go about your normal routine if you want, but I'm heading home after work, bolting my door, then hitting Craig's List for a deal on a gun."

"Still a newbie but catching on fast," Bill said. "They say what they have to say, we have to report what they say—however canned, inaccurate, or absurd—then we sell ads against those stories for tires and diapers. Then we all grow old and die."

Because we were busy writing stories that tried to capture the madness going on outside, I made no progress combing through Matt's notebooks. We were being bombarded by phone calls and emails demanding answers, providing tips, and blaming us for ruining Paducah.

I learned that more than a third of the 30,000 QuiltWeekers had left town, with many of them forfeiting the registration fees they'd paid for their seminars and having to eat the cost of the hotel and motel rooms they checked out of as soon as they learned of the latest two murders—of Heather Cain and Amy Thorstead. If the Paducah Police Department had made progress on the cases, Jane Galliski, the PPD public information officer, hadn't sent out a press release stating as much.

Greg, who wrote what he considered to be editorials, entered into the content-management system an editorial that would run in Friday's edition. I read it within the CMS. Under the headline— Murder is bad—the opening paragraphs, followed by others that were just as poorly written, read:

> As everyone who lives in Paducah knows, this city is paradise on earth, except you don't have to die to reach this paradise. You only have to exit I-24, heading either north or south, then drive any of Paducah's idyllic streets, minding the speed limit, of course.
>
> Except people are dying, being murdered, in fact. Right here in this paradise of Paducah. And it is our officially editorial stance that these killings are wrong. Murder is bad. Everyone knows that, regardless of whether you're a right-thinking conservative, a silly liberal or even a person whose sexual preference is not accepted around here (hint: Move to kooky California!).
>
> The fact is, murder is bad. Murdering with a gun is less bad, because as true

Americans we're pro guns. But, generally speaking, murder is bad, although we can think of a few exceptions.

So, we urge the police to solve these crimes. Crimes are meant to be solved, and our tax dollars say the police are the ones to do that solving. The great citizens of Paducah and all the many, many quilters in town for QuiltWeek deserve better then to be murdered.

Even thought most of the visiting quilters, who bring plenty of business to Paducah's businesses, are old and aren't likely to live too much longer, they shouldn't be stabbed to death, then wrapped in blankets.

Why not? Because murder is bad.

Did I correct the typos? I did not. Did those errors and the assaults on logic, on writing, and on the twenty-first century bother me? Absolutely. But correcting the minor issues without overhauling the major ones would be as pointless as me trying to teach Trapunto about mitered corners.

Despite giving our all, writing stories we could be proud of, and informing the *Chronicle* readers as best we could, the reporters felt kind of futile. We'd worked hard but had no solid news to report. Stories that concluded with some version of "the investigation continues" are not stories worth writing or reading.

I managed to slip away for a couple hours so Dakota and I could peruse some of the four hundred booths in the Convention Center called the Merchant Mall that displayed innumerable quilting wares. Fabrics of every quality, sewing machines whose ad copy all but promised to sew quilts without a quilter's input, and kitschy souvenirs such as coffee mugs adorned with every imaginable quilting pun, and many that shouldn't have been imagined, filled the enormous hall. In other words, the booths featured products that quilters couldn't live without. Dakota and I didn't know many of the products existed until we saw them on display, but then she knew she couldn't live without a coffee mug that said, *I don't always quilt past my bedtime. Oh wait, yes, I do!* And I might have disappeared if I hadn't purchased a T-shirt that said, *It began as a harmless hobby, I had no idea it would come to this.* I had to make peace with the improper use of commas on her mug and the comma splice on my shirt.

As she nearly always did, Dakota looked amazing. She wore a classy Brooks Brothers checked tweed jacket (sky blue with brown stripes), chocolate brown pants and boots, and a gorgeous, one-of-a-kind silk scarf that, after I complimented her on it, she said she'd purchased from SedoniasSilkCreations.com.

"Remember I told you I lost my necklace, the one you gave me?"

"Yes."

"I never found it. And now I can't find a scarf. Before I bought this one, I wanted to check if I already had one, or four, just like it, so I searched through my scarf drawers, and the one that's the most unlike the rest, the black-and-white one, isn't there. It can't be in the wash because I'm not an idiot. And I've never been one to forget to pick up dry cleaning, and they would have called if I'd left it, don't you think?"

"Probably."

"I'm really worried I'm showing signs of dementia."

A huddle of quilters scooted past us in the aisle, and one of them gave Dakota a nasty look when she heard her last comment.

"I haven't noticed anything. You're as sharp as a tack, but far more beautiful."

"Thank you, but it seems my looks are all anyone ever sees. I'm not sure people, mostly men, even hear what I say, so who would point out if I'm in the midst of cognitive decline?"

"I would, and you're not. To put your mind at ease, though, you should make an appointment to get checked, take the test, pass it, then sleep much better."

We wandered among the booths in amazement, even though we'd been to many QuiltWeeks. Each year delivered new features, and each year, I swore I had no need to buy more fabric. My finances that year dictated that I honor that commitment. Dakota offered to purchase a bolt of my choice for me, but I politely declined.

"Instead," I said, "I'd like you to answer if I call you in the middle of the night. I've been waking up in cold sweats. They've arrested Williams. . . . I didn't tell you he tried to break into my house."

"What? Oh, Hads. How awful."

"Officer Green told me he's concerned that Kramer, who stood and watched Williams beat me, could try to retaliate against me."

"Oh, honey, I'm so sorry you're going through this. Of course, you can call me whenever you have to. That's always been the case. I thought you knew that."

"I do, but I guess I needed to hear you say it."

I had turned my ringer down when Dakota and I entered the Convention Center because I thought, after the very long days I'd been putting in, I deserved a short break from whatever onslaught would slaught me that day. So, a few minutes later, when I sat in my truck, I looked to see if I'd received any calls. Poker-room manager Peter Yett had called. His message said, "Your suspicions have been confirmed. Donna Ackerman had a verbal altercation with Veronica Yarnell on the gaming floor that night. Security footage shows her leaving before Veronica left but after her son did. We've alerted Metropolis PD to these developments. Good luck—and be careful."

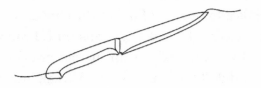

Chapter 29

Unraveling Seam

I had trouble settling my stomach. My body occasionally indicated I had a problem before my mind admitted the problem existed. Donna, my friend, fellow PQQ member, and the mother of the man I was supposed to marry could have killed Veronica. They'd argued that night, but when I'd asked Donna who she'd argued with, she said she'd just asked Justine why she hadn't been invited to her birthday party. If she was innocent and she'd had an argument with Veronica and knew it looked bad because Veronica was murdered soon thereafter, why wouldn't Donna admit to the argument? She could have said, "I feel doubly awful because our last interaction was an argument." But she hadn't said that or anything similar. She'd lied.

Donna was always broke, yet, apparently, she went to Harrah's frequently. She could have waited for Veronica to exit, then followed her to her car. Matt had taken a bloody blouse that wasn't mine to a dry cleaner that wasn't the one he and I normally used. I did my best to process this information, but it only resulted in an upset stomach. I'd have to think about how to proceed while also making sure I didn't lose my job, so I headed back to work, with no confidence that I'd be able to concentrate.

On my way to the office, I drove past City Hall. The number of protesters marching in front had quadrupled. The paper ran plenty of quotes from angry, frightened citizens, most of them involved in the extensive Paducah arts community. Understandably, Ed Colapinto doubled the press run to accommodate all of the people in town who wanted to stay informed (and he did so to make money, of course. I heard a rumor in the newsroom that the ad rates for the Thursday through Sunday papers jumped fifty percent, but I didn't care enough to confirm the rumor).

After a sleepless night, Friday brought more of the same deadlines, stress, and fear. The number of protesters at City Hall had tripled from Thursday's numbers. The reporters scrambled to make sense of what was going on. Greg once again proved that he couldn't hold a successful garage sale, let alone run a newspaper during a civic crisis. The above-the-fold photo on Friday's front page showed a nearly empty Convention Center. More than half of the four-hundred vendors who had paid significant amounts for their booths had pulled down their displays, then headed home. I didn't know how to calculate the economic impact that the mass exodus of quilters was having on Paducah's businesses, but I knew that many millions of dollars were involved. By the time I left work at 8 p.m. Friday, I was exhausted to the point of collapse. I walked Trapunto, brushed him, then fell asleep within an hour.

After waking twice in a cold sweat, I woke for good on Saturday morning to realize what a pigsty I was living in. I hadn't consciously planned to neglect my home, but as I looked around my kitchen and main room, I realized I hadn't cleaned at all since Matt left me. The women in the Paducah Quilters Quorum almost a week ago had obviously cut me slack by not mocking my lack of cleaning diligence. It hadn't seemed that bad on Sunday, but it certainly must not have been anywhere near clean.

After reading the paper, I drank enough coffee to jolt the heart of an elephant. I jogged three miles with Trapunto, then started cleaning. I dusted every surface, then swept, mopped, and vacuumed. I scrubbed the sinks, tub, and toilet, then did three loads of laundry, including the sheets that were on my bed. While the sheets were in the dryer, I decided to flip the mattress, so I lifted my side and was startled by a glimpse of navy blue where none should have been. My stomach flipped.

The sight of blue almost caused me to drop the mattress. I regained my composure, held the mattress up with my left hand, and grabbed Matt's journal with my right. I set the mattress back in place, sat on it, then tried to get my pulse to settle.

I knew Matt had written in his journal daily. We'd discussed some of his entries over the years, but he'd never offered to let me read any of them. I respected his privacy and loved him far too much to betray his trust by secretly reading his entries, however much I wanted to.

About a dozen of his blue journals lined one of the bookshelves in his house, which was even more rundown than mine was. I'd been curious about the journals, and I hoped that after he moved into my place, which he was supposed to have done in a month when his lease expired, maybe he would share those journals with me. If not, I'd make peace with that because we would be together—and sharing a life didn't mean sharing everything.

How long had the journal been under my mattress? I had a feeling he slid it there that last night, the one during which we laughed and played guitar and made love for the last time, the night before he broke up with me.

He left this journal where I'd hidden his Mike Schmidt baseball card that Christmas, when I'd forgotten where I'd hidden it. We'd laughed about my memory lapse. He knew I'd find the journal, but it was a safe bet I wouldn't find it on the morning he left or the next or the next. He had helped me turn over my mattress for the last five years, about every three or four months.

He wanted me to find the journal, but I couldn't open it. For five years, I'd wondered what he was writing each night and how many of his words were about me, and how many of those words were positive, and how many of those words were "I love Hadley."

I carried the journal from the bedroom to the main room, then sat in the brown reclining chair, the one I spent hours reading in with the good light perched behind it.

How long did it take him to fill a journal? If I opened it to the first page, which date would top the page? Did I want to start at the beginning, maybe a few months ago, maybe a year or more? Or maybe he'd just started writing in this one. I opened to the back page, then started flipping forward until I reached his last entry, about a third of the way from the back. I forced myself not to read any of his words until I reached the beginning of the entry, which was dated April 1. I thought I'd only have to struggle with his atrocious penmanship, but deciphering it was nothing compared to deciphering his meaning.

Dear Hads,

As you'll see when you read my earlier entries, which, knowing you, you'll do after you read this one, I don't address you directly in my journal, although I obviously write about you frequently, if not nightly. This journal entry, however, is different, so breaking form makes sense, even if nothing else does.

I left my journal where I knew you'd find it relatively soon. You probably guessed whenever you found it that I left it on our last night together, after I wouldn't let you come to my place. If so, then you guessed right, as usual.

As I'm sure you were shocked to learn, I left you the next morning. I can't say this more emphatically, Hads—I did not leave because of you.

I love you much more than I've loved anyone else; in fact, much, much more than I've loved everyone else combined, including my family. I definitely love you much more than I love myself, especially now that I'm doing what I'm doing. I can only guess the incomprehensible pain I'm putting you through.

But, after tossing and turning and even feeling nauseated all day long, day after day, I reached the only conclusion I could reach. The only other option was suicide, but doing that would take guts I don't have.

To try to prove to myself I do have some guts, though, prove I'm not a total coward, I poked the bear on your behalf by filing an Open Records request on Nick Stoddard and hassling him in other ways.

I didn't know what I'd find, and I mostly filed it and did the other stuff to annoy him, to pay him back for assaulting you and forcing you out of the newsroom. As you know, I hate bullies, although I never told you why, other than the Williams stuff.

I've never been man enough to confront bullies directly, and I don't think I'd fight very well if I had to. But I saw Stoddard berate one of his employees while the poor guy was drinking a hot chocolate in Pipers. It was the guy's day off, probably, and his two kids were drinking their hot chocolates next to him, but Nick lays into him, telling him he was an idiot, an incompetent fool, and something snapped in me.

I'm so tired of being a victim, and I wanted to play the hero, to see what that felt like, just once, so I went up to Stoddard and told him it was payback time. He looked shocked, like no one had ever told him off. No one but you, of course. I didn't hit him the way you did, but it felt really good standing up to him, and for a second or two, I swore I liked myself.

The Open Records request is in my desk drawer. I sent a copy to Suzanne Bigelow, so

I'm hoping she'll find something she can charge the bully with. I mean, he's a Stoddard, right? Saying someone might find criminal activity when investigating the Stoddards is like saying someone might find wetness when investigating water.

Sadly, that was the extent of my heroism. It ended with me trying to get revenge on that idiot for getting you demoted, even though heroism is what's needed now.

So, I NEED, NEED, NEED you to know this. I understand that knowing it could make things more difficult, not easier, and I truly apologize if that's the case, but I LOVE YOU and I'LL ALWAYS LOVE YOU, HADLEY CARROLL.

Please know I'm out there loving you from afar, but don't wait for me. I won't return. You'll meet a man who is far, far better than I am. Let's face it: Nearly all of them are. You're so amazing - intelligent, funny, gorgeous, sexy, adventuresome, creative, athletic, honest and loving. But you obviously have bad taste in men. Ha Ha. I hope you choose better next time because I'm sure you'll be able to choose nearly anyone you want.

So, please, I beg you, choose one of them. I truly hope he's the right one - but choose one. To be honest, I don't really want you to forget about me, but please don't pine for me and hope I'll come back. I won't. I can't.

I just couldn't do what I had to do, Hads. I couldn't. Other men probably wouldn't blink. But, sadly, as you'll see as you read this journal, I berate myself often because I'm not like other men. I'm just needy Matty Ackerman, the moron wearing the monocle or the ascot. At least I have the grace not to wear them simultaneously. That would be gauche. Ha Ha. But, none of that matters now, because I couldn't do what I needed to do. Please forgive me, even if that seems impossible.

I'm crying now, and, yes, those are smudged tears. I started to cry when I thought how much I'll miss your laugh. I miss it already, and I always will.

Again, Hads, please believe me: I left for a reason totally unrelated to you. I'm really screwed up, but I'm not stupid, and any man who willingly left you would be truly stupid. Screwed up and stupid. I left because I'm a coward. Again, please forgive me.

Instead of saying goodbye forever, I'll leave you with a poem I wrote for you.

Love, Matty

If All
If all the world were candy kisses
And all our thoughts were dreams
If everywhere were Disneyland
And all our tears were cream
If roses grew from all our anger
And all our fights were staged
If every thought became a lyric
And every fear uncaged
If songs would sing from words unspoken
And every wish came true
If the world believed in happy endings
Then I could stay with you.

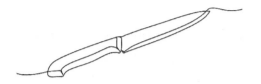

Chapter 30

Stack and Whack

I read the entry four times, then closed the journal and set it in my lap. Trapunto had seen me crying as I read, then put his chin on my right knee, looking up at me with his kind, brown eyes, wondering how he could help.

I should've been relieved. As Elaine had suggested, Matt hadn't left because I'd done something wrong or because of who I was or wasn't. In a journal entry as self-lacerating as this one, I had to take Matt at his word. Could he have lied in his parting words to me so I'd feel better about myself? Maybe, but in an entry in which he flayed himself, would he really be dishonest about the reason he was leaving? If I'd been lacking in some way, wouldn't he have told me that? Didn't I deserve that much?

As I sat there, trying to decode his message, I decided I had to trust that Matt was telling the truth. He'd grown up in a house "wallpapered with lies," as he'd put it.

On our third date, as we'd sat on the pebbles at Kentucky Lake's Moss Creek Day Use Area with our jeans rolled up and our bare feet in the water, he said, "I don't want to presume anything, Hadley, but if we move forward, there's something you should know about me."

That familiar "not-again" lump formed in my throat. We'd had three great dates—well, two and a half. He was so awkward during our first meal together, a veggie pizza at Mellow Mushroom, that I almost told him my stomach was bothering me so I could get out of there.

He'd told one awful joke, one inappropriate joke, and a weird story I think he thought was meant to be funny, so I thought, "Well, at least the pizza is great."

But I didn't give up. I knew the guy who'd asked me a couple of insightful questions at work was in there somewhere. So, I reached across the table and grabbed both of his hands. I didn't say anything, just looked at him kindly, and over the next fifteen seconds, I felt him relax.

"Matt, it's okay. The worst that can happen is that I reject you. Until two weeks ago, you hadn't seen me since high school, and we've only had a few short conversations, so you don't have a lot invested. You can relax."

He nodded and smiled.

"Or," I said, "I could stand up on my chair and scream that I used to have a crush on George Michael, shout that *The Princess Bride* was once my favorite movie, admit I cheated on a second-grade spelling test by looking at Melanie Gardenier's paper. I could take out a *Chronicle* ad saying I once dated a guy who insisted Big Foot was real. I dated another guy who was so self-absorbed that, after we'd been dating for six months, he admitted he didn't know what color my eyes are, and another who swore I'd made up the word 'denigrate.'"

Matt started to laugh when I said, *The Princess Bride*, and he was laughing hard by the end of my last statement, but I kept going.

"Then I could start to reveal my family's secrets. Or I could shut up so you can tell me who you really are. The worst that can happen is I reject you, but if you talk to me as you, instead of as the bozo you think is a better version of you, I'll probably stick around, at least for a second date."

My plan worked. He allowed himself to be the man he never allowed himself to be at work. So, on that third date, after getting my hopes up and feeling as though I'd met a man who wasn't just good on paper but who was similarly wounded, I was troubled by that "not again" lump forming in my throat.

"You're probably not presuming anything I'm not presuming, Matt, and, yes, I hope we move forward, so what do I need to know about you?"

Please don't be a married, heroin-addicted felon who roots for the Boston Red Sox.

He said, "I'll probably disappoint you in many ways, some of which I won't even understand, and I may not become what you need me to become—"

"Just tell me. What is it?"

"I will never lie to you. I will never cheat on you. I know a lying cheater would say exactly that, but I'm telling you the truth because, at the risk of blowing it all, this feels very different. You're very different. I grew up in a house wallpapered with lies. My parents cheated on each other back and forth out of revenge but had different versions of who stepped out first. It was like the Hatfields and McCoys. And my dad wasn't a good man."

"I'm really sorry, Matt. That sounds like a lousy childhood. I really wish I could tell you I have no idea what that must've felt like and tell you that my family was wonderful, but I never knew my dad, never met him, and my mom was, let's say, much less than wonderful. So, no, you didn't blow it all, not even close.

"In fact, most guys would reveal what you just did sometime after their seventh wedding anniversary, if they ever would. For many years I've said about myself, 'I'm broken, but I know it, and I'm willing to admit it.' That doesn't make me better or healthier than the people who aren't broken, but among those who are broken—I'd say seventy percent—I'm more self-aware and honest than they are, I think. So, I tell myself that that counts for something. As long as I don't hang out too frequently with the other thirty percent, the unbroken people, I manage to feel pretty good about myself, all things considered. As the saying goes, in the land of the blind, the one-eyed woman is queen."

He laughed, then said, "That's how the saying goes, huh? All these years I've heard it wrong."

"If you stick with me, you'll learn a lot."

"I'm sure I will." He leaned over and kissed me. I was pleasantly surprised to learn that Matt Ackerman was the best kisser I'd ever known. Among other things.

But I digress.

Saturday night was another rough one. After QuiltWeek officially came to an end—a tattered, torn, and sullied version of its usually gleaming self—I batted around Matt's possible motivations for leaving me. The only conclusion I could reach was that he thought his mother was a murderer, although he couldn't bring himself to turn her in.

Matt had rarely mentioned his father, so I thought it was odd when he suggested I meet his dad after Matt and I got engaged. I thought we might be heading to Philadelphia for some kind of father-son resolution: "Hey, Dad, how big a failure could I be if this wonderful woman agreed to marry me?"

The vibe between the two of them seemed strained, but I had no way to know if that was how they'd always been when together or if something else was going on. Barry Ackerman was nice to me, and I didn't spot any glaring character flaws. He treated me well and insisted on buying all of our meals, including cheesesteaks at both Geno's and Pat's.

Dakota had let me know she wouldn't attend this week's PQQ session at Donna's because, as she put it, "My sis needs me once again, as she seems to at least once a week. But anything for family, right? I'll miss you, Hads, and please give my love to all of them."

The rest of us greeted each other that Sunday afternoon with our usual pleasantries and teasing after we'd set the food on Donna's kitchen counters and set our hodgepodge of purses on her couch, ranging in size from the purple clutch that Janet carried that could hold little more than a phone and lipstick to the spicy-brown-mustard monstrosity Justine carried that a vendor at a ballpark should lug while shouting, "Dogs, get your piping hot dogs here."

The six of us settled into the positions we'd been in last week at my house, but at Donna's longer table, so we had more room to work on our traditional double wedding ring quilt with modern twists, especially because Dakota wasn't there.

We hadn't named the quilt we were working on. Unlike when I quilt on my own, we waited until we completed our Quorum quilts, then threw out suggestions for names as we looked at our completed creations. But I liked to name my quilts first, so I could curse at them by name when they misbehaved.

Despite our attempts to make PQQ that day similar to all of the ones that preceded it, the murders and the grip they had on Paducah kept elbowing in. Vivian and I repeatedly tried to change the subject when the murders came up. At one point, Justine said, "So much for Paducah being Mayberry. We're not safe."

"I know," Vivian said. "I can't believe he's still out there," to which Cindy responded, "And law enforcement doesn't have a clue."

"No one does. It's scary as all get-out," Donna said.

"Please, y'all, let's talk about something else," I said.

At one point, each of us mentioned the worst job we'd ever had, and, later, we each named our celebrity crush (one vote each for actors Bradley Cooper and George Clooney, two for actor Tom Hardy, and two for quilting heartthrob Ian Berry).

But the discussion kept coming back around to Natalie, Heather, and Amy. My fellow quilters had the class not to mention Matt in the presence of Donna and me.

When it was time to eat, I let them all head to the kitchen to prepare their plates while I stepped inside Donna's tornado of a quilting room. To the left, everything looked just as disastrous as it had the day I'd stopped by to tell Donna about Matt's murder, but the right side was different. Where the large pile of what I'd hoped had been clean laundry sat that day now stood a Horizon Memory Craft 8900 QCP Special Edition sewing machine.

My heart started to race. Donna was always broke and had borrowed money from Matt more than once, but suddenly she was in possession of a $4,000 sewing machine? I peeked into the main room, but they were still in the kitchen preparing their plates and talking. I looked at the machine. Pat DeLott had been stabbed to death during a push-in robbery, and one of the items Pat's daughter said had been stolen was an expensive sewing machine. I looked at the long, white boxes that I'd only glanced at last time. I stepped closer, bent down, then looked at the end of the boxes. The small green type read 'EMR Fabrics.'

"Aren't you going to eat?" asked Cindy as she reentered the main room.

"Of course," I said, stepping out of Donna's quilting room, then adding in a quiet voice, "I was just getting some decorating ideas." Cindy laughed so hard that her lasagna almost slid off her plate onto our quilt.

The others came back in, then sat down to eat, with their plates in their laps as we always ate to avoid staining the quilt. I went to the kitchen, ostensibly to prepare a plate.

The feeling of fear and nausea I had felt when I saw the Phillies watch on Matt's wrist in the water came back to me. I could posit many unlikely theories trying to explain why Donna had a $4,000 sewing machine on top of two dozen boxes of EMR Fabrics, or I could do what I'd done when I saw the watch on the male wrist in the water: admit the worst had happened, then try to make it through the aftermath.

I filled my plate, carried it to the main room, sat down, and started to eat for the sake of appearances. I couldn't look toward Donna, and I didn't know if I was eating fresh greens or Soylent Green. My mind was racing, but I did my best to pretend I was among them, listening to snippets of conversation between my panic attacks.

"A ballerina," Cindy said.

"A dolphin trainer," Janet said.

"A princess," Vivian said.

"A veterinarian," Justine said.

"An actress," Donna said, then added, "How about you, Hadley? What did you want to be when you were a little girl?"

"Safe."

They laughed, but I wasn't joking.

"We mean as a career, honey," Cindy said.

"A writer."

"Then you're the only one of us who became what you wanted to become," Vivian said. "Congratulations."

"Thank you," I said, feeling as though I was in the middle of an out-of-body experience, or maybe looking into this universe from a parallel one. I was being congratulated for a career choice I made when I learned very young that I could escape my alcoholic mother and the realities of my life by reading in the library and anywhere else I had a book. And I did my best always to have a book with me. But while they had that trivial discussion, I tried to convince myself that Donna didn't stab Pat DeLott to death, then steal her sewing machine.

If she did, though, then she must've killed Natalie, Heather, and Amy, too, because they were all stabbed to death.

It was a longshot, and I had no proof. I kept hearing Matt's words from his journal entry—"I just couldn't do what I had to do, Hads. I couldn't"—and his words convinced me that Matt had more than a hunch, too.

He'd written two names in his notebooks that didn't seem to be connected to stories: Veronica Yarnell and Pat DeLott. When he wrote those names, was he asking himself if they knew each other, if they knew his mother, if their deaths were related? Did he know they'd both died recently when he wrote their names?

He'd also written EMR Fabrics. All reporters juggle multiple stories at once, and fabrics fell into his A&E beat, so he could've written the name of that company down for a dozen reasons. Or he could've written it down for one purpose: He suspected his mother in the deaths of Veronica and Pat, and EMR Fabrics played a role. Was I reaching? Probably. But a drowning woman grabs anything thrown her way, hoping whatever it is will keep her afloat. However, I was pretty sure that desperation wasn't buoyant.

And if Matt suspected his mother of being a murderer, he would have confronted her, and when he did, she would have had a reason to kill him.

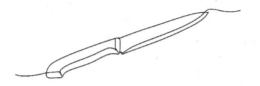

Chapter 31
Memory Quilt

While they discussed their biggest romantic regrets, I excused myself to use the bathroom, then wondered if my theory about what had happened made sense. Matt couldn't bring himself to turn his mother in as the murderer of multiple people, and she couldn't take the chance that he would change his mind, then turn her in, so it seemed as though she'd killed him.

He shouldn't have left me, but I thought I understood why he did. He'd never lied to me, and he loved me, so he didn't want to *start* lying to me. And there's a big difference between lying about whether you'd visited your favorite bar after work or about whether you knew your mother was a murderer. He understood me enough to know I wouldn't sit back and let Donna get away with murder, no matter how much I loved him and liked her. So, he *had* to leave.

I was surprised I was making sense of all of the chaos that had roiled me for the last twenty-five days, and I didn't want to believe I could be right because if this made sense, then what constituted senselessness?

I put my hand on the doorknob, intending to accuse Donna, in front of witnesses, of being the murderer. But I realized that if any proof of the crimes existed, it wouldn't exist for long, so I would've helped Donna avoid incarceration and maybe lethal injection. She would get away with all of it. I slowly counted to ten—okay, four—decided to think of another plan, then walked back into the living room.

They were tidying up. I looked at my phone: 4:30 p.m. For some reason, they were packing up early.

"We're calling it quits?" I asked.

"More weather's expected. Possible tornadoes," Vivian said.

"Good idea, then," I said.

As Cindy folded the quilt, then tucked it under her arm, the others put away their supplies. When Donna entered the bathroom, I stepped into her quilting room again. What was I missing? I looked around, but nothing registered that I hadn't noticed before. Then it occurred to me the door was open, so I couldn't see what was on the wall behind it. I carefully found places to squeeze my feet into, then closed the door. Behind it on the wall was a chart, about two-feet by three-feet. At the top in large green letters, it said 'EMR Fabrics Sales Success Checklist.' The chart was not identified as Donna's, just a nameless ledger.

Below the title, the hundreds of rectangular boxes looked like a giant Excel spreadsheet. The boxes stretching horizontally across the top from left to right were titled: Name; Address; Phone Number(s); First Contact; Second Contact; Third Contact; Success?; Products Purchased; Amount of Order; Re-contact date; Re-order date; and Products Purchased.

I quickly skimmed the names, drawing my left index finger from top to bottom. There were fifty-six names, according to the column of numbered boxes on the far left. Veronica Yarnell's name was number twenty-three; Pat DeLott's was thirty-one. I suddenly understood what had caused Matt to be suspicious, and my breathing became quick and shallow.

Donna had contacted Veronica and Pat three times each, based on the green checkmarks in their six contact boxes. Their Success boxes had a red X in them, as did those for all but eight of the fifty-six names.

Those eight boxes had green checkmarks in them. The sales ranged from $70 to $500, with only one above $300. Donna made a commission off those sales. Even if that commission were impossibly high—fifty percent, let's say—Donna didn't buy that $4,000 sewing machine with her EMR Fabrics commissions.

"Knock, knock," Donna said as she simultaneously knocked. "You playing hide-and-seek or stealing thread?"

I opened the door, stepped around it, and said, "Hi. Sorry. I saw those boxes and got curious. How's it going?"

"It's much harder than I thought," she said, stepping close to me. Too close. I was significantly younger and much more fit, but she outweighed me by probably a hundred pounds. If she tackled me, then simply lay on top of me, I would suffocate.

Had my life really come to this? I was worried about being killed by the woman who should've soon been my mother-in-law, a murderer who probably killed her own son?

By my side, I made a fist with my right hand. I wondered if there was a pair of scissors within reach on her sewing table. I hadn't seen one, and I didn't want to take my eyes off of her to check.

"EMR Fabrics are much less expensive than other fabrics," she said, "because we're the salesforce, and we aren't on the clock and don't get benefits. Straight commission. But I've learned people think the product is cheap. Of course, it's not Moda. Look at the prices, people. I've quilted with it plenty. No problems. I quilt because I like the process. Was surprised to learn everyone else cares that much about the finished product."

"I like the process, too," I said. "I'd rather end up with a nice quilt because it would show I wasn't just wasting time and I'd progressed as a quilter, but a poorly made quilt keeps me and everyone else just as warm as an award winner."

"Except no one would use an award winner."

"Which, if you think about it, makes shoddy quilts more valuable."

She laughed, and I opened my fist.

"Some people got so angry because I tried to sell them a product they don't like. Even got nasty. Personal insults, comments about my weight. It makes me so mad. EMR Fabrics has actually made me enemies. It's made me want to explode."

"I looked up EMR and learned it's a multi-level company. You get a commission on the sales of people you've recruited, right?"

"Supposedly. But when they make you spend all that bread for the initial pallet of product, they don't tell you how hard it is to sell this stuff. People who've been quilting a long time have their favorite brands. A couple nasty ladies touched the sample I handed them and told me to go sand furniture with it."

"So, you haven't sold enough to have salespeople downstream yet."

"Right. I heard eighty-five percent of the salesforce receive downstream income, but I did research I shoulda did before I spent all that money I didn't have, and I learned it's more like five percent. And I ain't never been in the top five percent of anything in my life."

"You're a great quilter and a great cook."

"Kris Vierra is a great quilter, and Emeril Lagasse is a great cook."

"They are, but that doesn't mean you're not, as well."

"Sure, thanks. But the dang company sells you a list of potential buyers. I got excited because it looked like they done most of my work for me. But then I started calling, and they sold the same list to every rep. They bought some list somewhere, then played us for fools."

I figured if she intended to smother me to death, she probably would've done it by then, but I didn't know what I was basing that homicidal timeline on. Probably hope, but it could've been stupidity because instead of being happy that my lungs worked as they were designed to work, I pressed my luck by saying, "That's a heck of a sewing machine. How'd you swing that with your money woes?"

I knew I could've triggered her murderous rage, but I needed proof that she was guilty. If she squashed me, conked me with something solid, or pulled a knife from behind her back, then ran it through me, I'd have my answer, and Vivian, Janet, Justine, and Cindy would testify that they'd left Donna and me alone together.

And the laws of probability had to apply, didn't they? How could this sixty-two-year-old woman with a bad knee go 7-0? An unblemished murder record without so much as a scratch?

For three seconds after I asked the question, it looked as though I had my answer, and the answer would allow me to stop worrying about everything forever. The skin tone on her face and neck went almost instantly from ruddy to deep purple, and the muscles in her neck, jaw, and forehead tensed up. Before she decided which method she wanted to use to end my life, I pushed her in the stomach as hard as I could, causing her to fall into a pile of fabric bolts; then I ran out of the room.

I grabbed my purse off the table, fished out my keys as I took the three strides to the front door, bounded the ten yards to my truck, and jumped in, glancing at the front door. She was standing in the doorway, glaring at me, her hands on her hips, her face having lightened a shade. I was glad she wasn't in good shape and had a bad knee because I jiggled the key for fifteen seconds before it would turn. If she'd been right behind me, who knows what would've happened?

I drove straight to Matt's house. I hadn't been there since a week before he left me. After he died, I meant to go there to help Donna deal with all of his stuff, but I couldn't summon the strength.

Matt and I had exchanged house keys within the first three months we were together, and he hadn't asked for his back on the morning he left me, so I parked in his driveway and opened the front door. I noticed that the mailbox, to the right of the front door, overflowed with mail. I stepped inside, and mustiness and stale air filled my nostrils. Maybe Donna couldn't bring herself to go to Matt's house either.

In the entryway sat four suitcases. His other possessions were in twelve large moving boxes, piled two-high in the living room. His old Mac desktop sat on the ratty carpet, next to the boxes. The contents of each box were listed in Matt's scrawl on the top flaps of the boxes in black Magic Marker. In one corner sat a bunch of stuff he'd found around town, along the roads, in dumpsters, or in alleys.

Where had he planned to go?

I felt woozy, but there was no furniture left to sit on. A sleeping bag on a sleeping pad was unrolled in one corner. I sat where I was standing, on the worn, faded, dingy-yellow vinyl flooring that lined the entryway. I pulled my knees toward my chest, then wrapped my arms around my knees and closed my eyes. When I finally opened them, I looked at the wall across from me for the first time since I'd been there. I saw something that looked familiar. I stood, walked to the wall, then saw a blow-up of a picture that Matt had taken of Donna's EMR Fabrics chart. It was about half the size of the actual chart, but I could still identify the green checkmarks and the red Xs. I looked again at the red Xs in the Success boxes of Veronica Yarnell and of Pat DeLott. Matt had obviously been as shocked as I was when I saw those names on the chart. And because he'd seen the chart, he almost certainly would have seen the $4,000 sewing machine. He'd seen his mother have an argument at the casino on the night Veronica had been killed, had probably confronted her about the argument, or about her gambling, or both. Then she'd probably asked him to take her bloody blouse to the cleaners. Or had he found it somewhere— hidden in her car, stuffed behind something in her house—then took it unprompted to the cleaners?

I sat down again, then thought, which had always been both my most beneficial and my most detrimental activity.

Was I supposed to be there? If Matt had wanted me to know where he intended to go, he would've told me or written the destination in his last journal entry, the one he'd intended for me to find. Did Donna know where he was heading? Did she know why?

He had to have confronted her, right? He wouldn't have broken his engagement off, sold or packed his stuff, then headed to another city without having said something like, "Mom, I've discovered what you've done. How could you?"

That's what I would've done, but I couldn't be sure Matt would have. "I grew up in a house wallpapered with lies," he'd said. Because his mother had lied to him regularly, big and small lies about everything and nothing, why would he believe her when she denied she was a murderer? The most honest person in the world—if she had somehow killed someone—would probably find it within herself to lie when faced with life in prison or lethal injection. Donna, obviously, was not the most honest person in the world, so, of course she would've lied when he confronted her. Why bother to confront her if his last interaction with his mother would almost certainly be a horrible argument?

That question made me jump to my feet and hurry to the front door to lock all three locks: the one in the knob, the deadbolt, and the chain. Just because she couldn't chase me on foot didn't mean she couldn't drive here to finish what she'd started in her quilting room. I looked around for a weapon. Matt's kitchen items, including his knives, were packed in one of the boxes, I assumed. It seemed faster to grab something from the pile of junk in the corner than to search for the correct box, so I hustled to the corner, then grabbed the object that would make the best weapon: a bowling pin—white with two fluorescent orange stripes around the neck and an orange triangular logo. I grabbed one of the three of them by the neck, lifted it, and it was much heavier than I would have guessed. My knees buckled and my stomach turned queasy and my heart raced, and I was transported physiologically back to the dock, when I saw the Phillies watch on Matt's wrist. I was all but certain I'd just figured out how Matt had been killed.

Not with the pin in my hand, necessarily, or with one of the other two still in the corner, but with a pin just like the one I carried across the room, then stood vertically beside me. The killer had grabbed a pin spontaneously, then had used it to end Matt's life. The heft and solidness felt up to the task, and nearly any size hand could grasp the neck, then swing the barrel of the club into an unsuspecting victim. The more than three pounds of menace I held in my hand would be enough.

Again, I tried to get my pulse to slow, but a thought was trying to bubble up, which kept my heartrate up. I tried to fight the thought off, but it popped into my head. If Matt was killed here, then his blood could be here, probably under one of the boxes. Would Donna have had the presence of mind to pull one of the boxes over whatever blood had been spilled so a casual observer wouldn't notice it, or had she cleaned it up from the vinyl flooring? The police had to have scoured this place, right? If so, wouldn't that mean a technician would have cleaned up any blood? I decided to go with that last assumption, so I didn't have to move the boxes to prove my assumption incorrect. I hadn't looked at Matty on the dock that morning, or in the morgue later, and I certainly didn't want the last image of "him" in my head to be a bloodstain.

When I'd arrived, Matt's door and deadbolt had been locked. Of course, Donna had a key to Matt's house, so she wouldn't necessarily have had to lock the door behind her with Matt's key as she lugged him to her car. She could have returned to the house to lock the door. If she didn't know he was leaving town before she arrived at his house, then killed him, she figured it out when she saw the suitcases and boxes. Did she decide to use his leaving to help her get away with murder? If she made his body disappear, and people who knew him knew he was leaving, then they wouldn't necessarily look for him— they'd just think he took off early. If his Honda was parked in the garage, no one would know otherwise, except the letter carriers who stuffed his overflowing mailbox. But they probably wouldn't say anything for a long time, if ever.

I sat, holding my knees, and rationalized my being there. Technically, Matt had broken up with me, but had he really? He did it under duress because he couldn't bring himself to turn his mother in, and, of course, he didn't know he was about to be murdered.

Or did he? Had Donna threatened him? Was that why he had to leave? Did he realize that anyone who could kill women might be capable of filicide? Probably, so instead of giving her the chance to kill him, he was going to take off. And that meant he wouldn't have told her where he was going, or even that he was leaving. But if she showed up at his door unannounced, found him packing, then responded violently to the news. . . .

Because of how Matt had explained his reasons for leaving in the journal entry, I thought it was reasonable to conclude that, if his mother hadn't been a murderer, I would still be his fiancée. Except for that homicidal fluke, we would have been married soon. I knew him well, or I thought I did as I sat there, and he would've wanted me to find out who killed him and why.

Although I was pretty sure I already knew those answers, I stood up, looked at the boxes until I found the one that said Journals on it, pulled out my keys, then raked one along the length of the packing tape that sealed the flaps. I carried a few journals at a time to the avocado-green built-in breakfast-bar, then opened the front flaps and organized them in chronological order.

Twelve journals contained Matt's thoughts about his life and the world, beginning the day he moved to Paducah when he was ten. If I waded into them, I had a long night of reading ahead. I'd been sitting a while, thinking, so I decided to stretch my legs before I settled in with the journals. I grabbed the bowling pin, walked through his kitchen to the side door, then opened it into his garage. I saw his old blue Honda closest to me and was surprised to see his bronze, convertible 1962 MG, an MGA.

He had bought it four years ago from a local guy who'd never fixed it after it had thrown a rod. That owner had parked it in his garage, then hadn't touched it for more than half a century. The car was a total mess when Matt had it towed to his house, then pushed it into the garage with my help. The interior had feces from at least three species in it, and the dust across the whole car was at least a quarter-inch thick. But the body was in great shape, with only a few small dings. To Matt's eye and mine, the body of the MGA was much more beautiful than that of the MGB.

Even though the owner wasn't asking much for the car, I'd tried to talk Matt out of buying it because he tended to convince himself he had more time and patience than he really had, and because he didn't know a thing about cars.

"Hads, listen. Very few people in the world can drive a car that spells out their initials exactly: MGA. Matt Gerard Ackerman. Come on, Hads. If that's not a sign, nothing is."

I'd always had trouble resisting his goofiness, and when he combined it with his smile, I was a goner. So, we found ourselves a couple of hours later pushing it into his garage.

Over the years, he cleaned the interior and replaced the cracked leather seats, but he never got around to fixing the engine, so we'd never driven the Woodlands Trace Parkway in Land Between the Lakes National Recreation Area with the top down as we'd hoped we would.

I'd only stepped into the garage, not walked over to the car. I glanced at the piles of gear and junk in the two back corners of the two-car garage. Next to the downhill skis and boots, the rock-climbing gear, and the easel and other painting supplies, none of which he'd used, sat more piles of junk he'd collected around town—scraps of wood, pieces of metal, parts of signs, a discarded purple plastic baseball bat. Matt must've seen the bowling pins in the dumpster outside Cardinal Lanes before or after his Monday-night league, then grabbed some of them, intending to turn them into something-or-other eventually.

I looked back at the car and wondered if he'd been unable to sell it because it didn't run. I walked to the front of it, just inside the big garage door, to take a look. I would have to get rid of the car because Matt only rented this house. The landlord would likely throw out Matt's stuff in a few days, at the end of the month. Because I didn't want the car to be junked, I added "deal with the MG" to my to-do list.

I looked at the car from the front. Two pieces of paper were stuck under the driver's side windshield wiper. I lifted the blade, then removed the papers. The first was the title to the car, signed over to me. The second was a hand-written note that said,

> Finish the job. You always had more
> follow-through than I did, Hads.
> Then drive the Parkway. Love, MGA

I was overwhelmed with happiness and sadness. His generosity clashed with his selfishness, or what I was calling selfishness because he couldn't simply do what was right: turn in his murderous mother, then marry me, build a life together, love our children, publish novels, or run our own newspaper or whatever else we wanted to do together—and drive the Parkway with the top down.

In his last journal entry, he said other men wouldn't have blinked before they did the right thing. If my mother had been a murderer, I would've begged the arresting officers to let me snap the cuffs on her.

But every parent-child relationship is unique, so I caught myself when I started to get angry at Matt, then I walked inside with the bowling pin to start reading his journals.

Within minutes, I understood why he couldn't turn in his mother.

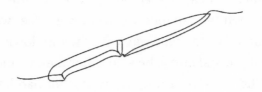

Chapter 32
Invisible Thread

"Sounds like you were triggered, which is to be expected after experiencing severe trauma," Elaine said. Even though I'd only been back at work for less than three weeks, I'd worked nearly every day, some of them sixteen-hour days, so I took Monday off, without asking permission. Elaine had an available 2 p.m. appointment.

"I know what to do," I said, "because it's the right thing to do, but Matt couldn't do it. For me to turn her in would be the ultimate betrayal, wouldn't it?"

"No. Because he left the journal for you to find and called himself a coward. No one ever has or ever will call you a coward, Hadley. Even though he couldn't provide the evidence to you because that would be the same as turning her in, I think he expected you to do what he couldn't. Go ahead, tell me again the message he left on the car, and listen to the words."

I thought for a second, then laughed hard. "I'm an idiot."

"No, you're not an idiot. Say the words."

"'Finish the job. You always had more follow-through than I did, Hads.'"

"He could've sold the car at a loss, given it to charity, or had it towed to his new city, but he didn't. He was asking you to do what he couldn't. If you want to fix the car, that's great, too."

"You're right. I should've gotten that. Oh, well. In his house yesterday, I started to read his other journals. He started the first one when the two of them were in a dumpy motel on their first night in Paducah. He was ten, and it was December 7. He ended his first entry by saying even though he didn't know anything about Paducah and would have to start at a new school and make new friends, he was glad they weren't in Philadelphia anymore because 'Dad can't hit me here.'"

I took a second to let my emotions settle.

"As I read, with the bowling pin beside me, I learned why they'd left Philly. His dad had been hitting Matt and abusing him emotionally since he was four. He hit Donna, Matt's mom, too, sending her to the ER twice, according to the journals. She protected Matt by taking him away. As horrible as what she's done is, he couldn't betray his savior."

"The torture he must've been in, the conflict."

"Could the abuse explain his social awkwardness, his wearing of armor in public?"

"Yes, I think so."

"Why wouldn't he have told me about that abuse? I mean, we were going to get married."

"Embarrassment, shame, humiliation, feelings of inadequacy. He was able to describe to you the torture he'd received at the hands of Williams because you brought it up—you mentioned that you'd seen Williams throw a can of pop at him in high school. He wasn't breaking a trust by adding facts to a narrative you were aware of. But turning in one's parents, even if they deserve it, can be seen as breaking a trust, particularly for someone as self-lacerating as you tell me Matt was. It's all very complicated. But I'm afraid that's our time." I cancelled the next day's appointment, we said goodbye, then she said, "You know what to do. Trust yourself."

The multitude of quilters had gone home because QuiltWeek had ended, and it had done so without further bloodshed. The protests continued in full force through Sunday in front of City Hall, but when I drove by on Monday on my way home from my appointment, only about twenty protesters, eighteen of whom were women, were slowly walking ovals. Three of them carried signs I hadn't seen. They read as follows:

Murder: The fabric of Paducah
Hell hath no fury like a woman stabbed
We put a man on the moon but can't stop women
from being murdered. Really?

When I got home, I tried to take a nap, but I tossed and turned because I was worried that Donna might come after me. I had resolved one of my biggest concerns: I hadn't done anything to cause Matt to leave me, and he hadn't left because he didn't love me.

Although I was almost certain Donna had killed him, I didn't know how to prove it. So, I tossed and turned until I admitted I wasn't a homicide detective and needed help.

"Hadley, I was hoping you'd call," Officer Brandon Green said when I called his cell.

"Why, do you have good news?"

"We're pursuing leads but don't have enough to make an arrest."

"You'll probably laugh at me, but I think I know who did it. I just can't prove it."

"Then you better come in."

"Can we meet somewhere other than the station? I don't want to deal with whatever abuse is on the menu today."

"Of course. Where do you want to meet?"

"How about Keiler Park, next to Midtown Market?"

"Perfect. Ten minutes?"

"Fine. Any chance you don't have to bring detectives?"

"I should, but if you let me record our conversation and take notes, I'm pretty sure they won't kick me off the force for meeting you alone."

"Good. See you there."

I rode my bike to the park. When I arrived, Officer Green was sitting on a bench in the shade, watching a boy of about six swing back and forth through the broken sunlight that the leaves created. His mom sat on a nearby bench.

Even though I'd be talking to a cop while I was there, I locked my bike to a tree. I know it's a cliché, but 'better safe than sorry' is a maxim worth heeding.

"Hello, Officer Green," I said as I approached, then sat on the bench on his right side.

"Hello, Hadley. How are you?"

"I've had better months."

"Yes. Hard to have a worse one."

"True, but I know four people who've had worse ones, and two who had a lousy March."

"What do you mean, lousy March?"

"You better start recording and taking notes. I hope you brought a backup pen."

He tapped his left breast, where two expensive pens were clipped. He pulled a small recorder out of his pocket, then hit 'record.' He removed a pen and picked up the notebook that sat next to him on the bench.

"Please listen all the way through without dismissing me as a crackpot. I've lived with this since April 2, the day Matt dumped me, which started me wondering. Then I found his body on April 9. What I say may not make sense, but I guarantee there's no one who's given all of this more thought, including your detectives."

"I'm sure that's true. One detective told me he has to remind himself he's working puzzles. If he thinks of the victims' families, he's done. Doing that case after case would cause PTSD, he said. Which reminds me—Williams will be brought up on federal charges for civil rights violations."

"That's great. Thank you. But why did mentioning PTSD remind you of Williams?"

"Because he suffers from it. He did two tours in Fallujah and should never have been hired by PPD. The brass like to beat their chests over how many decorated vets they hire, whether or not those vets are a danger to themselves and others."

"He's that bad?"

"I told my last partner I wouldn't bet against Williams being involved in a bad shoot within the year. Luckily, I was wrong, but I'm sure you don't feel lucky."

"Not overly so, no. Why'd you think that about him?"

"Sergeant Tarpley, an eighteen-year vet at the time, told Williams he was a Yankees fan. Tarpley opened his locker to show Williams a signed pennant from the 1978 season, their big comeback year, that his dad had given him. Tarpley closed the locker—probably too hard—and Williams attacked him as soon as he heard the sound. Tackled him. Screamed like a wounded animal. It's possible he's just a Red Sox fan, but that looked like PTSD to me."

"If that's what he's going through, I feel sorry for him, but that doesn't excuse—"

"No, Hadley. I'm not saying that. No one deserves what he did to you. Williams should've never been hired. Period. And Kramer only got a six-month suspension—the longest I've ever heard of—but he should've been fired and charged. You can't win 'em all."

"Except if you're Donna Ackerman."

He looked at me with the perplexed expression I expected, and then I told him what I knew, what I'd experienced, what I suspected, and what Matt had suspected.

I included all of it: Veronica had been shoved backward during a robbery after she won big at Harrah's; Pat had been stabbed to death during a push-in robbery, and her expensive sewing machine had been stolen; I'd interviewed Amy only hours before her death; the always-broke Donna had a $4,000 sewing machine in her house on top of stacks of EMR Fabrics, a product she sold through multi-level marketing; she had failed three times to sell her inferior products to Veronica and Pat, according to the chart on her wall; Matt had taken a bloody blouse to the cleaners a couple days after Veronica was killed;

and he had written many times in his journals about her temper, how she would often fly into a rage. Then I mentioned that Donna had blown a gasket when I asked her how she could afford such an expensive sewing machine.

I said I'd found three bowling pins at Matt's and that they'd make an effective weapon; I told him about Matt's last journal entry and how he'd called himself a coward for not being able to do something. I said that what Matt couldn't do sure looked like it was turning in his mother for murder. And I mentioned the note Matt left for me on the MG, telling me to finish the job.

I took about an hour to tell it all. At one point, Officer Green motioned that we should walk around the park, so we walked as I spoke until his recorder stopped recording because the batteries died. Then we sat back on the bench so he could take notes more easily.

"I'm not sure where to start," he said, "but I know I'm thirsty. You want a drink?"

"Yes."

We walked into Midtown Market, and he bought himself an orange Gatorade and me a cold, unsweetened tea. He didn't say anything during our short walk to the store, or as he bought the drinks, or on our walk back to the bench.

I wondered if he was contemplating how to commit me to a psych ward. What I'd said made sense to me, but what if the stress of the last twenty-six days—the traumas, the lack of sleep, my new medication, Matt's childhood abuse, and the possibility that my would-be mother-in-law was a multiple murderer—had made me delirious, delusional, despondent, desperate, and a few more d-words?

I turned to Officer Green, then asked, "I'm bonkers, right?"

"Definitely not normal."

"You keep saying that, but I'm starting to suspect it's not a compliment."

"Oh, it's a complement. Kind of the way one compliments Picasso's *Guernica*."

"Wait. I'm like a painting of a city bombed in the Spanish Civil War? Come on, seriously?"

"Relax. I'm teasing. You're under a ton of stress, but I'd bet a lot of what you told me will pan out." He looked at me. I must not have looked great because he asked, "You okay?"

"Compared to what?"

He laughed, then asked, "Is it possible Donna stabbed Pat to death, then stole her sewing machine? Yes, but it's also possible Pat was killed in a push-in robbery that went bad, then the perps sold Donna the machine for a rock-bottom price. It's obvious the other three stabbing deaths are related." He looked at his watch. "Gotta go. I'll pass along the parts of your story that don't make you sound crazy as a loon."

"If I weren't still in shock, I'd be offended on behalf of all women because there's misogyny in that comment." I smiled.

"Not misogyny, Hadley. Four younger sisters. It's called teasing."

"If you say so. Remember how you were willing to do a weak, helpless damsel a favor?"

"I remember helping you, if you're the one you're inaccurately referring to."

"Well, if you were willing to do me a similar favor—take a picture of or describe the necklace that was found at Pat's when she was killed—I'd be obligated to bake you the world's best peanut-butter cookies."

"You realize I'm an officer of the law, correct, and in a certain light what you've just offered could be considered a bribe?"

"But the cookies really are the world's best."

"Well, then consider it done. I'll call or text you a description or photo."

"I truly appreciate it. Oh, I almost have that list ready for you of short, fat, ugly, mean, and stupid women. But you're sure they have to be women, right? Because I could come up with a much longer list of men who fit that bill."

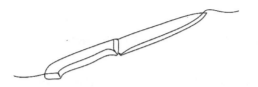

Chapter 33

Setting Triangles

Officer Brandon Green hadn't shot down my theory. He seemed skeptical, but skepticism in law enforcement is probably the norm. I hadn't provided proof, but it wasn't my job to provide proof. However, Matt was murdered nineteen days before, and, for all I knew, Justin Bieber could've killed him. Or Officer Green.

Monday night had arrived, and Mondays had been Matt's bowling night, when he donned his ghastly brown-and-yellow bowling shirt with the team's name, The Pathetic Fallacies, scripted across the back in orange, then joined his teammates, all writers, to roll three games against other poorly dressed and stupidly named teams.

Bill and Dan from the *Chronicle*, a playwright named John Rosenwasser, Dakota's ex and would-be novelist Freddie DiSalvo, and a poet named Niles McGuire rounded out the team. Whether they'd filled Matt's spot, I didn't know.

I strapped my helmet on, turned my front- and rear lights on, then pedaled to Cardinal Lanes. I locked up my bike, left my helmet hanging from the top bar, then went inside. The bowling alley was crowded, which meant very loud, with more than three-quarters of the lanes filled by league bowlers.

I found The Pathetic Fallacies on lane twelve. I'd met the guys I hadn't already known the previous year when I'd tried to be supportive of Matt by watching them bowl. But watching other people bowl is as interesting as watching other people quilt, except without a final product you could hold in your hand.

"Hey, Hadley," Bill said as I approached, setting his beer down.

"Hey, guys. Having fun?" I gave them all quick hugs as they said hello.

"Fun is not our objective. We're here to destroy the competition," John, the playwright, said in a tone that implied he couldn't care less if his team ever won a game, let alone a match.

The men standing or sitting nearby, all of them wearing blue-and-gold shirts that said The Stricken on back, acknowledged me with nods or a quick raise of their hands. I assumed the team's name was a play on the bowling term "strike," but I didn't care enough to ask.

"Anything new?" Dan asked.

"Williams has been arrested," I said, "and will have civil-rights charges brought against him. But as far as the murders go, the cops say they have a few leads, but I'm not holding my breath."

"Did they say what kind of leads?" Dan asked.

"No, not to me. Forensic, surveillance, a witness, who knows? They haven't officially ruled out the person I think did it."

"Freddie, you're up," Niles said. Niles was Black, early thirties, about six-one, and muscular.

"Oh, sorry," Freddie said, then found his ball, spotted his mark, maneuvered down the lane like a car with only three wheels, then threw a gutter ball.

"You owe us a round," Niles said.

"Yeah, yeah," Freddie said. "Add it to my tab. There're bound to be more where that came from."

"Who do you think did it?" Dan asked, then sipped from his Budweiser.

"I'd rather not say. I don't want the person named as a suspect, and I really don't want the suspect to identify me as the accuser if I'm wrong."

"You had to work hard not to use the word 'she,'" Bill said.

I smiled. "You're right. I'm an awful deceiver."

"Most people are," he said.

"How'd you know?" I asked.

"The default pronoun is 'he' when discussing a murderer. It's both a matter of probability and of cultural indoctrination. Men commit most murders. If you thought it was a man, you would've said 'he.'"

"You're such a pretentious twit, Bill," Freddie said. "'Cultural indoctrination.' My God."

"I'm pretentious?" Bill asked. "I heard you iron your underwear."

"That's a lie."

"Whatever, Harvard Law," Bill said.

"As if you haven't mentioned your Pulitzer forty-eight times this month," Freddie said.

To try to break the tension, I said, "How's the writing going?" I asked Freddie, but Niles said, "Great," and John said, "Great."

"Slowly," Freddie said. "It's much harder than I thought it'd be." He picked up his beer bottle, then took a swig.

"Isn't everything?" I asked.

Freddie, John, and Bill laughed while Dan rolled a strike. They cheered and gave him high-fives.

I watched them roll a few more frames. As I did, I couldn't remember if Freddie had attended Matt's funeral. The service, burial, and small gathering were a blur. I remembered specific details clearly—the black veil over Donna's face, the white gloves the pallbearers wore, the spray of roses draped over the dark-oak casket, the smell of dirt at Matt's gravesite—but I didn't remember who was there or whether I thanked them for attending. I couldn't even remember the words Father Sheridan had spoken.

"Nice spare, Freddie," I said, as he walked back to his seat. "I have a question for you. Did you attend Matt's funeral?"

He looked at me for three seconds. The funeral had been fourteen days before.

"Uh, no. That was a Monday, right? Yeah, I was sick that day. Food poisoning, I think. Missed that week's league. In fact, we forfeited."

"Too bad you couldn't make it. As services go, it was well-run."

"They're always tough. I liked Matt a lot."

In addition to eating many meals together, celebrating birthdays with each other, sharing Thanksgiving turkeys, and cycling as a foursome, Dakota, Freddie, Matt, and I had taken two overnight trips together: to Louisville and to Nashville. We'd had fun on both trips, but Freddie seemed only to tolerate Matt and his eccentricities. We drove separately because Dakota and Freddie wanted to stay an extra night both times. Matt and I couldn't afford to. Plus, I didn't like to miss the Paducah Quilters Quorum. Dakota didn't mind missing our sessions as much as I did.

On the drive home from Nashville, Matt had said, "Do you get the feeling Freddie thinks he's much better than us?"

"I know he does," I said. "He hasn't written squat but knows he can write circles around us. I saw your smirk when he called fiction 'real writing' and journalism 'just a way to pay the bills.' Tell that to Woodward and Bernstein. Don't take it personally, hon. He's jealous. On the other hand, maybe he's Tolstoy, so thinking he's better than us makes sense. We'll see when we read his work."

That was three weeks before Dakota left him, after she'd assessed his first chapter with "You can't go wrong with Times New Roman."

"On that last Monday Matt bowled with you," I said to Dan, "was anything different about him?"

"Like what?" Dan asked.

"I don't know. Did he tell you he was moving?"

"He said that would probably be his last night bowling with us, but when we asked why, he said it had to do with his mom."

Bill sat down next to us, after having knocked down five pins in that frame.

"Bill, did you notice anything different about Matt on his last league night?"

"It was weird he wouldn't tell us where he was going. I liked Matt. He could be irritating, but he had a unique perspective. He asked if I needed anything—appliances, CDs, golf clubs, a bike, a computer. I didn't, but Freddie took his stereo."

"You didn't?" Freddie asked. "You said you'd take his desktop."

"Changed my mind," Bill said. "We have two decent laptops, so we didn't need it. Did you take his stereo?"

"No," Freddie said. "Decided not to."

"He told me on Tuesday at work you were picking it up that night," Bill said.

"I was, but I called him and told him I didn't need it. I listen to music through earbuds."

"Did you notice anything unusual about Matt on his last night bowling, Niles?" I asked.

"He was more reserved, like he was somewhere else."

"Okay, guys, thank you. I'm heading out. I hope you vanquish your foes." They said goodbye. I looked up at the scoreboard, added the scores in my head, and determined that The Stricken had a 107-pin lead going into the ninth frame.

I texted Dakota and asked if I could come over. It was 7:54 p.m. She texted "of course," so I rode to her house. I needed some girl time. Dakota knew what to say and when to say it. I expected communication, compassion, and maybe commiseration. But what I got was one of the biggest scares of my life.

Dakota's house was huge and wonderfully appointed, filled with the best of everything. I felt uncomfortable sitting on most of her furniture, but not because the furniture was uncomfortable. It should all have been in a museum—and visitors are not allowed to touch art objects in museums. If Emeril Lagasse saw the quantity and the quality of her kitchen appliances and accoutrements, he would go home and kick his own collection up a notch. The irony of Dakota owning a kitchen that could have been featured in *Architectural Digest* or on the Food Network was that Dakota hardly ever cooked, or even went into the kitchen to do much more than to prepare a protein shake. She ate every lunch out and had nearly every dinner delivered. When Sunday rolled around and it was time to bring a food item to Paducah Quilters Quorum, she usually made sure to pick up something delicious on Saturday.

She and I sat outside on her veranda. The temperature was pleasant. "How's Cathy doing?" I asked. Cathy was her younger sister, whom Dakota sometimes called Troubled Cathy.

"Better. I hated to miss Sunday, but she's gotten herself in deep on some stupid multi-level marketing scheme, and I've been spending too much time helping her out. And by that, I mean selling for her."

"I'm going to go out on a limb and guess it's EMR Fabrics."

"Yes. Why'd you say it like that?"

Dakota was sipping a Kentucky cabernet, and I was drinking water. She'd offered food, but even though I hadn't eaten in hours, I wasn't hungry.

"Because EMR is overtaking Paducah like a dust storm, and it's following me around. Donna's selling it, too."

"I know. She's downstream from Cathy. It's not good fabric. The most expensive styles are decent quality, but the company markets itself as the least-expensive option in an otherwise very expensive hobby. But the inexpensive styles are garbage."

"Cathy's having trouble selling it, then."

"She finds ways to fail. It's her thing, like water flowing downhill. Selling EMR was supposed to build her confidence, give her something to be proud of, build positive momentum. But she manages to put obstacles in her way. She shies away from effort. The path of least resistance rarely gets us anywhere, Hads. Everything takes work."

I nodded. Dakota was the only family I had, even though we weren't related. She was much more of a sister than Jenny was. Despite this, I almost laughed at what she'd just said.

Yes, she'd worked very hard in high school, in college, and in law school, but she'd won both the genetic lottery and the parental lottery. No one who knew her could understand why she wasn't making millions as a supermodel. Her dad had invented five carbon-carbon nose cones for missiles, then sold the patents to McDonnell Douglas for enough money to buy most of Paducah. The family toured Europe every summer and snow skied in Zermatt, Switzerland, nearly every winter. Yes, succeeding in nearly every endeavor requires hard work, but some people start much closer to the finish line than other people do.

I thought about Dakota's pouting face last week when she arrived at my house for Paducah Quilters Quorum after Officer Green hadn't tried to become her man. I must have been forgetting certain occasions, but I couldn't remember when she'd suffered a setback. Within three months of deciding she wanted to become a cyclist, she completed a century ride. Riding one hundred miles doesn't come naturally to anyone; it requires dedication, discipline, and a whole lot of sweat, so I wasn't knocking her drive or her effort. She certainly knew how to succeed. I just wasn't sure she knew how to fail.

"Donna said she was having real trouble selling EMR," I said. "People were getting really mad at her."

"I'm sure I have a much better success rate than Donna has, but we did call many of the same people, and that doesn't sit well with them. They feel like they're being harassed."

"Do you have one of those sales charts?"

"Yes. It should be at Cathy's, but because I'm doing all the selling, I figured why not keep it here?"

She led me to one of her two sewing rooms, the one she sewed in, as opposed to her stash room. Donna's, Matt's, and my house could fit in one of the three wings that branched out from the huge atrium in the middle, topped by a twenty-foot-high glass dome.

We walked into the room that had the chart in it, and I went to the left wall, which was painted lemon yellow. The other three walls were a lighter shade of yellow.

Cathy's EMR Fabrics chart was pinned to a large cork board by four red pushpins. Next to it was a smaller chart that showed the multilevel-marketing aspect of the business. Donna was among the eight salespeople (all women) downstream from Cathy, meaning downstream from Dakota.

Ninety-eight of the one hundred numbers on the left side of the larger chart had names beside them. This chart was almost the inverse of Donna's. Nearly all of the Success boxes had a green checkmark in them, meaning very few of the Success boxes had a red X in them. Therefore, the red Xs stood out.

I suddenly felt my heartbeat in my temples. Dakota was standing behind me. Without indicating I was verifying specific information, I ran my eyes back and forth between the names and the red Xs.

Pat DeLott X
Natalie Loose X
Heather Cain X
Amy Thorstead X

Only about twenty other women had a red X in their Success boxes, and many of them had been contacted in the last few days.

I was afraid to turn around because I expected Dakota to be holding a knife, ready to stab me. I waited a few seconds and examined the column of items that had been sold so I could hide the fact I'd been looking at the names of the four women who'd been murdered and their corresponding red Xs. Then I thought I'd rather be stabbed in my stomach than in my back. That way, maybe I could take at least one eye that wasn't mine with me as I died.

I turned slowly, and Dakota was standing there, smiling, looking calm. She wasn't holding a knife. She didn't look suspicious, angry, or homicidal. She appeared to be the same Dakota I'd known and loved for years, the one whose arms I'd cried in when Matt dumped me, and after my mom died. She was the first person I'd called after Matt proposed, and the first one after he'd said goodbye. I didn't think there was a slight chance I didn't know who she was. But, as Matt's journals had proven, I also thought I'd known everything about him, but I hadn't known about the violence and emotional abuse his father had inflicted upon him.

"I need more water," I said, then walked out of the room, down the long hallway, and into the kitchen. I'd left my first glass on the veranda, so I grabbed another from a cupboard, then started to fill it from the filtered-water tap in the refrigerator door. I looked at her counter, where all of her high-end appliances sat, the ones she never used. A housekeeper cleaned twice a week, and yet she hardly ever had to wash a dish. I filled the glass, then turned to walk back to Dakota, wondering what I was going to say. I took two steps, then stopped and turned around. Something was missing from the end of the counter, the section bounded by the shelf of cookbooks, most of them never having been opened. What normally sat there?

A block of knives. I was sure they were J.A. Henckels.

I didn't want to go back to the sewing room. I thought for a second about which way to exit her Italianate labyrinth the quickest. Heading out the back would require me to climb an unclimbable fence that separated her backyard from the golf course. I could just start to sprint toward the front door, then hope I could fake her out if she tried to stop me. I hesitated for a second, then I heard her ask, "Hads, are you okay?"

She stood in the kitchen entryway at the edge of the formal dining room. The entryway was wide enough to drive a truck through, so I could probably slip by her, but I was sure I could sprint through the kitchen entrance nearest me, then beat her to the front door.

But I'd ridden my bike. What good would beating her to my bike do if she could just run me over with either of her $80,000 cars?

"What's wrong?" she asked.

It was fight or flight, and flight would only get me flattened, so I asked, "Where are your knives?"

"What?"

"You heard me."

"My knives? Where they always are." She pointed toward the far side of the counter, near where I stood and where the knives should have been. Her expression became confused, and she started to walk toward me.

"Hold it." I put my hand up, as if that would do something. "Don't come closer, or I'll run."

"Hadley, have you gone mad? What are you accusing me of?" She looked more hurt and confused than she'd looked at my door after Brandon had rejected her.

"I'm not accusing you of anything. I'm asking you where your knives are."

"I have no idea. You're really worrying me. I think you need a doctor. I'll call 911."

"I was thinking of doing the same thing. Your knives are missing. Henckels knives, the kind found at Pat's and Natalie's murder scenes."

"Oh, my God, Hads. What's going on?"

"I need you to walk ahead of me, back to the chart. Will you do that?"

"Hadley, I'm really freaking out."

"So am I."

"You think I killed Pat and Natalie?"

"And Heather and Amy. But I didn't quite say that. What I said was, I need you to walk ahead of me back to the chart."

She looked like a little girl who'd just been told that Santa Claus was as imaginary as unicorns and wedded bliss. She walked slowly back to the sewing room, then stood in front of the chart, about eight feet from it. I kept my distance, at least fifteen feet away, close to the door.

Then, I said, "I couldn't help notice how different your chart is from Donna's."

Dakota wasn't accustomed to rejection. She'd been truly shaken by Brandon not wanting a second date, as though being rejected was outside the scope of her imagination.

And every one of those red Xs was a rejection of *her*. She hadn't just been born with a silver spoon in her mouth—she had arrived wearing a tiara and a diamond necklace. When she was younger, she'd never worried that a boy she liked didn't like her because every boy did—and more than a few of the girls. She'd never called me or anyone else after she'd been dumped because no man had ever left her. Could her self-worth and her worldview be so warped that she couldn't abide any form of rejection? I'd never seen her be violent, but I'd only seen her be rejected once, and she hadn't processed that well.

"I'm pretty persuasive," she said. "The key is not to try to sell them anything over the phone. I call to set up an appointment, but I don't try to sell them a single swatch until we're face-to-face."

I'd gambled with Donna when I'd asked how she could afford such an expensive sewing machine, and I'd lost that gamble. Maybe she hadn't been about to kill me, despite looking as though she would. Maybe she was only furious because I'd poked her in her addiction, and addicts don't like to hear they're addicts. Maybe she thought I was about to accuse her of stealing the machine, which I was. It hadn't occurred to me she could've bought it from the thief or thieves who had stolen it.

Because my gamble with Donna had resulted in me shoving her then making a run for it, logic dictated I should keep my mouth shut, then let homicide detectives take a look at the red Xs on the chart to see which conclusions they reached.

Instead, I said, "Dakota, you're as smart as anyone I know, and your dad was literally a rocket scientist. You haven't looked at that chart and noticed anything odd?"

"No." She took two steps forward and looked at the chart. Three seconds later, she gasped, stepped back, and said, "Oh, no, Hads! What's going on?"

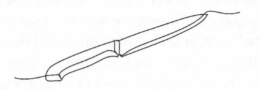

Chapter 34
Opportunity Quilt

About fifteen years before we stood in her sewing room that night, Dakota had played Nancy in a community-theater production of *Oliver!* at Market House Theatre. Dakota sang beautifully, and her looks alone probably filled the house, but her acting made me think of a frozen cyborg on stilts.

When she responded to the chart with, "Oh, no, Hads! What's going on?" I knew her shock was real. If she was the killer, I would have known it then. I didn't think I could know so little about both Matt and my best friend, but I'd still had my doubts about whether she could be the killer—until I heard her response. Even that simple question would have rung false when asked by a woman with less-than-zero acting talent.

"Now you see why I was studying the chart," I said. "You're as concerned as I am."

"Concerned? I'm horrified! Are you saying you think Cathy killed them because they wouldn't buy from her?" She staggered to a chair and sat down. Her face was red, and beads of sweat lined her forehead.

"She was the one who wrote the Xs of the victims?" I asked.

"Yes."

"Including Amy?"

"No, I wrote that one, after the awards ceremony. It seemed stupid to even approach her. She's sponsored by Moda. But Cathy asked me to because landing the Best of Show winner would be huge. Probably triple her downstream, so I asked. I barely got two sentences out before she said, 'I have to stop you. I'm a sponsored quilter.' She wasn't mean about it, and I knew it was a stupid idea."

"Who wrote those last Xs, the ones in the last few days?"

She stood up, walked to the chart, then looked at it. "We both did. I mean, those are my Xs, but we approached those women together. That's what I was doing Sunday, why I couldn't go to Donna's. Cathy and I had three appointments. Three more on Saturday." She looked at the contact dates. "Wait. One Friday, two Saturday."

I walked to a chair and sat down, and she did the same.

"I'm still shaking. This isn't possible, is it?" she asked.

"It's not *impossible*. Do you think there's any chance she could've done this?"

"No, none, for at least two reasons. One, she's not violent. I've never seen her in a rage. When she's really mad, she stomps her foot, maybe says something like, 'You make me so mad.' There's no chance she could stab somebody. Many somebodies."

"And what's number two?"

"I know this won't sound nice, but—"

"She's not smart enough to pull these murders off. It doesn't sound as unkind as you think it does. If someone says you don't think the way a murderer does, that's not an insult."

"You're right. But you know what I mean. She can't make a peanut butter and jelly sandwich without leaving two surfaces sticky. How could she not get caught in the middle of the first murder?"

"She would've gotten caught. Oh, I've been meaning to ask you something. I'm trying to give Donna the benefit of the doubt, but Matt left a bloody blouse of hers at the dry cleaner, and I can't explain it. I'm guessing, but have you ever known Donna to get a bloody nose?"

"That's right. You were visiting Jenny when PQQ was at my house. Donna's taking a blood thinner for her heart, and she had a nosebleed that day. Almost bled on our quilt. Said it was the second one she'd had, the first being when she sneezed on the way home from the casino. Said it just wouldn't stop."

"That helps, but I don't know if it's good or bad news."

"Why, you suspect Donna?"

"Yes, or I *did*. Or I still might. I don't know. I can't believe she'd kill her own son."

"But, Hads, the vast majority of murders are committed by family members, or at least by people who are involved in the lives of the victims."

"Which, if we can set aside Donna for a second, brings me to Freddie."

"Freddie?"

"Hear me out. I just saw him at the bowling alley. He hemmed and hawed when I asked him if he'd attended Matt's funeral. He said he hadn't, but said he liked Matt. Freddie isn't working, and we know he isn't writing, so what was he doing that prevented him from attending the funeral of a friend and bowling teammate who was violently murdered? He said he had food poisoning, but I don't think I believed him."

"He lies a lot."

"Why would he lie about that? Either he was having sex with someone he shouldn't have been that Monday morning, or he didn't want to appear in public. If we rule out the first possibility, why wouldn't he want to be seen? What if when he hit Matt over the head—"

"Wait, you think he killed Matt?"

"Possibly. If Matt managed to get in a punch to Freddie's face after he'd been hit, or maybe Freddie fell while hauling Matt to the river, then Freddie wouldn't want to show his face in public. Maybe he knows how lousy a liar he is—and if he had to lie to one person after another at Matt's funeral, with his victim in a box a few feet away, maybe he knew he'd blow it."

"Maybe, but he could've really had food poisoning. That's not what's tripping me up, though. Matt had nothing to do with EMR Fabrics. I don't get it."

"Matt was onto the killings. He figured out EMR had something to do with them—or he thought it did. He'd seen Donna argue with Veronica the night she was killed, had seen Pat's expensive sewing machine at Donna's, and took her bloody blouse to the cleaner. If Pat suspected Donna of killing Veronica and accused her of it, Donna could have killed Pat to keep her quiet, then figured she'd take the sewing machine. Matt saw Donna's chart, took a photo of it thinking maybe EMR had something to do with Veronica's and Pat's killings. He had most of it right, it seems, but maybe he just had the wrong murderer."

Dakota appeared to be thinking but didn't say anything, so I continued.

"Matt jumped with both feet before he even knew there was water beneath him. He bought the MG without knowing which was a crescent and which a socket wrench. He collected junk for projects he never started, and he had three unfinished novels in his drawer but kept telling me about the next one he was going to write.

"But he was diligent about his habits. He was a proficient cyclist and dedicated runner, he stuck with his journal every night for thirty years, and he was an excellent guitar player. He knew how desperate Donna was financially. He'd loaned her a big chunk of money more than once, which eventually became gifts. He was embarrassed by and frustrated by her being an addict, a compulsive hoarder. Her stash is worth I don't know how many thousands, and yet, on the absurdly low pay he was making at the *Chronicle*, he floated her money, enabling her, supporting her habit. And I've learned she gambles more than I knew she did. If her financial desperation and repeated rejection and humiliation turned to anger, she could've lashed out at the women she blamed, instead of admitting that her real problem was addiction."

Dakota nodded, then said, "I can see Matt believing that. Where does Freddie come in, if Matt thought his mom killed Veronica and Pat?"

"Freddie went over to Matt's to buy his stereo, I think. When I ran into Freddie after Matt's murder, he was obviously still bitter about you leaving him. And he was wearing new running shoes. I found a man's running shoe on the bank after I found Matt that morning. It could be nothing but, what if Freddie lost his temper with Matt—they had a history, remember?—clubbed him with the nearest weapon he could find, a bowling pin, threw him in the river, losing a shoe, then decided to frame you? The ultimate revenge. He could easily have found the key you naively hide under the rock fifteen feet from your door, could have seen the EMR chart on your wall, then set out to kill the women he thought rejected you. And your knives are missing."

She looked at me for at least five seconds, then said, "I'd like to believe you, if only to end this nightmare, but that theory doesn't account for the murders of Veronica and Pat."

"Yes, you're probably right."

I thought for a second, then remembered that I'd asked Brandon to send me a photo of the necklace that detectives found at Pat's murder scene. I looked at my phone. I'd received the photo. It was of the necklace I'd given to Dakota two years ago on her birthday, consisting of a series of silver whorls that created a seashell effect. My heart raced. Brandon's text said, "Hope this helps but doesn't get me fired."

I handed my phone to Dakota, who looked at the photo, and said, "Wait, where is it?"

"In an evidence locker."

"Oh, no."

"It was found with a broken clasp at Pat's crime scene, as though while she fought her attacker, it was torn off."

"No, no, no, no."

"I know this is a shock, but this is *good* news. If Freddie found the key, stole your knives, stabbed Pat—"

"Hadley, listen to me. Pat was killed late on Sunday, after PQQ was at my house. If Donna pushed Veronica while robbing her, stole my knives and necklace that day, and maybe my missing scarf—actually, I think there's more than one missing—then killed Pat to keep her quiet, she could have seen our EMR chart, then done what you say Freddie did—frame me."

I thought for a few seconds, then said, "Why? What's her motive to frame *you*?"

"I don't know." Her expression changed. I couldn't read the severity of the unpleasant thought that had popped into her head, but I knew it was significant. Two seconds after I saw her unpleasant expression, my face probably looked just as concerned because I had a thought that made my breath catch. I didn't want to believe it, but it stitched together everything. Donna didn't have a motive to frame Dakota, but someone else could have one, perhaps a jilted spouse. I said, "Does Freddie iron his underwear?"

"What? Why would you ask that?"

"Does he?"

"Yes."

"Do you have something to tell me, D, about your love life? Or at least your sex life?"

"No, why?"

"Dakota Crowley, please show me the respect I deserve and don't lie to me. I'll admit that twenty-five minutes ago I thought you might be a murderer, but I gave you the benefit of the doubt—and gave you the opportunity to stab me—had things played out that way."

"I really don't understand."

"Fine, I'll save you the trouble of saying it. You're sleeping with Bill Lang."

"Oh, my God, Hadley. I can't believe you'd say something like that!"

Frozen cyborg on stilts.

"Look, I'm upset with you for lying and thinking I can't see through your atrocious acting, but what you do in the privacy of your bedroom—"

And then it hit me.

When Bill called me at 2:15 a.m. during a storm to tell me another body had been found, wrapped in fabric, he hadn't said, "They've found another body." He'd said, "There's been another murder. Amy Thorstead."

When we'd been at the crime scene in Noble Park, Officer Green had told me who had been wrapped in the white fabric, and later, we received a press release from PPD confirming that it was Natalie Loose. After another body had been found on the Greenway Trail, we'd had to wait for a press release to identify her as Heather Cain. But Bill had known when he called me that Amy was the latest victim. He was the cops reporter, and he was well-liked and respected, so he could have had a connection on the force who'd filled him in. But my gut told me otherwise.

"You and Bill obviously poke fun at Freddie during pillow talk. How long have you been seeing him?"

"About seven months."

"Frequently?"

"Whenever possible. I feel so ashamed. I wasn't raised to be a homewrecker."

"No one is, but it happens. Have you wrecked their home?"

"I don't think so. He says he loves me, but what does that mean?"

"The unpleasant thought you had a minute ago was that Donna wasn't the only PQQ member to have access to your knives, jewelry, and scarves. Justine could have stolen all of them and stuffed them in that huge satchel of hers, and she has a reason to frame you."

Dakota started to cry. I went to her, scooched her over on her chair, then sat and put my arm around her.

She said, "Are you saying what I think you are? Justine did this?"

"*We're* saying it, D. You've filled in the gaps."

"So, everything Matt thought about Donna applies to Justine? I don't know how I didn't see it. Bill told me she had a gambling problem, had maxed out all their cards. That's why he didn't want to go to the casino on her birthday. She's been snippy with me lately at PQQ. She obviously knows." She dropped her head for a few seconds, lifted it, looked toward the EMR chart on the wall, then said, "I was with Bill on her birthday. I left the casino, and he told Justine he'd received a call about a house fire, so he had to go cover it. She said she'd get a ride home. But then he got a call at about 2 saying he had to go back to the casino because a woman had been murdered. Justine must've followed Veronica through the parking lot. Or maybe she knew where Justine had parked, then waited."

"Did Bill say anything about that night the next time you were together?" I stood.

"He said they'd had the biggest fight they'd ever had, by far. But he wouldn't tell me what it was about. I assumed it was about us because he's said, 'I love you, Dakota,' many times, and, let's face it, he spent the night with me on her birthday."

"If they confessed during their fight what they'd done—she admitted she'd pushed Veronica, accidentally killing her while robbing her, and he admitted to the affair—then she could have had it in her head to get even with you when she showed up here for PQQ. She excuses herself to go to the bathroom, then stuffs whatever she thinks she might need to frame you into that monstrosity of a purse."

I looked at the time on my phone: 9:55 p.m.

I dialed Cherie DeLott's number, then said, "Hello, Cherie. I'm sorry for the late hour. This is Hadley Carroll from the *Chronicle*."

"Hello. It's okay. Just finishing up the news."

"A quick question. Do you know if your mom knew Justine Lang?"

"Yes, they both volunteered at Paducah Cooperative Ministry, so they ran into each other sometimes. Mom didn't like her much. Said she put on airs. We ran into her at Kroger that day. I was getting apples, and I looked over and saw them talking. Well, more like arguing, on the other side of the produce section. When I asked what that was all about, Mom said, 'Proof warthogs don't learn a thing in finishing school.'"

"That's it?"

"Yup."

"Did you mention the argument to the police?"

"Yes, but don't know what came of it."

"Did your mom ever go to Harrah's Metropolis?"

"Most Friday nights. Why?"

"Do you know if she was there on March 21?"

"I don't but wouldn't bet against it. She loved the slots. You're asking for a reason. You think Justine did it?"

"Right now, all I know is that I know more than I knew before I called you. Thank you. You've been very helpful, and I'll keep you informed."

I hung up and looked at Dakota. She'd stood while I was on the phone, and now she was pacing. She looked at me and said, "The necklace, the scarf, the knives, they implicate me in the frame. They were stolen. You think the murder weapons are hidden here?"

"Probably. Justine must've been following you after the QuiltWeek awards ceremony when you approached Amy. I don't see how else she could've known Amy'd rejected your sales pitch. She saw the two of you speaking, then you walking away dejected, or at least not joyful. Then Justine got to her that night. Probably grabbed her outside the Museum." We'd been talking for hours, and I was only certain that no matter how much longer we talked, our talking wouldn't get anyone arrested.

"I'm going to call Brandon," I said. "We're out of our depths."

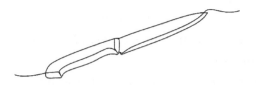

Chapter 35
Quilt Sleeve

Officer Green, a second officer, and three detectives arrived at Dakota's house not long after I called him. I told him that while we waited for them to arrive, we'd searched for the knives that had killed Heather and Amy.

"You won't find them here," he said. One detective walked down each of the three wings that radiated from the atrium, like spokes on a wheel, then disappeared into the rooms farthest from the atrium. Brandon admired the large expanse under the glass dome filled with carefully tended indoor plants. He looked down the three long wings. "Amazing home, Dakota. Ms. Crowley."

"Thank you. Doesn't exactly feel safe at the moment. Well, it does now, but you know what I mean."

"Yes. Officers are at Freddie DeSalvo's house searching for the knives."

"Wait, what?" I asked.

"Freddie did it?" Dakota asked.

"Shall we sit?" Officer Green asked, gesturing toward the seating area along the curved edge of the atrium at the end of the nearest wing. We sat, then he said, "No, Freddie didn't murder anybody. Bill and Justine Lang did." Dakota gasped, then shook her head slowly.

"Wait," I said. "You solved this but didn't tell anyone?"

"Hold on. We arrested Bill in the Cardinal Lanes parking lot when he walked out. Picked Justine up at their house at about the same time. We're gathering evidence that will guarantee convictions."

I said, "You let me blab on for an hour in the park, but you were about to arrest them?"

"You knew plenty about what happened that we didn't. And you were very close to putting it together. Plus, I don't mind listening to you talk." I shook my head.

"How do you know Bill and Justine did it?" Dakota asked.

"Because we're still making our case, I shouldn't discuss details at this stage."

"But I can, right?" I asked.

"Your speculations proved to be mostly accurate, so knock yourself out."

"Officer Green, perhaps you'd prefer to use another phrase, considering?"

"Yes. Sorry. Please present your theory."

"Justine robbed Veronica in the Harrah's parking lot, probably killing her accidentally. She stabbed Pat, making it look like a push-in robbery because Pat either saw Justine kill Veronica or accused her of the murder. But between those two killings, Justine and Bill had a major fight, in which Justine confessed to accidentally killing Veronica while stealing her winnings that night—I'm guessing Justine has a major gambling addiction."

"As big as gambling addictions get," Brandon said, "before the addict heads to loan sharks. According to Bill, she tapped out their credit cards' cash advances and forged his signature so they could take out a second mortgage on their home—then she lost all of it."

"Yikes," I said. "In their fight, Bill admits to his affair with Dakota. Then at PQQ at Dakota's, Justine slips the knife block into her purse along with the necklace that she salted Pat's murder scene with—and the scarf she left at Natalie's scene."

"We kept the scarf we found at Heather's scene from the press," Brandon said, "so we'd know if we were dealing with the murderer or a copycat if he contacted us. We didn't know what we were onto at Natalie's, but we knew it was a setup as soon as we found the second scarf. As some kind of bizarre calling card, sure, but as something accidentally left behind at more than one site? No chance. At three scenes? Forget it."

"Good thing you're not revealing details of the case," I said, "because doing so would be inappropriate. Don't ever become a spy."

He blushed. "Darn, that was my next career choice," he said, then smiled.

I said, "Armed with Dakota's knives, necklace, and scarves, Justine set out to get revenge. She looked at Cathy and Dakota's chart, happened to get lucky, if I can call it that, when she saw that Pat hadn't purchased EMR fabric from her—"

"The fabric was helpful," he said, "so thanks for encouraging us to consider it carefully. But the witness was essential."

"To what?" Dakota asked.

"I may as well tell you now. The cat's out of the bag and running down the street. A homeless man trying to sleep at the top of the boat ramp at the end of Broadway saw a truck drive down the ramp to the water's edge. The driver dragged a body out of the bed and into the river. Bill's mistake was leaving his lights on. He only planned to take a few seconds to dump Matt, but he slipped on the mossy ramp, lost his shoe, and scrambled around, struggling to regain his footing. If he'd turned his lights off, he'd have been fine because the homeless man wouldn't have been able to see his plate. The plate light stays on when the headlights are on. Because he recognized what was happening, he knew he should memorize the license plate. But he didn't want to get involved. He was high and had stolen items in his possession, so he tried to forget about it, go back to sleep. But when he heard about the women getting killed, he thought they might be connected, so he reported what he saw. And the thing is, if you're going to be stupid enough to commit a spontaneous murder, I guess I shouldn't be surprised that Bill was stupid enough to dispose of the body in a vehicle with a vanity plate: STET. I looked it up. It means, leave it alone, correct as is."

"Copyediting term," I said. "Writers don't like to be edited. Bill is great at his job, and many editors aren't at theirs. But, apparently, Bill's not a great murderer. He must have figured out that Justine had killed Pat, or she told him, including her plan to frame Dakota."

"Close. He figured out the frame when he saw the necklace. He came to the house, the station, in his role as the cops and courts reporter, and asked to see the necklace. Unlike Matt—sorry, but it's true—Bill hadn't alienated most of the force."

"I have," I said.

"Well, let's say you've exacted justice, or are in the process of it. I hope your civil suit against Williams, the department, and the city is underway."

"It is. So, Dakota and I had it mostly right?"

"Yes. You two putting this together without any resources is impressive."

I said, "But we didn't count on Bill sabotaging Justine's frame of Dakota, which is why you're looking for the knives at Freddie's house."

"You're good. Bill gave a full confession instantly, filled in all the blanks."

"A natural storyteller," I said.

"Please don't tell me it was because of me," Dakota said.

"It *was* because of you," he said, then smiled. She shook her head. "He said he loves you and wouldn't let you go to prison for life, or worse, for crimes you didn't commit. He was wrestling with turning in his wife for the murders of Veronica and Pat. He couldn't bring himself to do it, he said. They'd been married for twelve years. He was almost ready to turn her in, though, when he—'like an idiot' in his words—stopped by Matt's to accept a free desktop he didn't need. Thought he could sell it for a few bucks. That's how bad their finances are. Matt had put a lot of the pieces together, and Bill said Matt mentioned seeing Bill and Justine at Harrah's that night. Then Matt said he thought Veronica's and Pat's murders were related, cause and effect, but he didn't say he thought his mother did it, didn't say why he was leaving. Matt was probably trying to show Bill that he was the better cops reporter.

"Bill panicked, he said. Matt was half a step away from implicating Justine, and he might still make the connection. Bill realized they were cooked, and he snapped. He grabbed the pin, hit Matt full force when he was wrapping the computer cord up, then realized he couldn't turn in Justine. He was now a murderer, too. He said a heated, recent argument that Freddie had with Matt flashed in his head. He realized that Freddie had motive to hurt Dakota by framing her, so he formed his plan to frame Freddie, without telling Justine, of course.

"By the way, with Metropolis in Illinois, out of our jurisdiction, we had no reason to link Veronica with Pat, and that slowed down our investigation. But you linked them by yourself, Hadley. Great job. When Bill visited you, Dakota, he removed the knives Justine planted here. Justine hauled off fabric when you were at work. You really need a better place to hide your key. You have a palace like this, but you keep your spare key under a rock."

"It's worse than that," she said. "I have a great security system that I find too troublesome to use. That changes tonight."

"Good," he said. "While you were asleep, Dakota, Bill searched your house for the knives. He didn't say if Justine told him she hid them here, but he found them, then planted them at Freddie's, one at a time. Freddie's hiding place for his key was a little better than yours, but Bill found the key in one minute, he said. People are too lazy to hide keys far from their front doors. Hadley, it turns out you have a good friend in Garrett Hunt."

"Really? What do you mean?"

"He told us you were a heck of an investigator, and he knew you were on the right track at Harrah's, long before we connected those pieces. He rethought the evening he tailed Matt there. He wasn't willing to disclose how he did it, but he got access to the surveillance tapes, the eye in the sky, as casinos call them. He recognized that Bill and Justine were together. He saw her return to the gambling floor, to the dollar slots, after the time Veronica was suspected to have been killed, after appearing to have argued with Veronica earlier, presumably about money. But Justine suddenly had money, and Hunt said she lost a great deal of it, based on how frequently she stuffed bills into the machine. He said it looked like she lost everything because she looked really dejected, then started approaching people, probably to ask for money. Bill eventually returned, chewed her out, then they left, shouting at each other. As it turned out, he'd just been reporting on the murder of the woman his wife had killed."

"Wow," Dakota said. "What did Garrett do with that information?"

"He started to tail them, alternating between the two. He didn't want to alarm you, Hadley, with all you'd been through. And he was pretty sure he was just seeing a marriage unravel, but while he was watching their house, he saw Justine drive away one day. He followed her and watched her go straight to your hidden key, Dakota, while you were at work. She carried something in a small duffel. She carried it differently, crumpled in her hand, when she left. Now he knew this wasn't just a domestic dispute, so he contacted us. It took some maneuvering, but after we put some pieces together, which we couldn't do until our witness told us what he saw at the dock, we got a warrant.

"It turned out both Bill *and* Justine killed Natalie, Heather, and Amy. Much easier to subdue victims with two people, although Bill swore Justine did the stabbing. Hunt got video of Justine planting the knife in this house that they used on Amy. Said he needed sleep, so he missed Bill transferring it to Freddie's. Bill and Justine figured they were both murderers, so they should team up to pin the murders on someone else. They just weren't trying to pin them on the same someone."

"Ain't love grand?" Dakota asked.

"Did they find the bowling pin?" I asked.

"Probably while we've been talking. Bill said he tried and tried to figure out how to get Freddie's DNA on it. Couldn't think of anything. Finally, he dunked it in Freddie's toilet."

"Ewwww," I said.

"Thankfully, we wear gloves at crime scenes, which reminds me—I should probably pretend to do my job."

"One more question. Were you right about Donna buying the sewing machine from robbers who ransacked Pat's house after Justine stabbed her?"

"Yes. She paid $150 for it. We found the Marketplace ad. Arrested the seller. Don't think she'll be charged, but she won't get to keep it, I'd bet."

"Maybe we should swear off betting for a while," I said, "considering that Justine's gambling started all this."

A week later, I was sitting in a booth at Mellow Mushroom, waiting for my Holy Shiitake pizza and reading Michael Connelly's *Lost Light*, when I heard, "Hello, Hadley."

I looked up to see Brandon Green, out of uniform. He wore jeans and a royal-blue button-down dress shirt, untucked. We smiled at each other, and I said, "Please join me."

He sat across from me, pointed to my book, then laughed. "I'm reading him, too," he said.

"Which one?"

"*The Poet*, about a reporter. For some reason, I'm more interested in journalism than I used to be."

"Weird. I chose this one from the library because it's told in first person, and I wanted to learn more about how a cop thinks."

"Any particular cop?" He smiled.

"Harry Bosch, the narrator, obviously." I smiled. "Did you catch flak for passing along information during an investigation?"

"No, or at least not yet. How's work? Hectic, I'd imagine."

"Only if you define roller-skating chimps playing chess in ice cream as hectic."

He laughed. "That's how Merriam-Webster defines it, right?"

"I was in the CIA with Merriam Webster, and she could barely spell CIA."

He laughed. "Grade inflation. What can you do?"

"Apparently, more than I think I can. But I'm having trouble getting comfortable with having lost a great friend, and the paper's lost an excellent reporter. I never liked Justine, but Bill and I were really close."

"It's sad. I'm sorry. Addiction destroys lives, no matter the addiction. Lost my father to alcoholism. He was a brilliant lawyer, but the bottle won."

"The bottle beat my mom, too."

The server arrived and set the large pizza on the rack between Brandon and me.

"Thank you," we said together. "Please, dig in," I said. He nodded, then did.

While we ate, we talked about our upbringings, our mutual fondness for the McCracken County Public Library, and our near obsession with cooking shows.

After eating one slice too many and asking the server to bring a box for the leftovers, I asked Brandon, "Are you a car guy?"

"Yes. My dad and I, when he was sober, rebuilt a convertible 1972 Corvette Stingray. Took us about a year, but then he wrapped it around a telephone pole. Why do you ask?"

"I think I mentioned the new-to-me, 1962 MG, a defunct MGA. I know only enough about cars to know I know nothing about cars."

"Are you asking if I'd like to help you restore it?" He wiped his mouth with a napkin.

"I'm not sure what I'm asking."

"Then the answer is yes."

"Look, I shouldn't have. . . . I've been through a lot."

"Hadley, we're talking about restoring a car together. If you'd like to break out the wrenches in a year, great. Two years, fine. Whatever time you need."

"I'm not sure time's what I need. What if I need something else?"

"Such as?"

"I don't know. Maybe if I tell you more about myself, you can tell me what you think I need."

"Okay, what else should I know?"

"Favorite color is Sagittarius. I'm pretty sure I'm a quilting addict. I'd like to be banned from at least one continent, I've never been in a Turkish prison, and I think silence is overrated."

"Good to know. Anything else?"

"I'm not normal."

"No, you're not. What would you like to know about me?"

"You don't own a monocle, do you?"

Acknowledgements

I would like to thank my wife, Sedonia Sipes, without whom *Quilt City Murders* would not have been published. If I started to list the countless other ways in which she shows her love for me, I would double the length of this book.

I could not have written this novel without the insightful comments made by my beta readers: Jessica Carroll, Colleen Friesen, Barbara Leonard, Brigette Leonard, Biz Lyon, Jennifer Mauerman, Veronica Piffer, Alyxander Rowan, Eva Spring, and Janey Wells.

I owe a very special thank you to Robert Bigelow and to Andrew St. Laurent for their sage legal advice. I truly appreciate their insights.

I'd like to thank my diligent, astute editor, Kim Coghlan, and publisher TouchPoint Press.

I owe an enormous debt to Paducah, Kentucky, and to its stellar arts community, which welcomed me when I lived among its creative artists, including the numerous quilters who taught me about their world. And I thank the *Paducah Sun* for everything I learned while covering the A&E beat there.

And I'd like to thank my mother, Barbara, my brother, Brett, my sister, Brigette, and my late father, Bruce Sr., affectionately known as Pops, all of whom inspired me to write *Quilt City Murders*.

Thank you so much for reading *Quilt City Murders*. If you've enjoyed the book, we would be grateful if you would post a review on the bookseller's website. Just a few words is all it takes! ♥

Made in United States
Troutdale, OR
10/09/2023

13550033R00170